"As pleasant as it is, imagining you in your lingerie, I think it's time we discussed a little business," The Ghost began.

"It appears we're at an impasse," Allison responded coolly.

"Perhaps we should work together...."

The proposal startled the hell out of him. He had always worked alone, always.

Although he couldn't see her eyes, he could feel her stare. What astonished him as much as his impulsive suggestion was that she didn't reject it out of hand.

"I've always worked alone," she said after a lengthy pause. Turning her head, she appeared to watch an Italian luxury liner leaving port, but he doubted she saw it.

"So have I. But this is an unusual situation."

"My first instinct is to refuse. But there might be certain advantages in joining forces." She let another pause develop. "I'll have to think about this," she said finally, speaking slowly.

"You do understand that I'll have to know a lot more about you before I agree to work with you." The statement was partly backpedaling, seizing the opportunity to pry more information out of her. "We have to trust each other completely, or any joint venture will be doomed to failure."

Weddings by De Wilde™

Weddings by
De Wilde™

PREVIOUSLY AT DeWILDES

Unexpected hijinks at DeWildes, London...

- Tessa Montiefiori, a DeWilde cousin working incognito at the London store, has managed to turn the press and the family on its ear once more.
- The news of a new DeWilde offspring has caused even more complications.
- A bridal contest that ran afoul of two adorable American children and their matchmaking grandmother has yielded record media attention and an English bride for the children's daddy.
- The heirloom DeWilde pearl choker may have been responsible for it all!

But, in Monte Carlo, a clever jewel thief named *The Ghost* is on the loose.

Maggie Osborne is acknowledged as the author of this work.

ISBN 0-373-82542-0

TO LOVE A THIEF

To Love a Thief

MARGARET ST. GEORGE

Harlequin Books

TORONTO • NEW YORK • LONDON
AMSTERDAM • PARIS • SYDNEY • HAMBURG
STOCKHOLM • ATHENS • TOKYO • MILAN
MADRID • WARSAW • BUDAPEST • AUCKLAND

INTEROFFICE MEMO

From: Monsieur DeVault, Chief of Police

To: Monte Carlo Police Force

Gentlemen: As you are aware, the cat burglar, internationally known as The Ghost, struck the Monaco region this time last year. As The Ghost appears to operate on a cyclical basis, all units will henceforth conduct regular drive-bys of high-ticket residential areas. We will discreetly advise selected residents to increase security measures.

The Ghost is skilled and exceptionally clever. He or she has eluded detection for years. It's unnecessary to remind you that apprehending The Ghost would be a significant coup for this department. I urge you to remain alert.

CHAPTER ONE

DESPITE YEARS of experience, Allison always suffered a case of nerves before a big caper. Like stage fright, her tension dissolved into cool efficiency once the job began, but waiting for evening to arrive had resulted in a long, tense day. Now that the waiting had ended, she was beginning to feel calmer.

After concealing her Renault within a leafy copse and double-checking that the car couldn't be observed from a nearby access road, she opened the trunk, then inhaled a deep breath of soft, sea-scented air. She flexed her shoulders, beginning her warm-up routine as she studied a huge lemon moon.

A moonless night would have been better. On the positive side, the moon's silvery glow made it easier to spot the pitons she'd set in the cliff face last week, which would make the climb to the Waldheim villa a fraction less dangerous.

Before shouldering her rope and climbing gear, she tucked a curling mass of honey blond hair into the dark hood she pulled over her head, careful to capture every strand so only her face showed. A long-sleeved black T-shirt covered her torso, and black pants and dark climbing shoes concealed her lower body. If someone on the lighted yachts rocking gently on the Mediterranean chanced to notice her clinging to the rock face—an un-

likely event at this distance—she would appear to be a
shadow or a cleft in the stone.

Muscles loose now, she followed a narrow rocky strip
that separated the base of the cliff from the water, looking for her chalk mark. When she located the mark, she
carefully rubbed it out, then donned her belt and gear and
examined the daunting vertical rise.

"You are Spiderwoman," she murmured firmly. The
remark was a prelude to the speech she gave herself whenever she embarked on a difficult climb alone. "You are
invincible."

Hands on slim hips, she rotated her upper body in a circle, gazing steadily at a glow of light rimming the distant
lip of the cliff. Baron and Baroness Waldheim had illuminated the grounds for the convenience and pleasure of
any guests who might choose to stroll along the cliff edge
and enjoy sweeping vistas of moonlit sea.

Strolling guests meant the Waldheims had kenneled the
Dobermans that ordinarily patrolled the estate.

Easing back her cuff, Allison checked the radiant dial of
her wristwatch. It was almost ten-thirty. For nearly an
hour, a steady flow of headlights had been twisting up the
serpentine road to the villa. Each vehicle would be stopped
at the iron entrance gates where tuxedo-clad security
guards would match invitations against the number of
guests in each automobile and insist on looking in the
trunks. Limo drivers and chauffeurs were required to leave
their driver's licenses with the guards at the gate before
entering the estate.

Invitations might or might not be rechecked at the door
of the villa. That possibility didn't concern Allison.

She opened and closed her hands, flexed her knees, then
stepped up to the cliff face. Although every nerve ending
urged her to haste, she willed herself to climb slowly,

carefully, placing each hand and toe securely, making certain her grip was comfortable before she rose another few inches.

As she climbed, her thoughts drifted to the jewels that would be flashing and twinkling from ears and throats tonight. The Waldheims' annual fund-raiser for the Opéra Monaco brought out the crème de la crème of European society. The usual names and faces would be present, masked for the ball, plus a sprinkling of international film stars, the winner of last year's Grand Prix and a couture designer or two. Princess Caroline would represent the Grimaldis, and rumor whispered that Princess Di would attend the ball this year.

Allison had also learned that Gabriel DeWilde and his pregnant wife, Lianne, would be present, and possibly Gabriel's twin sister, Megan DeWilde.

Her fingers slipped and small stones skittered a hundred yards down the face of the cliff.

Gulping a quick breath and listening to her heart pound, Allison closed her eyes and pressed against the rocks, clinging to the warmth retained from the day's heat.

Nine months had elapsed since she had last seen Jeffrey DeWilde, but the pain was still as bright as the moonlight. If it had been Jeffrey attending the Waldheims' fund-raising ball instead of his children, she would have . . .

What would she have done? What did one say to an ex-lover? *Why couldn't you love me as much as I loved you?* Or: *Why didn't you phone me after your wife left?*

For weeks after the announcement of Jeffrey and Grace DeWilde's separation, Allison had stared at her phone, waiting for a call that never came. Adrenaline flooded her body, riding a wave of pride. It was over. If Jeffrey DeWilde hadn't called immediately after Grace left him, he wasn't going to call nine months later. He didn't want to see her again. She needed to forget about Jeffrey and get on with her life.

"How could you have been so stupid?" she muttered, sliding her fingertips toward a narrow ledge.

Getting involved with a married man was the dumbest and most painful thing she had done to herself in recent years. She had never before involved herself in an extramarital affair and never would again. It continued to shock her that she had thrown reason and principles out the window less than twenty-four hours after meeting the legendary head of the DeWilde corporation. And she had pursued him even though he'd mentioned that he was married and had children as old as she was. She must have been crazy.

Pressing her lips tightly together, fueled by anger and a bitterness that increased rather than diminished over time, Allison completed the climb with cool, concentrated efficiency. This was not the moment to flog herself about Jeffrey DeWilde, not the moment to think about paying him back for breaking her heart. She needed her wits and a focused mind to pull off tonight's heist.

Pushing Jeffrey firmly out of her thoughts, she cautiously raised her head above the edge of the cliff and scanned a sweep of manicured lawn, relaxing only when she discovered the grounds were nearly deserted. Music and light cascaded over the nearest stone terrace and flowed over ornate urns spilling fans of crimson blossoms. As this terrace was farthest from the ballroom, few guests had yet discovered the stunning view it offered of sea and rock and moonlight. Only one couple stood beside a stone balustrade flanking wide steps that led to the gardens and lawns.

Allison waited while the couple toasted each other with flutes of champagne, waited until they finally lowered frilly domino masks over their eyes and noses and reentered the villa, arm in arm.

While she waited for the couple to depart, she inched along the cliff ledge, moving closer to the trees where she had concealed her costume. A wig, mask, collapsible panniers, slippers and a designer replica of an eighteenth-century gown were packed carefully inside a large green plastic bag, which Allison had tied in the branches of a chestnut tree.

When she was certain the couple on the terrace had departed, she crawled over the lip of the cliff, scrambled to her feet and darted like a shadow into the thick foliage at the foot of the garden. Here she paused, listening and scanning the lawns and three-story exterior of the villa. When nothing stirred, she moved unerringly to the correct chestnut tree and lowered the plastic bag to the ground. Nothing inside had been disturbed.

Moving with lithe, fluid motion, she quickly peeled off her black climbing garments, then strapped the panniers to her hips and dropped the voluminous gown over her head. The gown's low, ruffled bodice skimmed the lacy top of the bustier she had worn beneath the black T-shirt, exposing an expanse of breast she was unaccustomed to displaying. Since people remembered jewelry, she deliberately wore no necklace or earrings.

Before she closed a cleverly concealed zipper that ran down the front of her gown, she checked the harness clasped around her waist. Everything was in working order.

The wig she had chosen, coiffed high in the style of the eighteenth century, was auburn and studded with faux pearls and diamonds. One edge of her domino was sewn to the left side of the wig, the other was secured by a hidden snap on the wig's right side. She could reveal or conceal her face in mere seconds, and there was no possibility of losing the domino or leaving it behind.

Plum-colored lipstick, applied before she left home, matched the brocade gown, but she had drawn her lips thinner than their natural shape. A black beauty patch glued a half inch from the corner of her lips also drew attention away from her mouth. To complete her disguise, she wore brown contact lenses and heavy, obviously false lashes.

She would have liked to wear her climbing shoes instead of the silver-buckled slippers. To do so would shave three minutes off the time she'd need to get out of this rig and back into her climbing outfit. Plus, the hem of the gown covered her feet and she felt reasonably certain that no one would glimpse her shoes.

But if she were wrong... Sloppy guesses could get her arrested—an embarrassment and a nuisance to deal with—or perhaps provoke an attack by a zealous servant.

Sighing, she pushed her slender feet into slippers dyed to match her gown. After looping the ribbon on the end of her fan around her wrist, she stood still in the darkness, mentally trailing a finger down a checklist. Confident that she had overlooked nothing, she packed her black clothing and gear into the plastic bag and reattached it to the pulley she had rigged earlier. Silently, the bag moved upward into the branches of the chestnut tree.

There was a break in the foliage at the foot of the garden only a few yards from the tree, and she stepped through, then smoothed down her skirt and adjusted the domino, which was ruffled around the outer edges to conceal as much of her face as possible.

A sudden tremor shot through her body, and her heart raced with a thrill of apprehension. Before she returned to this spot, the mix of danger and excitement would create an adrenaline high unlike anything possible through artificial means. And maybe, she thought, that was why breaking and entering had become so addictive.

Raising her fan to cover the lower part of her face, she stepped into a pool of low subdued lighting. In case anyone watched from the upper-story barred windows, she bent slightly at the waist, keeping her features in shadow, and pretended to examine a bed of spiky scarlet blossoms.

Although Allison had lived in Monaco for four years and the flowers were common to the area, she didn't have a clue as to the name of the blooms. She could recognize thorny foliage that might be hazardous to her line of work, but unless a plant had grown in the backyard of the Ames home in the Berkshires, where she had grown up, she didn't know its name and could care less. Gardening was for people who had unlimited leisure time and no interest in adding an element of danger to their lives.

Forcing herself to proceed at an idle pace, she strolled through the gardens then wandered across the lawn toward the back terrace, twitching slightly when two men and a woman stepped out of the interior doorway and walked toward the stone balustrade. They saw her at once.

"Just what we need," the man dressed as a Harlequin called gaily, "another woman to make this a foursome. Join us, Marie. It is Marie Antoinette, isn't it?" He waved a champagne bottle as Allison lifted her skirts and mounted the staircase.

"Perhaps some other time. I'm afraid I've left my escort alone too long as it is." She answered in faultless French. Hearing her accent, no one would guess she was American. She spoke Italian, Spanish and German with equal facility, a definite asset in her line of work.

The Harlequin clutched his heart and pretended staggering dismay at her rejection. Laughing, the man's companions, a pirate and his harem girl, bowed to Allison as she passed by them, on her way to the villa. A world-famous pendant swung between the harem girl's breasts, and Allison recognized it immediately as belonging to an Italian actress whose third husband liked to shower his wives with obscenely expensive jewelry. She wondered if the Waldheims had security guards disguised as guests, alert to a slippery hand here or a quick snatch there. She'd check.

Once inside the villa, she released a low breath. She found herself in a long room furnished with heavy, beautifully polished antiques. Pausing only long enough to confirm her appearance in a mirror that hung above a sofa upholstered in watered silk, she followed the sound of music through a labyrinth of wide airy corridors. Guests had drifted away from the ballroom and congregated here and there in salons opening off the corridors. Several times someone called to her to join their group, but she sank into a graceful bow, covered a smile with her fan and continued toward the main part of the house.

For her purposes, it was satisfying to note that the guests were spilling into all parts of the villa. This made her job easier. But she couldn't help wondering if Gabriel, Lianne and Megan DeWilde were among those gathering in the salons.

"Not now," she cautioned herself firmly. With everyone wearing masks, she wouldn't recognize the DeWildes, anyway. Besides, she had only seen their photographs. She hadn't met any DeWilde in person except Jeffrey.

Jeffrey, who had let her fall in love with him. Jeffrey who had said goodbye with the terse finality of a man more comfortable with facts and figures than emotions. Jeffrey, who had pushed one of the distinctive blue leather DeWilde boxes into her shaking hands as if a piece of jewelry would compensate for a broken heart. He had actually looked surprised when she threw the box at his chest, then slammed the door behind her.

Jeffrey, whom she had loved helplessly, hopelessly.

Jeffrey, whom she now hated for letting her hope, however briefly, that he might love her in return.

A tiny ripple of shock flowed over her skin as she realized she had reached the main entrance without fully being aware of her route. Thinking about Jeffrey was not only futile and stupid, in the present situation it was dangerous.

Focusing sharply, she moved to stand beside a wide sweeping staircase and observed the entrance. Invitations *were* being double-checked at the door. If she had attempted to enter through the front, she would have been apprehended at worst, turned away at best.

A tiny satisfied smile curved behind the lace trimming her fan. The arduous climb up the cliff had been worth it; she was inside the villa and free to roam.

The entry was noisy and crowded; no one took notice as she paused to scrutinize the ballroom before she started up the stairs. Midway up the staircase, she stopped and looked down at the crowd in the foyer as if searching for someone. Gorgeous costumes representing a dozen time periods met her eyes, and a multitude of jewels flashed beneath the light of an immense chandelier.

At the top of the staircase, a man wearing an obviously rented tuxedo intercepted her. "May I help you, *madame?*"

"Please." Lowering her fan, Allison smiled fetchingly. She let the lace on the fan trail across her exposed bosom. "The man downstairs directed me to a ladies room, but

I'm hopelessly lost. I hope the powder room on this floor is easier to find?"

She assumed he had been instructed to bar access to the family's living quarters. She also knew the instructions would become harder to uphold as the evening wore on and champagne flowed and hundreds of guests sought the nearest facilities. Long before the last guests departed near dawn, some would have wandered all over the villa's three floors.

"I'm not supposed to..."

Allison spotted a woman wearing a Roman toga in the corridor behind him. Wiggling her fingers in a wave, she pretended delighted recognition then lifted her skirts confidently and stepped forward.

The guard gave her a weak smile. He couldn't deny Allison access when he had obviously granted it to an acquaintance of hers. "Down that corridor, and take a right," he said with a sigh. "It's the second door to your left."

"Thank you." Touching her gloves to her lips, she blew him a plum-colored kiss, then twitched her skirts around his legs.

At the end of the corridor, she glanced back, prepared to blow another kiss if the guard was watching. But he was engaged in attempting to persuade two Regency gentlemen to seek the facilities on the ground floor.

Instead of turning right as instructed, Allison darted left down the corridor. Moving quickly, glad the woman in the toga had disappeared, she headed toward to an unobtrusive door set into the wall at the top of three narrow stairs.

Although the villa had been built to appear as if it had graced the hills above Monte Carlo for at least a century, the structure was only about thirty years old. The blueprints were on file, and Allison had thoroughly familiarized herself with the house long before tonight.

When she opened the narrow door set into the wall, she knew it would reveal a servant's staircase and knew the stairs led to the third floor and opened only steps from Baron Waldheim's study.

The third-floor lighting was dim. A silent corridor draped in shadow stretched toward a distant balcony. But it was the heavy carved double doors to her left that occupied Allison's attention. Picking an interior lock was child's play, and she had the doors unlocked in less than forty seconds.

Slipping inside, she quietly closed the doors behind her, then paused to inspect the room. Moonlight streamed through gently billowing draperies that veiled the entrance to a stone balcony. A lamp shone down on papers scattered across the surface of a massive cherry-wood desk. Aside from two groupings of well worn leather chairs and footstools, the room could be considered almost empty when compared to the proliferation of furniture crowding the downstairs salons.

Smiling, she studied Baron Waldheim's huge desk and decided the little baron suffered delusions of grandeur. Heads of nations had plotted wars from desks smaller than this one.

Still not moving, she let her gaze roam the paneled walls, seeking the small exquisite Rubens that was the object of her own plotting and careful planning.

Once she spotted it, Allison sucked in a low breath of appreciation and wondered why she hadn't noticed it immediately. The painting depicted an old Flemish couple seated on a wooden settee before a kitchen hearth, their shoulders touching.

Drawn forward, her gaze riveted, Allison decided the couple had been married for half a century. They did not look at each other in the painting, but their touching shoulders spoke volumes. Wrinkled faces betrayed a lifetime of hardship; they had shared obstacles, perhaps tragedy. But a weathered contentment softened the firelit pleats on ancient cheeks, and they leaned against each other with an affection undimmed by decades.

Inexplicably, sudden tears sprang into Allison's eyes and she dashed them with a gesture of annoyance. She was not here to indulge in weepy sentiment—or to applaud Rubens's genius. She was here to steal the damned painting. The sooner she did what she had come to do, the sooner she could get safely away.

At this point, she was most vulnerable. There was no reasonable explanation should someone discover her standing inside the baron's study on the third floor.

Since the only light in the room came from the lamp on the desk, and since she didn't dare turn on the table lamps, she withdrew a straw-thin penlight from her cleavage. Leaning over a wall table, careful not to bump any of the objets d'art carelessly arranged on the surface, she directed a small, intense beam of light at the gilt frame of the Rubens, looking for evidence of a trip wire that would sound an alarm if the painting were removed from the wall.

"There's an alarm laser at ankle height in front of the floor safe, but no trip wire or laser on the painting. There may be a pressure alarm, I was about to check when you arrived."

Allison whirled, and the penlight dropped from fingers that turned suddenly boneless. Rigid, aware of her heart hammering in her ears, she gripped the edges of the baron's desk and peered into the shadows beyond the pool of light cast by the desk lamp.

A man stepped away from the draperies fluttering beside the open balcony doors and sauntered toward her. He wore a black cowboy hat above an amused smile, black pants and cowboy boots and a black shirt, partially covered by a vest, with pearl buttons at the sleeves and running down the front. Two pearl-handled toy pistols hung from a wide belt that cinched a lean, narrow waist. A black domino concealed the upper portion of his face, but not the amusement she saw twinkling in his eyes.

"Looks like we're poaching in the same woods, Chéri," he commented in a light voice, rounding the desk.

Before Allison could recover from the shock of his presence, he tilted her chin toward the desk light and studied what he could see of her face. He was reaching to lift her domino when they heard two men laughing just outside the study door.

For an instant, they both froze, staring into each other's eyes. "Quick," the cowboy said in an urgent whisper. The door latch rattled. "Under the desk."

Allison's paralysis was broken by a rush of adrenaline. Gathering her voluminous skirts as close to her body as she could, and silently cursing the wide panniers at her hips, she dropped to her knees, shoved the baron's chair aside and crawled into the space beneath the massive desk top.

"My penlight!" she muttered, suddenly remembering.

"Got it." The cowboy swept up her flashlight, then dived into the cubby after her, switching off the flash.

Allison's elbow cracked against one side of the desk, but she didn't think the men heard, since they were still laughing when they entered the study. She prayed they were loud enough, intoxicated enough, not to overhear the mad rustling emanating from beneath the desk as she and the cowboy silently struggled to twist themselves into the pretzels they needed to be to fit inside the space. The desk was huge, but the hole beneath it was only slightly larger than average, flanked on each side by double rows of drawers.

To accommodate her elaborate wig, Allison twisted her head at an awkward angle down and to one side. She shifted her legs across the cowboy's lap, felt them pressed against his chest by his own drawn-up knees. The butt of one of the toy pistols dug into her calf. He wrapped one arm around her waist, the only place it could go, and his cheek rested against her shoulder.

For the first few seconds they paid no attention to the men chatting in front of the desk. Frantically, the cowboy used his free hand to grab handfuls of Allison's skirts, jerking the material away from the opening of the desk. Allison managed to catch his hat before it rolled out, and she stuffed it behind a pannier frame that had broken and was pushing into her side.

"I'm not at all concerned about the cat burglar," Allison heard Baron Waldheim say. During the ensuing pause, in which she fought to catch a deep breath, she sniffed the scent of cigar smoke.

"You should be," answered a voice that she didn't recognize. "He's skilled and clever. I've heard he can scale walls like a fly."

Allison rolled her eyes toward the head on her shoulder and lifted her brows. "You?" she mouthed silently. A dumb question. Who else could it be? The cowboy shrugged and winked.

Immediately she noticed three things. It was insufferably hot in the cramped space beneath the desk. The cowboy had a hand on her thigh. And his warm breath flowed across her breasts in a tantalizing manner that made her acutely aware of the way they were intimately wound around each other's bodies.

She also realized that he was trapped in a position where he was looking straight down her cleavage, and there was nothing she could do about it. Nor could she do anything about the fact that her lips were less than an inch from his forehead. She was practically kissing him.

The clink of a decanter touching the rim of a glass sounded on the other side of the desk, then the splash of liquid.

The baron puffed noisily on his cigar. "I'm utterly confident of the villa's security."

"I was equally confident, my friend, but the cat burglar managed to relieve me of a small fortune in uncut gems. With a thief in the area, you're taking a large risk hosting tonight's fund-raiser."

The baron launched into a lengthy discussion of the security measures he and the baroness had authorized for tonight's event. While he spoke, Allison's mind raced.

Undoubtedly the man breathing on her breasts, whose lap she was sprawled across, was the cat burglar. Journalists had breathlessly labeled him The Ghost because he came and went without leaving a trace and there was no hint when or where he might next appear. All that could be said with certainty was that wherever the rich played and frolicked, in whatever city, on whatever continent, The Ghost was likely to appear and skillfully help himself to art, hidden cash or, his favorite target, jewels.

"I understand perfectly," the baron said, leaning on the front of the desk. Only inches separated him from Allison. "I don't mean to imply that I'm ignoring the problem or placing myself at unnecessary risk. I have, in fact, engaged the services of Alliance de Securité Internation-

ale to examine the estate's systems and either reassure the
baroness or advise improvements.''

At the mention of the security firm, Allison's attention
focused intently on the baron's conversation.

Then something happened that abruptly shifted her
thoughts.

The cowboy slid his free hand along her thigh, then up
the flat front of her gown to her breast. She glared and
made an almost inaudible hissing sound, and for a second
his hand stopped on her breast, cupping its fullness in se-
ductive warmth. She drew a sharp breath, shocked that her
nipple rose and a wave of heat flowed through her body.

Her own hands, unfortunately, were both trapped. One
arm had been caught behind his shoulders, the other was
pressed hard and immobile against the side of the desk.

She could do absolutely nothing to stop him. She could
not swat him away, and dared not utter a sound.

His hand rose almost to her chin, then she smothered a
gasp as she felt a startling coolness in the cleft between her
breasts. It was an odd sensation. Something cool and slim
sliding between her breasts, with his fingers hot at the top.

Her penlight. Obviously he had watched her remove it
from her bustier, and now he replaced it. Clearly this action which he might justify as thoughtfulness had in-
spired him to take outrageous advantage of their situation.

Gently, his fingertips teased along the plunging line of
her bodice, following the warm curve of her breasts. When
Allison stiffened and narrowed her eyes in a warning glare,
he blinked in a parody of innocence then smiled.

It was the oddest sensation to have a stranger caressing
the swell of her breasts, as peculiarly and as thrillingly
erotic as she suspected he intended it to be. Fighting the
onslaught of the wild-heated sensations he aroused in her
didn't help much. In fact, she became aware that his other

hand lightly stroked her waist and the top of her hip, leaving a maddening tingle.

When his lips brushed across her bare shoulder like a whisper of flame, she almost gasped aloud.

The cowboy had more freedom of movement than she did and he lifted his head slightly. Warm breath flowed over her ear. "Shh."

To her fury, the soft sound contained amusement as well as a warning. Grinding her teeth, Allison tested her range of movement and discovered what she already knew. She was pinned in the corner of this space beneath the desk, rendered totally immobile by her cumbersome wig and the damned panniers. But The Ghost could move his head and one hand.

"You smell like rose-scented soap," he whispered, the sound in her ear only marginally louder than a breath.

Her heart rolled in her chest. She could feel perspiration rising beneath her wig. He was crazy, a risk-taker like none she had previously encountered. Holding her breath, trying desperately to concentrate on the baron and his guest, for any sign of alarm, Allison struggled to ignore the feel of the cowboy's arousal against her legs in his lap.

There was nothing she could do as he nudged aside an auburn curl with his nose, then caught her earlobe gently between his teeth. She drew a sharp breath as he sucked at her earlobe and ran his tongue along the edge. Before this moment, Allison would not have believed that an earlobe could be so sensitive, or that a man's tongue there could be so wildly exciting.

But between his fingertips caressing the tops of her breasts, his tongue stroking her earlobe, his warm breath in her ear and the crush of his body, he was driving her crazy. As, she suspected, he intended to.

"Stop that!" She moved her lips against his cheek, forming the words without sound. He wasn't wearing cologne, but she too could smell the soap he used. The fragrance was expensive, musky, strongly masculine. An exciting scent that reeled through her senses.

"So then I...did you hear something?" the baron asked, only a few feet from where they struggled beneath the desk.

The cowboy, clearly a man who courted danger and liked living on the edge, chose that moment to turn his face so his lips were now merely a fraction of an inch from Allison's. He touched his tongue to her bottom lip, and, feeling frantic inside, she closed her eyes, trembling and unable to believe he was doing this.

Acutely aware of the baron standing mere feet away, she didn't make a sound as the cowboy explored her mouth with his tongue, teasing her, making love to her. When she tried to push him away with her own tongue, she discovered to her horror that all she accomplished was to intensify the arousal she was pretending to ignore.

Then the cowboy kissed her. His mouth was full and surprisingly soft when it claimed hers. His hand slipped to lightly cup one breast, and he kissed her deliberately, thoroughly, leisurely. When she struggled to find an inch to pull back from him, his hand moved from her breast and he caught her chin, positioning her mouth firmly for his exploration.

As if he made love to women beneath a desk every day, as if he had planned it this way, he nipped her lower lip playfully, then covered her lips fully with his own and kissed her so deeply and so passionately that for one crazy instant she thought she might faint. Whoever the cowboy was, he was no stranger to kissing. If he was half as skilled at burglary as he was at kissing, it no longer surprised her that he hadn't been caught.

Leaving her shaken to her toes, he dropped his hand from her face to her thigh and slid his fingers beneath the voluminous folds of her gown. Warm fingertips followed her stockings to the strip of skin at the top then played there at a teasing game of advance and withdrawal that made her feel wild inside.

On one level, Allison was furious that he was taking advantage of her and their perilous situation, knowing she didn't dare make an audible protest. On another, utterly helpless level, what this stranger was doing was crazily, dangerously exciting. He seemed to sense exactly what she would find most arousing, seemed to know her trembling body as if he were following a map to her most sensitive and vulnerable points.

Because her arms were pinned and she couldn't move her head, all she could do was helplessly submit while he lightly explored and teased, then shifted intensity to drink ardent, intoxicating kisses from her mouth. It was the wildest, most erotic thing that had ever happened to her.

"I love the taste and the feel of you," he murmured huskily against her lips, speaking in a normal tone.

"You idiot!" Allison gasped. Her eyes widened and darted to the desk opening.

They were seconds away from being discovered, minutes from being arrested.

CHAPTER TWO

THE COWBOY'S THUMB traced the contour of her lips, and he peered into her dismayed eyes as if trying to see past her mask. "The baron and his friend left several minutes ago," he murmured in a husky voice.

"What? You bastard!" Allison couldn't believe that she'd been so rapt, so lost in his kisses that she hadn't noticed the baron's departure. Embarrassment and anger flamed on her cheeks.

The cowboy laughed as she dug an elbow into his side and struggled fiercely to untangle herself and crawl out from beneath the desk. Once she was on her feet, a quick inspection revealed that one pannier hung like a broken wing from her left hip, her wig tilted precariously, and, what irritated her most, a rosy flush of arousal glowed across her breasts.

Swearing in three languages, Allison furiously adjusted her wig and the bodice of her gown. She checked the snaps on her domino then pressed the mask firmly across her eyes and nose.

When the cowboy straightened beside her, shaking his head at the crushed state of his hat, she whirled on him and would have slapped the arrogant smile from his face except he caught her wrist and used her momentum to pull her close to him.

The shock of feeling herself pressed to the hard heat of his body momentarily paralyzed Allison. When his gaze dropped to her lips and it appeared that he might kiss her again, she jerked her wrist free of his grip and backed away from him.

"You... you..." For the first time in years, she was stuttering. None of the friends who marveled at her coolness under fire would have recognized her. "What in the hell were you thinking of! We could have been—"

His laugh was low and genuinely amused. "Just passing the time in a pleasant way, *chérie.*" Still smiling, he sat on the edge of the desk and folded his arms loosely across his chest. "I want to see you again."

"Well, I don't want to see you!" Turning, she glared at the Rubens, remembering his comment about a possible pressure plate.

"We need to discuss our relationship."

"*We* don't have a relationship," she snapped, leaning to peer behind the frame. He had a nerve the size of Gibraltar.

"Ah, but we do. We're geographically incompatible. We have a territorial dispute."

Lifting her skirts to her thighs, she found a length of industrial tape and removed it from the pocket at the top of her stockings. To annoy her, the cowboy whistled softly as her long legs came into view. But then he'd felt along the length of them, and he knew about the pocket and the tape, of course. She scowled fiercely, then stepped forward to examine the items on top of the baron's desk. It was only a guess, but she thought the phone directory would approximate the weight of the framed Rubens. The trick lay in switching one for the other without tripping the pressure alarm.

As if he had read her mind, the cowboy nodded. "The directory looks about right. What are the chances that you'll break the circuit?"

"None," she said sharply, irritated by a question that implied she was a novice.

"If you have any doubts," he commented, watching her heft the directory in her hand to judge its weight, "I'll be happy to make the switch." After pausing a beat, he added in a pleasant drawl, "After all, I was planning to do it myself, anyway, since I was here first."

Allison lifted her head with a frown and studied the challenge gleaming through the eyeholes in his domino. To test him, she switched from French to English. "I see your point about a territorial dispute," she conceded after a minute.

His English flowed as flawlessly as his French. "As it appears we're both working this area," he replied, "we need to discuss the situation or we're likely to encounter each other in this same situation again." He continued in German. "Tomorrow. Lunch in Cannes at the Hotel Bonaparte across from the little park. Do you know it?"

Allison nodded slowly. "I know it." Tucked away on a side street, the Hotel Bonaparte was a perfect choice for a discreet meeting. "It will have to be late," she answered in Spanish. "I have a morning appointment in Monte Carlo. We'll meet in the park at, say, one-thirty?"

"Agreed. How will I recognize you?" His gaze steadied on her mask, then dropped to a long, lazy sweep across her breasts. She told herself that his Spanish carried an accent, but she admitted her judgment might be biased by wishful thinking.

"You won't." Her jaw tightened and she unfurled her fan to cover her cleavage. "I'll recognize you." He said something but she didn't understand, and it made her furious that he'd one-upped her. "I don't speak Russian," she said between her teeth.

His grin raised a flush of pink to her cheeks. "I said that I doubt you'll recognize me."

Time was passing. Allison didn't think the baron would return to his study, but he could, and she was aware of that. What she wanted now was to get out of here, descend the cliff and return home to analyze everything that had happened tonight.

She nodded at the Rubens. "How do you propose we decide who takes the painting?" This was a critical moment. If the cowboy insisted on first rights, she would have to make some quick decisions. One thing she had already decided: she'd rather trip the alarm than let him walk off with the painting. That wasn't going to happen. The Rubens was priceless.

The cowboy studied her for a lengthy moment during which Allison examined him, too. She was tall, but he was taller by a good three inches. The domino concealed his upper face, but the mask couldn't disguise the fact that he would be a very good-looking man without it. Still disturbed by his kisses, she didn't inspect his mouth too closely. Instead, she tried to decide if his hair, dark and on the longish side, was a wig or his own. If he wore a wig, the wig was expensive and well-made. She couldn't be certain.

As one would expect from a man who had probably climbed three stories to reach the stone balcony opening into the study, his body was taut and muscular, a classic wedge shape that tapered to athletic hips and thighs. His hands, which she had come to know very well, were tanned, square shaped, and ended in long, elegant fingers.

And he thought she wouldn't recognize him? Allison smiled. She would spot him within three minutes of entering the park.

When the challenging silence had stretched into discomfort, the cowboy suddenly swept low in a bow and twirled his hat in a flourish toward the Rubens. "I cede to beauty and charm, *chérie*. This prize is yours. The next, should we again meet professionally, is mine."

Suspicion narrowed Allison's gaze, but she accepted the offer with alacrity. "Your gallantry and generosity take my breath away, monsieur."

Withdrawing the penlight from between her breasts, she turned and pushed back her cumbersome skirts before she directed a thin, intense beam behind the gilt frame. He was right. The painting was protected by a pressure-plate alarm.

"Would you hand me the directory?" she called in a low voice.

When he didn't respond, she turned with a frown toward the dim light shining down on Baron Waldheim's desk. The cowboy had been standing there a minute ago; now he wasn't.

Slowly, Allison scanned the room. The only movement came from the draperies fluttering gently in the moonlight streaming past the balcony.

The sobering thought crossed her mind that he was very, very good. She had not heard a footfall, not a rustle. It was as if he had simply vanished into the soft, moonlit air.

Glancing at her watch, she realized she was running seriously behind schedule. Thrusting the cowboy out of her mind, she worked swiftly but meticulously, concentrating fully on easing the baron's phone directory onto the pressure plate as she eased the painting off. Once that was accomplished, she lowered the painting to the table conveniently set below it. Holding the phone directory in place, she taped it against the wall. Not breathing, she stepped back and stared until she was certain the tape would hold the directory against the pressure plate.

There was satisfaction in observing her success, in realizing the fruits of seemingly endless hours of practice.

A slight smile of triumph curved her lips before she raised her brocade skirts and fit the Rubens into the harness suspended from her waist. When she was certain the painting was secure, she flashed her penlight beneath the desk to double-check that she and the cowboy had left no incriminating traces behind them.

Next, she propped up the broken pannier as best she could, then dropped in on the ball for an hour before strolling through all the rooms on the first two floors of the villa. Finally, she exited the way she had arrived, from the back of the house. At the chestnut tree, she changed clothing, shifted the harness holding the painting to her back, clipped the plastic bag containing her costume to her waist, and edged over the cliff.

It wasn't until she had stowed the Rubens inside a false car door panel and was backing her Renault out of the dark copse that she let herself remember the cowboy and his outrageous behavior beneath the baron's desk.

A grin curved her lips, then she laughed out loud. What a rogue he was. He had kissed and teased her, but he hadn't really crossed a line that she couldn't forgive. In retrospect, she could even view his actions as a boyish prank, dangerous at the time, but rather charming from a distance.

While driving down the twisting road, she idly wondered who he was. Actually, and she hated to admit this, she was intrigued enough that she looked forward to seeing him again tomorrow.

It had been a long time since any man had piqued her interest. Nine months, to be exact.

Suddenly, Jeffrey DeWilde returned to her thoughts. She wished there was some way to strike out, to revenge herself and cause him just a fraction of the pain he had caused her.

FOR HER EIGHT O'CLOCK meeting with the baron and baroness, Allison chose a Dior suit of crisp white linen, worn over a sunshine yellow silk blouse. She had dressed her hair in a businesslike French twist and wore no jewelry except small pearl earrings.

Leaning forward, she placed a thick report on Baron Waldheim's desk, then relaxed into her chair and sipped coffee from a gold-rimmed china cup. When she thought about the romantic tussle that had occurred beneath that desk only hours ago, she almost laughed aloud.

Baroness Waldheim gazed at the stack of pages and released a sigh. "When on earth did you find time to write your report?" She still wore her ball costume, and her eyelids drooped with fatigue. Lifting both arms, she removed a diamond tiara from her graying head and placed it on the small table beside her chair.

"I wrote most of the report earlier in the week, then finished it last night and early this morning," Allison answered.

The baron, who had changed into a dark green silk dressing gown, glared at the spot on the wall where the Rubens had hung. "I don't believe it," he muttered. Pushing back from his desk, he stood and ripped down the tape and phone directory.

Somewhere, Allison knew, a silent alarm was sending a signal to a security service in Monte Carlo. Earlier, she had phoned the service and warned them this would happen. Almost instantly the phone rang on the baron's desk. He answered and barked confirmation into the mouthpiece, then handed the telephone to Allison.

"This is Mademoiselle Ames," she said quietly. "No, you don't need to dispatch someone to the estate. Speak to Monsieur Gris, he'll explain."

Baron Waldheim returned to his chair and dropped his head in his hands. He stared down at Allison's thick report. Finally, he raised his eyes. "The guards at the gate and at the door swore that no one entered the premises without an invitation."

"They're wrong. I did." She didn't mention the cowboy, or The Ghost, as she believed him to be. Why she said nothing was something to ponder later. She hesitated, then added, "If I managed to get past the security guards, others may have done so, also."

The baroness turned the Rubens between her long fingers, idly picking at the string and brown paper in which Allison had wrapped the painting. "I would have sworn you couldn't steal this painting. How did you do it?"

"I can't tell you that," Allison demurred. "Suffice it to say that once I gained entry into the house, the actual theft was child's play." She looked at both of them. "You were lucky. I'm sure you're aware that a cat burglar is working the area. If he'd reached the painting first..." She shrugged the lightly padded shoulders of her suit jacket. Their faces confirmed that her point was made; she didn't need to belabor the issue by revealing how close they had come to actually losing the Rubens.

Rising, Baroness Waldheim opened the package, then rehung the painting. She touched her husband's shoulder before she returned to the chair beside Allison. "My husband and I are tired, and we're shocked that you succeeded in stealing the target item. We'll need time to read and digest your report. Could you give us a brief summary of your findings and recommendations?"

"Certainly."

For the next hour Allison shocked them again by relating the security infractions and omissions she had observed, and they both winced as they contemplated the expense of the additional measures she recommended.

At the end of her recitation, the baron exchanged a long look with his wife, then sighed heavily. He waved a hand and watched it drop back to the desktop. "All right, please proceed. Make the arrangements for the measures you've recommended."

"I'm sorry, but my job is only to test existing systems," Allison reminded him. She nodded at her report. "I've included a list of contractors and installation experts. I can attest to the discretion and excellence of each. Any of them can supply or build the devices and systems I've recommended. They may, in fact, suggest additional measures."

The baron and baroness rose to their feet as Allison did. "Thank you, Mademoiselle Ames," the baron said, managing a smile. "This has been an interesting and invaluable experience." He glanced at the Rubens from the corner of his eye and shook his head. "When may we expect to see the bill for your services?"

Allison returned his tired smile. "Soon. My secretary will deliver an invoice later this week," she said as he walked her to the double doors of his study. A servant waited in the corridor to show her out.

"Will I groan when I see the amount?" the baron inquired, bringing her hand to his lips.

"Oh, yes." Allison laughed and her blue eyes twinkled. "I hope you haven't forgotten the bonus in the event I succeeded in stealing the target item." The bonus was a standard feature of her contract. "But even with my bonus, the fee will be much, much less than replacing the painting would have cost."

Baron Waldheim smiled, his weariness almost vanishing. "The Rubens is irreplaceable, and so are you, young lady." He pressed her hand between both of his. "The Baroness and I are grateful for your stunning demonstration and for your recommendations. We thank you."

Her eyes sobered. "Don't delay upgrading your system. And don't forget to fence the cliff face. I advise letting the Dobermans patrol between the fence and the cliff."

They chatted for another minute, then Allison glanced at her watch. She had just enough time to alter her appearance, drive the Corniche to Cannes, and meet The Ghost in the park across from the Hotel Bonaparte.

PAUL COURTWALD ARRIVED twenty minutes ahead of the appointed meeting time. Well-honed instinct warned that his mystery woman would arrive early, too; as a professional, she undoubtedly thought much like he did, which was one of the reasons she had captivated his interest and his curiosity.

"It's a lovely day, isn't it?" he inquired, smiling and instigating a conversation with a couple standing near the gate to the park. Since he would have wagered his professional reputation that they were American tourists, he addressed them in English and laid on a heavy French accent.

The woman stared. "I swear, you're the first Frenchman who's said a civil word to us! Isn't he, Fred? Isn't he the first and only one?" she demanded of her husband.

"Have you viewed the Navarre Fountain?" Paul inquired, nodding toward the park's leafy interior. "It's said you haven't seen Cannes if you haven't made a wish at the Navarre Fountain.''

The couple took the bait and together they entered the park, a chatting threesome instead of Paul arriving by himself. Once inside, sauntering alongside the American couple, he casually scanned the grounds.

It wasn't unheard of to borrow a child for a surveillance assignment, but his mystery woman was too experienced to bring a child to an actual meeting. Therefore, he immediately dismissed the young mothers strolling or playing with toddlers.

But a baby wasn't out of the question, he decided, watching a nursemaid pushing a baby carriage. He studied the woman without appearing to do so. No, she was too plump in the face and legs. If he knew nothing else about his mystery woman, he did know the curve of her legs and the shape of her luscious body.

Taking a seat on the lip of the fountain, he let the spray dampen his hair, which was pulled back into a short ponytail, and listened absently to the American couple bicker over the wishes they wanted to make while they searched their pockets for spare change.

All the while he examined the few people in the park who appeared to be alone, although he didn't believe she would arrive alone any more than he had. On the other hand, she might assume that he would assume that she wouldn't arrive alone and try to foil him by doing it that way.

He grinned at the tortuous path his thoughts followed, enjoying the challenge his mystery woman presented.

Among the people alone, he noticed two elderly ladies who seemed to be gravitating toward each other. A middle-aged man sat alone on a bench, and he spotted a woman on the grass, reading and nibbling a pastry. The woman was too skinny, although she continued to glance up from her book as if expecting someone. He moved to the other side of the American couple for a better view before he concluded her legs were too thin and her chin too pointed.

"Do you live in Cannes?" the American woman asked brightly. She'd been babbling since they'd sat on the edge of the fountain as if she hadn't spoken to anyone in weeks. This worked well. To an observer, it would appear that Paul and the couple were definitely together.

"Not far from here," he answered vaguely.

"I thought you were American until you spoke. Probably a college basketball player." She ran a glance over his University of Southern California T-shirt and ragged cutoff jeans and smiled at the baseball cap he had turned backward on his head. She didn't notice the lifts in his shoes, didn't know that he wore dark contact lenses or that he had thinned the hair on his legs and arms to create a more youthful appearance. He'd applied a couple of pimples to his chin for the same purpose.

While they talked, he continuously scanned the people entering the park or strolling along the pathways or sitting on the benches. He even studied the men, although he didn't believe for an instant that his curvaceous mystery lady could convincingly impersonate a male. A Catholic sister caught his eye and he almost laughed aloud, thinking he had her, but he was wrong. When the sister fully faced him, he realized she was too old and her face was too wide.

He checked his watch as the minute hand passed one-thirty. She had to be in the park now; he could dismiss anyone who entered from this point forward. Why he thought she would play fair and be on time, he couldn't have said, but he sensed that she would, and he was a man who lived by his instincts.

Standing and stretching, he slowly, intently examined everyone in the small park, even those he had previously dismissed. Absently he fingered the small gold hoop in his ear. The earring gave the impression of piercing his lobe, though it didn't. It did, however, pinch like hell.

He spotted her at almost the exact moment that recognition flared in her eyes. They stared at each other and she nodded slightly before she moved toward the entrance facing the Hotel Bonaparte. Damn, he thought, frowning. She'd been right in front of his eyes for fifteen minutes.

"Excuse me," he said to the American couple. "I've been waiting for my grandmother, and I just saw her."

He had underestimated her. Several times he had considered the two elderly ladies but had dismissed them each time. Irritated with himself, he followed and watched her lean convincingly on a wooden cane, then shuffle across the street. She moved slowly, tossing glares at the cars she passed, walking as if her hip pained her. It was a performance calculated for his benefit and Paul knew it. She was very, very convincing.

Walking up beside her, he opened the door to the Hotel Bonaparte. "Arriving alone was clever. I didn't expect that. But your hands are too youthful," he commented, searching for something to criticize. "And the sweater gave you away."

"Older women have circulation problems," she murmured, stepping inside the lobby. She sounded indifferent to his critique, but her eyes narrowed in annoyance. "Even on a warm day they may feel chilly."

"Agreed. And just for that reason, they would not perspire."

His comment raised a ghost of a smile as she conceded his point. "How rude of you to notice." She didn't pull away when he lightly touched her elbow, guiding her toward the entrance to the restaurant. "I made you when you stood and stretched," she remarked. "Then the lifts in your shoes became obvious." She glanced at him. "Plus, without facial hair, it's difficult for a man to disguise his mouth."

Ah, so she remembered his mouth, did she? Hiding a smile, he gave a false name to the maître d' and followed his mystery woman to a secluded booth. Locally famed as a trysting spot, the restaurant at the Hotel Bonaparte positioned its tables with the utmost discretion. No one in one booth could see or overhear the occupants of another. Dim romantic lighting softened the plastic wrinkles on his mystery woman's face. Had the wrinkles been genuine, he would have looked at her and glimpsed the beauty she once had been. Instead, knowing they were as false as his pimples, he wished he could see her without the stage makeup. He suspected she was a dazzler.

Paul ordered from the wine list, then, when the steward had departed, he lifted a hand and began ticking down his fingers.

"You're American, but you've spent several years in Europe."

"Justify," she demanded, crossing her arms on the tabletop. She gazed at him with amusement twinkling in her eyes, but also, he was pleased to see, confirmation.

"You didn't learn to speak flawless French, German and Spanish in a classroom. You've had hands-on experience. I'm guessing American because there's a directness about you, a willingness to meet a person's eyes, and you're obviously self-motivated, ambitious and daring, qualities I associate with Americans."

"Go on."

He ticked down another finger. "You live in the area, you're not just passing through." When her steady gaze challenged him, he explained. "Very few tourists have heard of this hotel, and then only by accident, but you knew it at once. You also knew the layout of the Waldheim villa, and where the Rubens was hung. A novice or a newcomer would have targeted the guests' jewels. They wouldn't have known about the Rubens or where it was located."

"The same could be said of you. But it wouldn't be true."

He ignored the remark and lowered another finger. "You're unmarried—no tan line around your ring finger. I'd say you're in your late twenties, but that's strictly a guess. You're a careful planner, but resourceful when you need to be. You're athletic, that's obvious. You enjoy strenuous sports, and you work out regularly."

"Justify."

"You entered the estate by climbing the cliff." When she lifted an eyebrow, he laughed. "I used your pitons on the way down."

A gleam of admiration flashed in her eyes. "Which you did for the mere hell of it, because you entered through the front door and you could have departed the same way."

The conviction in her voice startled the smile off his lips, and his eyes narrowed. "How did you guess that?"

She reached into a worn tapestry purse and removed a cream-colored square of paper. "Here's your invitation. I lifted it from your vest last night, Mr. Courtwald. You were a bona fide guest at the ball. I think you entered the study from the balcony because you weren't familiar with the villa and didn't want to risk wandering in areas where you weren't supposed to be while you searched for Waldheim's study. I suspect you did know it was on the third floor, however. I doubt you make a move without first doing extensive research.''

In a reflex action, he lifted his hands to his chest, where the pockets on his vest would have been. Damn. A heavy scowl lowered his eyebrows. He'd been so intoxicated by a few kisses, so amused by finding the Rubens, then letting her steal it and walking away empty-handed, that he hadn't missed the invitation. He hadn't committed such a glaring error in ten years.

She raised a hand and pulled down one finger. ''You've been in the area for a while, but it's not your natural habitat. You've used your time to familiarize yourself with targets and safe places, but you've only recently gone back to work.''

He stared at her, pulling his gaze away only when the waiter arrived to take their order.

She didn't continue speaking until they were alone again. ''I think you're English, but I won't swear to that one. You were educated in Germany, though. German and English are the languages that came most easily to you, but you've traveled extensively and you have a gift for accents.''

''What else?'' he asked tersely. The game wasn't as pleasant when he sat on the receiving end.

''Despite looking like a student right now, I'd say you're thirty, give or take a couple of years on either side. You're also unmarried, and also athletic. You're a risk-taker and an opportunist. You come from a privileged background.'' Her voice held a faint note of surprise when she mentioned his background.

''Justify.''

''There's the invitation, for one thing. The baron and baroness don't invite peasants to their fund-raisers, and

only large contributors were invited to last night's bash. I
don't doubt that your profession earns enough that you
can donate generously, but the guest list was compiled
from old-line society names. That says the Courtwalds are
socially prominent, and wealthy enough to be regulars on
fund-raiser lists."

It galled him that she knew his name. He should have
disposed of the invitation the instant he passed security at
the front door of the villa. It was a stupid mistake.

The makeup she wore had required a couple of hours to
apply, and she'd mentioned a morning appointment. That
meant she probably had not had time to research his family name. But she would. He knew that as well as he knew
her discovery of his name changed everything.

She ticked down another finger. "You're the jewel thief
they call The Ghost. I suspect Paul Courtwald's movements will align precisely with The Ghost's activities." She
shrugged. "Paul Courtwald appears in Rio de Janeiro and
so does The Ghost. Paul Courtwald decides to try his luck
at the tables in Monte Carlo, and The Ghost appears in
Monaco."

There was no smile in his eyes now. "So how do you
plan to use these assumptions?"

Leaning against the tucked leather back of the booth,
she studied him as the waiter served their lunch. "I don't
know," she said finally. Her gaze flicked to his mouth.
"I've been thinking about the problem all morning."

He had been thinking about her, too, but in an entirely
different regard. He'd been remembering the satiny feel of
the skin above her stockings, recalling the heat and sweet
taste of her mouth and the full curve of her breast. What
had begun as an impulsive prank had ended in full-blown
arousal. Remembering made him shift uncomfortably, as

if the temperature in the restaurant had suddenly risen several degrees.

Now the power had shifted. She had the upper hand, and he didn't like it. Aside from the very real threat she posed, she had taken control of this meeting, and he was placed in the uncharacteristic position of reacting instead of instigating.

She smiled, and he realized she had been watching him for several minutes. "The earring and ponytail are nice touches. You really do look like a college student. If I didn't know better, I'd guess you were about twenty years old."

"Do you know better?" he challenged. "You're just guessing."

"I'll know for certain by this time tomorrow," she said softly. There wasn't a nuance of doubt in her tone. "I'll know everything there is to know about Paul Court-wald."

"You won't find much information."

"We'll see. This wine is very good, by the way."

Leaning back, he tried to appear relaxed. "What shall I call you? You have the advantage, *mademoiselle*. You know my name, but . . . ?"

"Nice try," she said, smiling across the table.

"I have to call you something."

"Why?" The roots of her lashes were pale; she was a blonde, he decided, examining the gray wig she wore. The information was paltry compared to a name, damn it. He needed to level the playing field by learning her name.

"I'd like to know your name in case we run into each other. It could be by accident or by design," he added smoothly. "Which do you prefer?"

She stirred sugar into her coffee. "Aren't you worried that I'll expose you as The Ghost?"

"That would be...inconvenient. Is that your intention?"

She gazed into his eyes, and it was an effort to appear unconcerned. He was, of course, prepared for the possibility of problems with the authorities. Should suspicion focus on him, there would be no record of Paul Courtwald being in Rio de Janeiro, as she had put it, at the same time as The Ghost. Still, he wasn't eager to call attention to himself regardless of how well he had covered his activities. No one was so good or so careful that he didn't make a few mistakes. Frankly, he wasn't eager to invite that kind of test.

"I should turn you in," she said finally, speaking slowly, thoughtfully. "Perhaps an anonymous tip..."

Hearing a hint of indecision, Paul suddenly knew that she wouldn't. The tension eased out of his shoulders and thighs. "Have I mentioned that you're the sexiest grandmother I ever saw?"

A startled look widened her eyes, then she laughed. "You're outrageous, do you know that? Are you ever serious?"

"Oh, yes. I'm serious about wanting to know your name."

"It's Allison."

"Allison what?"

"For the moment, just Allison."

"Is Allison your real name?" When she didn't answer, he heaved an exaggerated sigh. "All right. What will you do with the painting, Just Allison?" If he could learn the line of people she worked through, he could learn a lot about her. Loyalty was for sale. All he needed was the name of one fence.

For an instant it appeared as if she didn't understand the question, then she looked away. "You know I'm not going to answer that question." She wasn't going to give up anything.

"Do you consider yourself a fair person?" he asked in a teasing voice. Her mouth was fuller than she'd drawn it last night, he noticed. He'd thought she had full lips when he kissed her. Now he knew for certain that she did.

Her head snapped up and she glared at him. "I'm the fairest person you're likely to ever meet."

"Then tell me your full name. Let's equalize the threat. Right now, you say you can persuade the authorities that Paul Courtwald and The Ghost have a suspicious facility for appearing in the same places. Doesn't it seem fair to give me the same power over you? How can we trust each other otherwise?"

She laughed, a charming, light sound. "Sorry, cowboy, I'm not handing anyone the power to incriminate me in anything." Her smile gradually faded, and she studied him seriously. "Tell me something. Was I correct that you're not married? Or do you have a wife and family stashed somewhere?"

He raised an eyebrow. "I'm not married, never have been." After a brief hesitation, he decided it would do no harm to mention his family. She'd find out, anyway. "My father is Stanford Courtwald."

She released a low whistle. "Courtwald Industries. I just made the connection." She stared at him. "Mining and development. Steel. Construction. International real estate holdings. What the hell are you doing pilfering from your family's friends?"

His gaze hardened. "That's really none of your concern, Just Allison."

"Have you thought about the scandal you'll cause your family if you're caught?" Suddenly, she sounded genuinely angry. "Do you have any idea what you'll put them through? The embarrassment? The humiliation? The tabloids will have a field day ripping apart you and your poor family."

What kind of button had he pressed? She was getting angrier by the minute. He could see it happening—sparks flashed in her eyes, circles of color brightened her cheeks.

"Allison, wait!"

But she was sliding out of the booth, reaching for her cane. To his astonishment, she looked as if she wanted to hit him with her walking stick.

"We haven't settled anything. We need to finish talking."

She whirled in the aisle and glared at him. "If I want to talk to you, I'll send you a message."

By the time he summoned the waiter, paid their check and dashed out of the hotel doors, she had vanished.

"Damn it!"

What the hell had happened in there? As he strode toward a rented Porsche, he pulled off the painful gold earring and jammed it in his pocket.

He didn't calm down until he was whizzing along the Corniche, taking the curves at dizzying speed. Eyes on the road in front of him, he didn't spare a glance for the sparkling Mediterranean or the villas climbing the cliffs to his left.

If and when she decided to talk to him again, she would send him a message, would she? She was that confident that she was in control and could find him at will? Well, he'd give Just Allison a little surprise.

God, she was a fascinating woman. And it wasn't just the mystery about her that intrigued him. She was mentally quick, a careful observer, and his equal in a solitary profession that could get lonely. His eyebrows rose when he realized he had never before thought about the loneliness inherent in the life he had chosen. It was more pleasant to recall that her disguise hadn't hidden her sensuality. She really had made a sexy grandmother.

Grinning, his optimism returning, he stepped on the gas, eager to return to Monte Carlo and arrange his little surprise.

CHAPTER THREE

SURPRISE DIDN'T BEGIN to describe Allison's reaction when she opened her mail two days later and discovered a note from Paul Courtwald. She stared at the creamy ivory envelope in profound shock. How could he possibly have discovered her last name?

Carrying the mail out onto a balcony overlooking Europe's richest coastline, she sat at a wrought iron table, took another sip of her morning coffee and, frowning, read his note again.

Dear Allison,
I apologize for whatever distress I may have caused you. Since we didn't discuss solutions to future encounters, it's urgent that we meet again.
   Wednesday. Cosmopolite. Same time.

P.

Several items impressed her about the note. He didn't have any idea why she had gotten so upset. In fairness, how could he? Second, he correctly reminded her that they had resolved nothing. Third, this time he had chosen a long-established restaurant situated behind the Monte Carlo railway station. Due to location and a low-priced menu, it was unlikely they would encounter anyone either of them knew. Or perhaps this was merely a meeting site and he didn't intend to have lunch.

Most shocking was that he had addressed the note to Allison Ames at her correct home address. Once he had her name, the address was no mystery, of course. She was listed in the principality's telephone book. But how had he discovered her last name, and how had he accomplished it so swiftly? According to the postmark, he had mailed this note early yesterday morning.

Lifting her face to the morning sunshine, enjoying the cool breeze fluttering the hem of her silk wrapper, she considered the problem. No immediate answer leapt to mind. However, she knew she'd figure it out eventually. Grudgingly, her admiration for Paul Courtwald's abilities rose another notch.

After reading the rest of her personal mail, she glanced through the newspaper, intending merely to browse the headlines. But an item in the business section caught her attention, as the name DeWilde always did, and she read the article slowly and carefully, feeling a flush burn her cheeks.

After Grace DeWilde had left both her husband, Jeffrey, and her position within the DeWilde empire, the corporation had wobbled a bit, but despite rumor and speculation, the writer of the article suggested that DeWilde's now appeared to be operating smoothly again.

According to the article, Grace DeWilde was currently living in San Francisco, about as far from Jeffrey as she could get, and had opened a full-service bridal shop there. The DeWilde Corporation practically held a monopoly on the bridal wear industry with its five international stores, and though Grace DeWilde was a woman of enormous charisma and expertise, her store did not, in the writer's view, pose a serious business threat to the retail giant.

Leaning back in her chair, Allison rubbed her temples. If the writer was correct, then Jeffrey rolled on unscathed. His wife might be gone, but his wealth, position and his corporation remained solid and unaffected. Moreover, she doubted Jeffrey DeWilde would remain unattached for long. He was attractive, sophisticated, wealthy and charming. Women would line up to apply for the position left open by the departure of Grace DeWilde. Any other man would undoubtedly revel in his newfound freedom and eligibility.

But Jeffrey loved his wife.

"Damn it!"

It wasn't that Jeffrey was a man who claimed to love his wife while jumping from one affair to another. Allison would have wagered everything she owned that he had not violated his marriage with any other woman before her. And it wouldn't have happened with her except that she had pursued him, and they happened to meet at a moment when both were particularly vulnerable and needed someone or something to fill a lack that most likely neither could have defined or explained.

But the affair had been based on false assumptions. Jeffrey had assumed that she was accustomed to affairs; maybe he imagined that everyone her age jumped in and out of bed on a whim. For all she knew, he could be right. But he was dead wrong in her case.

For her part, Allison had assumed that he was experiencing serious problems in his marriage to Grace and was looking for someone to love him, someone to admire and praise his success in business and in life.

How could she have guessed that the last thing he wanted was for her to fall in love with him? Or that it would appall him when he discovered she had known from the first who he was, that he was *the* Jeffrey DeWilde? How could she have guessed that her praise and admiration of his success had been the reason behind his periods of coldness? Too late she had realized that he wanted to be Jeffrey the man and not Jeffrey the international corporation. And last of all, she couldn't possibly have intuited that a man who allowed himself to be seduced by the respect and admiration in a young woman's eyes could possibly be in love with his wife.

In retrospect, she had met Jeffrey DeWilde during a period of great confusion in his life and during a need for stability in hers.

Standing abruptly, Allison moved to the edge of the balcony and leaned on the stone railing, frowning at the yachts and luxury liners moored in the harbor. She lifted her gaze to the hazy line where sea met sky, then closed her eyes.

It still hurt to think about Jeffrey. It hurt when she drove past DeWilde's Monte Carlo on the way to her office. It hurt to read about a wedding where the bride's gown was described as a DeWilde creation. It hurt to remember Le Bristol hotel in Paris, or La Lune Ascendant in Montmartre, their favorite restaurant. It hurt to know that she had been nothing more than a tiny ripple on Jeffrey's pond, while he had created a tsunami in hers.

Allison had pursued Jeffrey, that was true. But it was also true that he had been easy to catch, she thought defensively, and he had used her. Maybe he had needed her to bolster his ego, or maybe she'd been an unknowing weapon in a war with his wife. Maybe he'd used her as a diversion or a midlife fling. Whatever the reason—and she doubted that she would ever learn the truth—once she confessed her love for him, he had discarded her like a spoiled peach.

It continually gnawed at her that Jeffrey had gone on with his life as if Allison Ames had never existed, as if she had made no impression in his life whatsoever. Unemo-

tional, unflappable, unscathed, that was Jeffrey De-
Wilde.

It wasn't fair that he had turned her world upside down
and hurt her deeply, but she had made no impact on his
life. She longed to even the scales. She yearned to do
something that would say, You can't do this to me. You
have to suffer a little, too.

Lifting a shaking hand, Allison rubbed her forehead. It
wasn't like her to be so obsessed. Why couldn't she get it
through her head that it was over with Jeffrey? Why
couldn't she simply forget him and move on with her life?
Wishing for revenge simply wasn't like her.

Spinning from the balcony rail, she returned to the table and picked up the note from Paul Courtwald. The
Ghost didn't know it, but he had arrived at a perfect time,
just when she needed something or someone to challenge
and engage her mind. He certainly did that. And not only
her mind, she thought with a rueful smile, recalling his
skilled touch and teasing hands. Paul Courtwald did
strange things to her body, too.

Thinking about him, she dressed for work, then drove
to her office in the Monte Carlo *quartier*. This was the
section of Monaco that housed the ornate Casino and the
luxury boutiques that offered five-hundred-dollar scarves
and couture fashion. Unavoidably, Allison's route took her
past Dior, Chanel, Henri & Co. and DeWilde's.

As always, her gaze was drawn to the elegant facade of
the DeWilde store. The peach-and-navy exterior hinted at
the exquisite jewels, gowns and bridal accessories artfully
arrayed on the other side of the brass and leaded-glass
doors. For the curious, a piece of jewelry from the De-
Wilde family's famed personal collection was on display
inside each DeWilde store. At the Monte Carlo branch it
was a tiara once owned and worn by Catherine the Great,

Empress of Russia, and equally priceless pieces could be found at the DeWilde stores in London, Paris, Sydney and Manhattan.

The DeWildes had it all, wealth, success, international respect. Unquestionably, fortune had smiled on Jeffrey's family. Unlike Allison's family, no public scandal tarnished them. If there was a skeleton in the DeWilde closet, no one knew about it. No DeWilde had to apologize for being a DeWilde.

Unreasonably angry, her thoughts firmly in the past, Allison wheeled her Renault into her parking space, narrowly averting a collision with Monique, her secretary, who was backing out at the same time Allison pulled in.

Monique rolled down her window. "The coffee's made," she called cheerfully. "I'm on my way to the *pâtisserie* for croissants. Or would you prefer something else?"

"Croissants will be fine." Allison's hands shook on the wheel. It wasn't like her to be careless, wasn't like her not to pay attention to her driving. It wasn't like her to let a man prey upon her mind like this.

But she had loved Jeffrey, she thought helplessly, staring at a palm tree in front of her bumper. If only he hadn't ended their affair by trying to give her a piece of jewelry. She couldn't forgive that. She couldn't forget how cheap and small it had made her feel. The instant he had placed the jewelry box in her hands, he had reduced their relationship to something tawdry and sordid. He had to pay for making her feel used.

She banged a fist on her steering wheel. "Stop it, stop it, stop it!"

Furious at herself, she flung open the car door, then walked up one flight of stairs to her suite of offices. This, at least, was something in which she could take pride. Al-

liance de Securité Internationale was her baby. Allison had
built the business step by step, scrupulously nurturing her
skills and her reputation.

The last required a delicate balancing act. She wanted to
be known well enough to garner referral accounts, the
backbone of her business, but not so well known or recognizable that she ceased to be effective. The security
business was built on discretion, particularly her area of
expertise.

"Good morning, Mademoiselle Ames."

"Good morning, Gina." She stopped at the desk of her
top researcher. "Anything more on the Courtwald family?"

Gina pushed a pencil behind her ear and leafed through
a pile of notes. "There's a wealth of information about the
father and the two oldest sons. Then it starts to get sketchy.
Paul Courtwald isn't involved in the family businesses, so
there isn't much information about him."

Allison tapped an impatient finger against the edge of
Gina's desk. "Give me a quick rundown on what you
have."

"Paul Courtwald, born in London on June 10, 1965, to
Stanford and Cornelia Courtwald. He's the youngest of
three sons, the last child in the family. He was privately
tutored until the age of ten, when he was sent to school in
Munich, and later in Bern. He returned to England, to
Oxford, but left shortly before completing his studies. His
field was international banking. His older brothers are
CEOs in various family-held businesses, but Paul is not
involved in any of the family corporations, at least not that
I've been able to ascertain."

"What about personal information?"

"He plays amateur tennis, he golfs, climbs, skis, he's a
yachtsman. Name a sport and he's participated." She

smiled. "He's never married, but his name has been linked with at least a dozen beautiful women, starlets, singers, socialites. If he owns a home, I haven't found a record of it. He's usually on the move, traveling from one posh watering hole to another, renting or staying with friends." Gina sighed. "This is a playboy *extraordinaire*. He's got it all, looks, charm, a wealthy family. Why can't I meet guys like this?"

"Any problems with the law?" Allison inquired.

Gina's eyebrows rose. "None that I've found so far." She frowned and sifted through her notes. "Did you have something in mind?"

"Just curious."

"He's had a few speeding infractions, but no serious brushes with real trouble. At least none that I've found yet."

"Keep digging. I want to know everything about him." She glanced at her watch. "I'm especially interested in tracking his exact movements over, say, the last year. I'd like to know where he's been and when, and I'd like that information by tomorrow morning if possible."

The windows in her private office overlooked the park facing the harbor. Monique had opened the draperies and placed a china cup and saucer on a napkin on Allison's desk next to her appointment book. Allison poured herself some coffee from the coffeemaker on the credenza, then walked back to her desk. She glanced at the list of appointments, then at a stack of phone messages, before she carried her coffee to the window.

What was she going to do about Paul Courtwald?

They were on opposite sides of the law. Her business, her life for that matter, was committed to stopping thieves like him. Philosophically, Allison detested everything Paul Courtwald stood for.

He preyed on others. He took. Although he stole only from the very rich, she couldn't picture him as a Robin Hood type. She was willing to be surprised, but right now she doubted that anyone benefited from his thievery except him. She suspected he used his ill-gotten gains to finance an idle and extravagant life-style, which was something else she found less than attractive. With Paul Courtwald's intelligence and observant eye, with his background and family connections, he could have been successful at banking or any other profession. But he'd chosen burglary as his life's calling.

"Daddy must be very proud," she muttered sarcastically.

Stanford Courtwald was very much on her mind this morning. Allison didn't know the man, but she could guess his disappointment in his youngest son. And she knew the devastation an honorable man would experience if his son were exposed as an international thief. Oh, yes, she knew that kind of catastrophe very well. Been there, done that, she thought bitterly.

If she had an ounce of sense, she would pick up the telephone and call Monsieur DeVault, chief of Monaco's police force. Considering Monaco's minuscule crime rate, and how DeVault had complained of boredom the last time Allison had been seated next to him as his dinner partner, he would thank her forever if she gave him an internationally known jewel thief. DeVault would fan the flames of publicity to his glory and dine out on Courtwald's capture for the next decade. He would refer more business to Allison than she could handle.

But as a result, Paul's family would be flogged in tabloids on at least three continents. If there were other family secrets, they would be dredged up and inflated for maximum titillation value. None of the family would es-

cape the tabloid's attention. His parents, his brothers and
their families . . . all would be pilloried by the lowest form
of journalism.

Still, despite her genuine sympathy for Paul's family,
Allison was committed to justice and fair play, both of
which demanded that she phone Monsieur DeVault and
turn The Ghost in to the authorities.

Turning back to her desk, she put down her coffee cup
and placed a hand on her telephone.

How had he learned her last name, and subsequently her
address?

Five minutes later she had convinced herself that it really wasn't reasonable to speak to Monsieur DeVault at this
point. It made better sense to wait until Gina had tracked
Courtwald's movements and she herself had correlated his
travels to the international appearances of The Ghost. The
proof wouldn't be long in coming, and proof was always
more persuasive than mere suspicion. DeVault would
thank her for her thoroughness.

QUIET, AND KNOWN primarily for plain, inexpensive fare,
the Cosmopolite was located in the rue de la Turbie behind the railroad station. If a man tilted his head toward
the sky, it was possible to gaze up a steep incline and
glimpse the top of the palace walls; otherwise, there was no
view to speak of outside the Cosmopolite and none from
inside.

There was, however, an interesting view in the street directly in front of the restaurant. A sad smile touched Paul's
lips as he counted the women lingering around the restaurant's perimeter, trying not to appear too obvious as
they searched each face that approached the restaurant
doors. That they would respond to a stranger's message
saddened him. As he had specified a time in his note

known only to *his* Allison, they might have been waiting here for several hours.

The problem he should be focusing on was how to recognize his mystery woman. It amused him that he had met her twice, had exchanged passionate kisses with her, had lunched with her, and he still didn't know what she looked like.

Leaning back in the seat of his Porsche, he peered through the windshield and wondered which, if any, of the waiting Allisons might be *his* Allison. And, of course, it was possible that Allison wasn't her name at all but a name she had plucked out of thin air. If that were true, then he was back to square one.

Frowning, he tapped his fingers on the steering wheel and tried to decide how to proceed in the worst-case scenario. If her name wasn't Allison, then she hadn't received his note. Or, she might have received the note but decided not to meet him. Or, it was remotely possible that her name was indeed Allison, but his computer had failed to flag her.

As he was trying to unravel these tangled threads while studying the women clustered near the restaurant, the door opened on the passenger side of the car and a long-legged woman wearing a hat and dark glasses slid into the seat next to him. She wore a pink Chanel suit, adorned by the signature braid and gold buttons, and dyed-to-match pumps. Her perfume smelled like money and success, mystery and sex.

Paul inhaled deeply and grinned. This came close to being every man's fantasy, that a beautiful, mysterious woman with shapely long legs would slide in next to him and calmly buckle her seat belt as if she knew it was going to be a wild ride.

She placed a small purse on the floor, then gazed at him through the dark glasses.

"How?"

"Computer search," he replied, knowing at once what she was asking. He studied her for a long, appreciative moment, then turned the key in the ignition. "There's a company in Nice that sells disks of phone books with listings for just about any city you can name." He tried not to sound smug, but it pleased the hell out of him that he had one-upped her.

Nodding slowly, she scanned the women near the restaurant door as he drove past them. "You mailed the same note to every Allison in Monaco."

"And in Nice and Cannes and...well, you get the idea."

"Very impressive."

He sensed the moment when she understood that he still didn't know her last name or where she lived. He'd mailed more than a hundred notes. He didn't have a clue which of the Allisons she might be. When that realization struck her, she crossed her long legs and relaxed against the leather seat, her incredible mouth curving in a knowing smile that told him he might be a tad premature in his self-congratulations.

"Your turn," he said, heading toward the Corniche. "How?"

"Easy. The license plates signify a rental car, you were studying those women like you wanted to memorize them, you were alone, and finally, this time you wanted me to recognize you."

He laughed. "Right on all counts."

"Where are we going?"

"There's a place by the water in Imperial that has the best steamed mussels you ever tasted." He glanced at her, keeping his voice casual. "Did you bring your passport?"

"Sorry," she answered in an equally bland but pleasant voice. "I'm not carrying any identification. We'll have to save Italy for another time. Nice try, though."

"Foiled again." He glimpsed perfect white teeth when she smiled. "Are you ever going to tell me your name, Just Allison?"

"I haven't decided yet."

"Right now I think I'd settle for the name of your perfume." At the next stoplight, he turned to look at her fully, wishing she would remove her dark glasses. But he'd been correct about blond hair. Sun blond tendrils fluttered at the nape of her neck, teased by a light breeze floating through her opened window. "That's a potent scent. Unforgettable."

"Sorry again, but I don't know the name. I have a box of sample vials. Every morning I reach inside and wear whichever hits my fingers first."

"No signature scents in our business, right?" He had already guessed that she wouldn't have a favorite perfume or one she wore regularly. This was a pro; she wouldn't overlook any details no matter how small. He wondered what she knew about him. She'd had two days at her computer—he didn't doubt that she owned one—to search for him among public records.

He thought for a minute. "How about Le Louis XV?"

"Ah, barbecued scallops and crushed truffles."

So she had dined there. But then, a glance at the Chanel suit told him that she had expensive tastes. And if her usual target fell in the range of the Waldheims' Rubens, she could afford to indulge them.

"Actually," she said, "I don't usually eat lunch. There's a place on the quai, not far from Loews casino, that serves coffee and light pastry...unless you're really hungry?"

"Sounds fine." He wasn't about to argue with her at this juncture. But it amused him to realize that she was the only woman he almost knew who would turn down a meal at Le Louis XV.

As he'd expected, the little café she suggested offered no interior seating, and hence no reason for her to remove her sunglasses. He held out her chair, then seated himself at a sidewalk table that offered a fine view of the port and a picturesque glimpse of the palace atop a jutting promontory on the opposite side of the bay.

The air was moist and slightly cool but warm in the sunshine. A light breeze rattled the fronds of palm trees shading the street. Paul couldn't think of any place he would rather be right now than here, sipping café au lait with a beautiful, intriguing woman wearing a wide-brimmed straw hat and a pink suit. Not a person passed them who didn't look at her, no doubt wondering if she was a model or a film star or visiting royalty.

"There's been no mention in the newspapers about our mutual friend's recent loss," he remarked, watching her blow lightly on the hot foam topping her coffee. The sight of her pursed lips paralyzed him, and his abdomen tightened. She radiated a high-voltage sexuality without even trying. His palms grew moist when he considered what she would do to him if she ever actually wanted him to want her. He stared at her, aroused by the thought.

"Did you think there would be any publicity?" she asked curiously.

He shrugged and forced himself to look away from her mouth. "Sometimes people report the loss. Sometimes they don't want any public notice, don't want to alert others in the area to a treasure trove awaiting further plunder. But you know this already."

The dark glasses lifted toward the palace on top of The Rock. "Ever think about that one?" she inquired after a minute. A slight challenge drew her lips into a smile.

He laughed, enjoying the sunshine, the conversation, the cool beauty beside him. "Of course. Don't you?"

"The palace security is excellent. It's a stimulating exercise to contemplate, but a waste of time. Unless you *want* to end your career in lots of publicity. Which I don't think you do. At least not yet."

He couldn't see her eyes, but he watched her smile harden and her body momentarily stiffen. Gradually he was forming an impression that getting caught was an upsetting subject for her. Something along those lines had set her off at the Hotel Bonaparte. He wished he could recall exactly what they had said.

"Take off the dark glasses," he said softly.

"Not yet," she answered, not missing a beat.

"I want to look at you."

She let a silence build before she spoke as quietly as he had. "You neglected to mention that you're a magician. That's a neat trick, being in two places at the same time."

He followed her reference, of course, but he pretended ignorance.

She waved a pink-tipped hand. False nails, he noted idly. "Oh, you know exactly what I mean. Late last year, Casper the Friendly Ghost was on the Italian Riviera while you were skiing in Switzerland. Isn't that amazing? Quite a feat."

"Well, well, so there's a crack in your proof?" He grinned. "Maybe the playing field isn't so lopsided, after all."

A cool smile twitched her lips. "It's easy enough to explain. As a matter of curiosity, how many different passports do you have?"

"Why? Are you running a tape inside your purse?"

Instead of answering, she opened her bag and showed him the bottom seam. She wasn't carrying lipstick or a wallet or even a tissue. Her purse was empty.

"How about the pockets that don't show? The ones that must be sewn on the inside of your jacket?"

She wiggled a teasing finger at him. "Naughty boy. I'm not going to remove my jacket and sit here in my lingerie just to satisfy your curiosity. You'll have to take my word that I'm not recording our conversation."

"Interesting image." Grinning, he signaled for fresh cups of coffee. "As pleasant as it is, imagining you in your lingerie, I think it's time we discussed a little business." After the waiter departed, he sprinkled extra chocolate on top of the foam in her cup. "Why haven't I heard about you? There isn't a whisper that another pro is working the area."

She shrugged eloquently. "I'm careful."

That she was. Careful not to carry a single item of identification, careful not to allow him a glimpse of her eyes, very careful to reveal no personal information. She was a tantalizing mystery that begged to be solved. A mouth that begged to be kissed. A body that begged to be stroked and caressed. He had to concentrate on not touching her just to see if her lightly tanned skin was as firm but as soft as he remembered.

"So, how do you propose we settle a certain professional difficulty, Just Allison? While there is abundant opportunity for both of us, two professionals working the same small area could lead to a repetition of a certain awkward situation. Not to mention that a doubled crime rate could bring unwanted attention and publicity."

She gave him a dazzling smile, danced her fingernails across his wrist, then leaned back in her chair. "My suggestion is that you leave at once for fresher fields where your expertise won't be challenged and your activities will draw less attention.''

"Cheeky little thing, aren't you?" he asked, laughing. "Odd, but I was about to suggest the same thing to you."

He couldn't believe that the playful touch of her fingernails on his wrist could be so exciting.

She shook her head, still smiling. "Sorry. As you guessed, I have a home here. And I was here first. You're the newcomer, the poacher, if you will. Fairness demands that you should be the one to move on down the road."

"I don't agree, *chérie*," he said pleasantly. "I've invested a lot of time in research and planning, I've leased a villa for the remainder of the season, and I find the climate invigorating. I'm staying."

"It appears we're at an impasse."

"Perhaps we should work together...."

The proposal startled the hell out of him. He couldn't believe such a suggestion had fallen out of his mouth. He had always worked alone, always. Working alone was safer and smarter.

Although he couldn't see her eyes, he could feel her stare. What astonished him as much as his impulsive suggestion was that she didn't reject it out of hand.

"I've always worked alone," she said after a lengthy pause. Turning her head, she appeared to watch an Italian luxury liner leaving port, but he doubted she saw it.

"So have I. But this is an unusual situation."

"My first instinct is to refuse. But there might be certain advantages in joining forces." She let another pause develop. "I'll have to think about this," she said finally, speaking slowly.

"You do understand that I'll have to know a lot more about you before I agree to work with you." The statement was partly backpedaling, partly seizing an opportunity to pry more information out of her. "We have to trust each other completely, or any joint venture will be doomed to failure."

"You can't trust me until you know my last name?" she asked in a teasing voice.

"I can't trust you until you trust *me* enough to tell me your name." He let his tone reflect his seriousness. "I suspect you know a lot about me by now, but I know next to nothing about you. That's not how partnerships work, Just Allison."

She considered for several minutes, watching the parade of people strolling along the quai. He couldn't be certain, but it appeared that her dark glasses followed two women, one of whom carried a large box stamped on the side with the DeWilde logo.

"You know," she said in a soft, musing tone, "you may have hit upon the perfect solution. Together, we might be able to accomplish...things...neither of us would attempt singly."

His practical side insisted that he should withdraw his suggestion of a partnership. But the reckless side of his nature was intrigued by the possibilities.

"Such as?" He glanced at the sunwashed walls of the palace on the far side of the bay. "Surely not...?"

Rousing herself from a private reverie, she followed his gaze and laughed. "No, not the palace. I told you, as far as we're concerned, it's impregnable. If not for security reasons, then from the standpoint of sheer good sense."

"I have a feeling you have something in mind, though."

"Perhaps. Something just occurred to me, but...no, it would be too crazy. I don't know what I was thinking of. Never mind."

"Now I'm curious. Were you thinking about a caper?"

"Seriously, I don't want to talk about it." Tilting her head, she directed the dark glasses toward his face. "Don't push, Paul."

He folded his arms on the table and examined his reflection in the lens of her glasses. "Nothing happens until we trust each other. That means I need to know as much about you as you think you know about me. And frankly, we're off to a bad start in this area. By now you have reams of computer paper on me, but what I know about you wouldn't fill your inside pocket. That changes or we don't have a deal."

"Slow down, cowboy. I said I'd think about your proposal. I haven't made a decision yet."

But she would. And she gave him reason to think she might decide to join forces when she offered the first gesture of trust by removing her dark glasses and folding them into her empty purse. Lifting her head, she gazed fully at his face.

Paul drew in a deep breath. She had stunning blue eyes of a particular changeable shade that he didn't recall having seen before. The shade would subtly alter depending on what color she wore near her beautiful face. In candlelight, he suspected it would appear that her eyes were violet; on a rainy day, friends would swear her eyes were as gray as his. At the moment, lit by sunshine, the color was a clear azure blue.

And she was a beauty, a stunning, absolutely unforgettable woman, as powerfully exciting as her fragrance. Seeing her now, he found it utterly amazing that she had played such a convincing grandmother.

"You are very lovely," he said simply, staring at her.

"It's a trick," she said, laughing. "Done with mirrors and makeup."

"No."

The quiet conviction in his voice appeared to make her uncomfortable. After glancing at her wristwatch, she sipped the last of her café au lait, then set her napkin aside and stood.

"I have an appointment. . . ." she said crisply, suddenly businesslike and giving the impression that she was running behind schedule.

Paul placed some bills on the table. "What are all these appointments you have?" he asked lightly. He still knew nothing about her.

"I'm a busy woman," she answered, telling him exactly nothing.

"Two things, Just Allison . . . if we're to start trusting each other, then I want to know your last name—now— and we need to set up another meeting."

One eyebrow rose and a teasing sparkle lit her eyes. "Patience isn't your long suit, is it, cowboy?"

"Not where you're concerned." He touched her back, feeling the warmth of her through her jacket and remembering the slightly apricot taste of her skin when he had kissed her bare shoulder under the baron's desk. "The car is this way."

She shook her head. "No, I'll be leaving you here." Deftly, she stepped away from his hand. In about two minutes, the hat would come off, and perhaps she wore shorts and a tank top beneath the pink suit. Whatever, he suspected she would vanish into the flow strolling along the quai, a disappearing act calculated in case he decided to follow her. He was tempted.

"Your name," he reminded her. "And when shall we meet again?"

"Tomorrow, same time, right here. Have you been to Eze yet? You bring the wine, I'll bring a picnic. Bring climbing gear."

The waiter tapped his shoulder to give him change that he had intended as a gratuity. When he turned around, she was gone.

Frowning, he scanned the quai, zeroing in on a blonde with long, purposeful strides. It wasn't Just Allison. Frustrated and fascinated, he walked toward the Porsche. By the time he reached the car, he was laughing and shaking his head.

He'd been crazy to suggest that they work together. But what a team they would make! He'd never met anyone like her.

It occurred to him that he was half in love with a woman he knew nothing about. He'd been determined that she wouldn't get away without revealing something of herself, but he'd failed. He still didn't know her last name.

CHAPTER FOUR

AFTER ALLISON COMPLETED dictating half a dozen letters, she leaned back from her desk and reached for a tumbler of seltzer. "I think we're on top of everything," she said to Monique. "Henri will handle the film star in Rome, and Dominique will take the Rochlund case in Paris. Have I overlooked anything that you can think of?"

Monique checked her notes, then shook her head, sending her cap of shining dark hair swinging. "The Waldheims' bill went out in this morning's mail. We received the final check from the Harts in London."

She cast a quick glance at Allison when she said London, but Allison didn't alter her expression. There was a time, Allison knew, when the mention of London had made her face light up like fireworks, and then a time, shortly thereafter, when the same word had plunged her to the depths of despair. Now the word *London*—and its association with Jeffrey DeWilde—did nothing more than fan the flames of the anger that burned in the pit of her stomach.

"Good," she said, turning to face her window and the view of the harbor. "We've pared away everything that isn't absolutely essential."

"You're practically on vacation," Monique agreed, smiling.

"I'll phone the office every day, of course, and come in once a week. And I'll handle the Trazakis job." She returned Monique's smile. "But you're right. Considering the pace I'm accustomed to, a reduced schedule will feel like a vacation."

"What you need is a *real* vacation."

They repeated this conversation every few months, whenever Monique fell into her mother hen mode. Allison nodded and folded her arms across her chest. Already her mind had leapt from the office to Paul Courtwald. "Have you ever done something that you knew was truly stupid... but you did it, anyway?"

Monique laughed. "That kind of statement can refer to only one thing—you've met a man," she said, not a doubt in her voice.

Allison gave her a rueful smile. "And he's an absolute disaster. Mr. Wrong if ever there was one." Like a moth to a flame, she seemed drawn to unsuitable men, first Jeffrey and now Paul Courtwald.

"But good-looking?"

Tapping a finger against her lower lip, Allison thought about Paul sitting at the outdoor café, wearing a bronze-colored Armani shirt, opened halfway down his chest. She remembered gray eyes with a roguish twinkle, dark hair that shone like strands of silk in the sunlight. His athletic body tapered in the classic male shape; he had a sensual mouth that laughed and whispered and, she recalled from the first night they'd met, tasted faintly of peppermint toothpaste.

"Oh, yes," she said softly. "You'd swear he was a film star, he's that handsome."

"Charming?"

"Perfect manners, knows the best restaurants, a bit reckless... his eyes twinkle with little-boy mischief, and... he makes me laugh," she added helplessly.

"Somehow I doubt we're talking about a waiter or one of the pretty boys who hang around the beaches and hotels," Monique commented, her smile growing.

"His background is impeccable, his family is on the A-list socially, and—he doesn't know that I know this—but one of the yachts out there is his. He's...he's..." She spread her hands.

"He's Paul Courtwald," Monique supplied softly.

Instantly, Allison's eyes narrowed. "Justify," she said sharply.

Monique shrugged. "Why else is Gina researching him? He doesn't own a house and therefore has no need for us to test his security. It follows that your interest is personal." She stood and gathered her notes and notebook. "Frankly, I couldn't be happier. You worried all of us after...London. I'm glad you've finally taken an interest in someone else."

"Paul Courtwald couldn't be a worse choice!"

"Really?" Monique looked skeptical. "Handsome, charming and rich doesn't sound all that bad to me." At the door, she glanced back and grinned. "It's hard to see how this guy could be a disaster." A knowing look came into her eyes. "Enjoy your vacation."

"It isn't a vacation, just a reduction in my schedule."

It was on the tip of Allison's tongue to tell Monique everything, how she had met Paul and who he really was. A minute later she was glad that she hadn't, glad that she had personally done the research on The Ghost's activities and whereabouts instead of asking Gina to do it. So far, Allison was the only person who knew Paul and The Ghost were one and the same.

As long as that was true, then her options remained open.

Angry with herself, she returned to her desk and pushed papers around the surface in a haphazard manner. There was only one option open to her, just one. And that was to pick up the telephone and call Monsieur DeVault at once. It wasn't her job to provide irrefutable proof that Paul and The Ghost were the same person. It would be enough, more than enough, to tell DeVault that Paul had been after the Rubens and that he had all but confessed that he was The Ghost. Let DeVault prove it. He was a careful man, he would build a slow but airtight case; if Allison could deduce that Paul held passports in different names, so could DeVault.

Turning Paul over to DeVault was what she *should* do. There was no question on that point, not an iota of doubt.

So why didn't she reach for the telephone?

Irritated, she stood and paced across a faded Oriental rug, glancing at her desk phone from the corner of her eyes.

The answer was complicated. Part of the reason that she hadn't turned Paul in had to do with his family and the pain they would suffer when his crimes became public knowledge. And part of the reason was that she hadn't actually seen him do anything illegal; it was she who had stolen the Rubens, not him. He would have taken it, she argued with herself, but the fact was, he hadn't.

She made a face. This was a very marginal reason for not turning him in.

But the reason that carried the most weight—and was also the most illogical—was that Paul Courtwald intrigued her. She was attracted to him. He had made her feel again. The numbness that had encased her heart since that terrible night when Jeffrey said goodbye was dispelled by Paul's presence. He challenged her; he interested her. His reckless charm excited and attracted her. He was a dangerous man because he represented all the things that she did not want in her life. There was no doubt whatsoever that he was absolutely the wrong man for her.

But he made her laugh and he made her feel again. When she was with Paul, she was aware of the sun's warmth and how the air smelled and tasted. She was aware of her body and how it moved, and the twinkling of his eyes when he thought he had bested her and the way he gestured with his hands. For far too long her world had been painted in shades of gray. But when she was with Paul, her surroundings seemed to sparkle.

Concerned about the impression she would make, she had spent two hours deciding what to wear for their last meeting, something she hadn't done in ages. But Paul was the first man who had stirred her interest since Jeffrey. In fact, if she didn't count Jeffrey, Paul Courtwald was the first man who had aroused her interest in a very long time.

She couldn't turn him in to DeVault. Not yet.

But she could not work with him as he had suggested. Allison was not a thief. In fact, she was fiercely opposed to dishonesty of any kind. The only reason she had not rejected his proposal out of hand was that for one minute—for one insane minute—an image of Catherine the Great's tiara had flashed through her thoughts. And she had wondered what would happen to Jeffrey DeWilde's empire if the priceless tiara were stolen?

It was a crazy idea and she had shoved it away at once.

But during that brief hesitation while ludicrous thoughts teased her mind, Paul had assumed she was considering his suggestion that they work together and burglarize the very people who were Allison's clients.

And she had told him that she would consider his suggestion.

Well, she decided, checking her watch, she would consider his proposal just long enough to recover from her infatuation with him. Then she would turn him in to Monsieur DeVault.

On her way out of the office, she stopped at Gina's desk. "Anything new?"

"There's nothing more on Courtwald that amounts to much," Gina replied, looking up with a smile, "just little things that will be in my final report."

"Actually, I want to ask you about myself."

Periodically, Allison instructed Gina to run a background check on her in order to discover what other people would be able to find if they were so inclined.

Gina frowned. "We ran a check on you about two months ago."

"I'm not suggesting another," Allison said hastily. "I'd merely like to refresh my memory. How easy is it to connect me as the owner of Alliance de Securité?"

"It can be done, of course," Gina answered slowly, curiosity gleaming in her dark eyes, "but not easily. The company is incorporated in the Bahamas, there's a lot of red tape...." She shrugged. "If you're asking if your association with the company appears anywhere that's easily accessible, the answer is no."

"How about banking records?"

"If a person is determined enough and persistent enough, he can find out just about anything he wants to know about another person. Someone good with computers could, if he were a hacker, find your personal account here in Monaco." She smiled. "But he would have to be *very* determined to find your business account in Paris."

Allison's business checks were signed by her accountant, so her name did not appear on most checks drawn on the company account.

She felt her shoulders begin to relax. "So, if someone knew my name, it doesn't automatically follow that he'd connect me to my business?"

"Well," Gina said with a grin, "he could always follow you to work...."

"Not if I'm on vacation," Allison answered. "That's covered."

"As I said before, a determined and persistent person can dig out a lot of information, and, yes, that information will eventually lead from you to Alliance de Securité Internationale. But the threads are so tangled, this persistent person will need a lot of time, a little luck, and he'll have to know where to look in the first place."

"Thanks."

Allison's drive to bury personal information was a legacy from her father. Andrew Ames had been a powerful man, successful, wealthy, a Wall Street wheeler-dealer *extraordinaire*. He'd also been closemouthed, secretive and, in the end, on the wrong side of the law.

Her father had died six months before Allison met Jeffrey DeWilde. Her feelings had been conflicted then, and they still were. She didn't know if she would ever reconcile loving Andrew Ames with hating him for the humiliation he had brought on her mother and herself.

She blinked hard, gazed around her suite of offices, then gave everyone a wave and walked out the door to begin enjoying her pared-down schedule, which was the only vacation she had allowed herself in four years.

She had two weeks of minimal business demands to make the most of her brief time with Paul Courtwald.

That should be enough to get him out of her system.

FOR TODAY'S OUTING, Paul had rented a convertible. They sped along the Corniche, taking the curves at high speed, enjoying the sunshine sparkling on the Mediterranean and brief glimpses of perched villages high on the cliffs. Wind and traffic noise made conversation difficult, but Allison found the high speed relaxing.

"You're a good driver," she commented as he slowed, turning into the village of Eze. Shops accommodating tourists had swelled the village from the size it used to be, but it was still not much larger than a postage stamp.

He pulled over near a roadside stall that sold color posters of the medieval castle rising from the top of the cliff and rested an arm across the back of Allison's seat.

"Is there anything you're not good at?" Allison inquired curiously. Suddenly, she was very conscious of his mouth. He habitually wore a half smile as if the world amused him, a smile that proclaimed an assured, optimistic nature. She knew the excitement he could generate with those confident lips.

"I'm not good at guessing last names," he said, his eyes as teasing as his voice.

"It's Ames."

"Allison Ames," he said, his voice deep with pleasure. "Now, why didn't you tell me in the first place?"

She couldn't decide if his eyes were gray like a stormy sea, or gray like the hills and cliffs around them. "Maybe because I wasn't certain if I wanted to see you again."

"Some women handle that by saying, 'Paul, I don't want to see you again.'"

She laughed. "I don't imagine many women say no to you." Pushing back a wave of hair that had blown in her face, she smiled. "Maybe I didn't want you busily rummaging in your computer, digging out information about me."

"You know I'm going to." He caught a strand of her hair between his thumb and forefinger. "Silky," he commented.

She smiled, then gave him directions to a little-used road that would take them to the water and near the base of the cliff atop which the medieval castle sprawled in majestic splendor.

Once they had parked and unpacked their climbing gear, Paul leaned back from the waist, shaded his eyes and scanned the rugged cliff face. "No pitons this time, right?"

"Right," Allison confirmed, pulling her hair back and securing it with clips and a rubber band.

"What is this, a test?" He grinned at her, then began strapping on his harness.

"Nope," she said honestly, "just recreation. Since you've been climbing from about age fourteen, I thought you'd enjoy it." She gave him another smile, knowing her days of smugness were about to end. By this time tomorrow, he would know that she too had been climbing from about the same age. "Lunch at the top is your reward." Stepping back, she made a sweeping bow. "After you."

"You want me to go first?" He stared at her a minute, his eyes skimming down the form-fitting spandex top to her shorts, then slowly down the curve of her legs. "My, my. When we begin to trust, we really begin to trust."

"I'm not a halfway person."

"No, I didn't think you were." Surprising her, he kissed her on the nose, then turned to study the cliff face.

It was a pleasure to climb with an experienced partner. The cliff was challenging enough to be interesting, but not difficult enough to pose a real risk to a veteran climber.

As she climbed, Allison thought of Jeffrey. Although he liked to relax by watching action-type films, he wasn't particularly athletic.

It occurred to her that he was one of the most intellectually exciting men she had ever met, but they were ill-matched physically. Part of the problem was an age difference of nearly thirty years, but a larger part was preference. Jeffrey preferred pursuits of the mind, whereas she enjoyed testing her body. She liked flirting with the danger of fast skiing, climbing, spelunking, sports that required swift and furious action coupled with careful planning and maneuvering.

She and Paul emerged at the top of the cliff not far from the entrance gates to the castle. "Bravo," she said as they peeled off their climbing gear. The climb had gone well; neither of them was even winded.

He gave her a pitying look. "A piece of cake. Next time, select something with a challenge, will you?"

Allison looked up at him and laughed. "That kind of arrogance can get you in trouble, Courtwald."

A grin curved the mouth she now knew so well. "I'm trying to impress you. You're supposed to think, Wow, he thought that climb was nothing, he must be very, very good."

She hadn't laughed this much in almost a year. "Actually, that's exactly what I was thinking. Wow. This guy is really, really good. And he's got a cute fanny, too."

"Fun-ny," he said, grinning at her. "Next time, you go first. Hmm. Maybe not. I could get so wrapped up watching your behind that I might fall off the cliff."

"It would serve you right for taking liberties under the baron's desk. I still owe you for that."

Bantering and laughing, they adjusted their backpacks and approached the gates to Eze castle. They paid an en-

trance fee, then wandered around, peeking into shops occupying ancient castle rooms, visiting the great hall and the
private rooms of the lords and ladies who had once re-
sided there.

Paul squinted out of an archer's window, looking down
a sheer stone wall. "Our kind would have had a tough time
making a living back in the old days."

"Thieves always find a way," Allison said lightly.
"Come on, let's locate the common area. I believe there's
a place to picnic there."

He dropped behind her as they climbed stone steps set
in a narrow passageway, then came up beside her as they
emerged into the open air. "Is that how you think of us?
As thieves?"

She looked at him in surprise. "Don't you?"

He pushed his hands into his pockets and looked around
at an acre of grassy ground. Beyond crumbling stone walls,
the sea sparkled as if a sun god had strewn the waves with
diamonds.

"I suppose in a literal sense we're thieves. But I seldom
think of it that way. Our mutual friends, for instance, can
afford to lose a half-dozen Rubens without wincing. Most
items are insured, anyway."

Allison chose a spot with a fine view of the sea and the
castle. She shook out a checkered cloth, then began pulling items out of her backpack. Roast chicken, cold lobster, grapes, a container of pasta salad. She handed Paul
a corkscrew, then noticed he'd brought his own. He
opened a bottle of Chardonnay.

"Thieves drive up the cost of insurance," she said, again
keeping her voice light. "That doesn't count?"

"Whose side are you on?" He took the plate she handed
him.

"How did you get started in this?" Allison asked, side-stepping the question.

"Good chicken." He took another bite, then blotted his lips with a checkered napkin. "Do you want the short version or the long version?"

Allison shrugged. "We're not in a hurry, are we?" He looked so handsome sitting cross-legged on the checkered cloth with the sea and the sun behind him. She decided she could look at him and listen to his deep voice all day.

"The short version is that when I was at university, I accepted a dare issued by some bored friends. I stole my mother's favorite earrings." He shrugged. "I discovered I liked the excitement, the challenge, the thrill, if you will."

Allison paused with her fork midway to her lips. She stared. "You stole some earrings from your own *mother*?"

He rolled his eyes in a pained expression. "I returned the earrings. It was only a prank. But that's how I happened to set out on the road that led to here."

"I think I'd also like to hear the longer version."

He set his plate in his lap and studied the castle ramparts over her shoulder. "Do you have any brothers or sisters?"

"I'm one of those spoiled only children."

"Then you don't know how it feels to never be first at anything." His eyes gazed into the past. "The first bicycle, the first car, the first job, the first girl . . . by the time those experiences reach a third son, they've been mastered by the two older brothers. No matter what I did, Eric or Peter had done it first and, to hear them tell it, done it better or smarter or quicker or longer, whatever.

"Don't misunderstand, I love my brothers. I don't have a doubt in the world that I could pick up the phone and say I need you, and they'd be on the next plane, no questions asked. But they're way ahead of me in life and always have been. Peter is seven years older than I am, Eric is five years older. When I was just starting university, Peter was already managing one of Dad's companies. That's a big head start."

"So, you steal because Eric and Peter don't?" Allison inquired softly. "You're first at stealing?"

"That's part of it," he admitted frankly, looking at her. "Part of it is the thrill, and doing something I'm good at. And maybe part of it is that I haven't decided what I want to do with my life. I know I *don't* want to be in any of the family businesses. I don't want my performance to be judged against the meteoric rise of my brothers."

Allison looked down at the piece of chicken she was turning between her fingers. "I suppose it's occurred to you that time is passing. If you plan to enter another line of work, you should probably do it soon."

"Tactfully put," he said, smiling. "Maybe I'm just lazy."

"Are you?"

"No," he said finally, setting aside his plate. "But, as you know, what we do is addictive... the challenge, the risk, that rush of adrenaline when something goes a little bit wrong." He smiled at her with shining eyes. "Or even when things go perfectly right. The truth is, I like what I do. I'm good at it."

Allison studied him with regret. "Then you haven't considered retiring?" She wanted him to tell her that he planned to go straight and turn his talents toward a legitimate business. She didn't want to make that phone call to Monsieur DeVault.

"Of course I've considered stopping. Haven't you? I know the statistics. You do, too. The odds are against us. Eventually, we'll get caught. The trick is to stop before we reach that point."

"No, the trick is to recognize that point."

He laughed. "Now it's your turn. How long have you been breaking into other people's houses?"

"Professionally? Four years, almost five." It was a truthful answer. Except she referred to an honest business.

"I've been at it longer. Statistically, I suppose my time is running out." A frown crossed his features before he placed a hand on her arm. "You aren't going to go weird on me, are you? And run off?"

"No," Allison said slowly, "but it does upset me to talk about getting caught, and everything that follows."

"And why is that, exactly? Aside from the obvious."

She drew a deep breath. He was going to discover her background. "Because my father was caught. He died last year. In prison." Now it was her turn to look toward the sea and peer into the past. "You can't imagine what it was like for my mother and me when he was arrested. I was sixteen, going to school in Switzerland, but I was home for the summer when the police came and took my father away in handcuffs like he was a common criminal."

"Was he?" Paul asked gently.

She almost laughed. There had been nothing common about her wonderful, elegant father with his hand-tailored suits and imported cologne, or the string of polo ponies and the limousines. "Andrew Ames belonged to an elite group. My father was one of the first big names to be implicated in insider trading. The next big fish to get caught was Ivan Boesky."

"Ah. Your father was a Wall Street guru."

She nodded, looking down at the piece of chicken in her hands. "He was a partner at Little, James and Dalton. We had an estate in the Berkshires, a co-op overlooking Central Park, a house in Nassau in the Bahamas. It was the

American fairy tale. Poor boy claws his way through Harvard then catches the gold ring."

"But in this case, the gold ring belonged to someone else?"

"I guess you could say that." She looked at him. Most of what she was telling Paul had appeared in headlines around the world. Little of it was a secret. But this was the first time that *she* had told the story, and that made a huge difference. "You must have read about Andrew Ames's arrest and subsequent trial when it happened."

"Yes," Paul said simply.

"Then you know he was convicted and sent to prison." A long pause followed. "The tabloids had a heyday. They made my parents' lives sound frivolous and shallow. They hinted at affairs that never existed, at a life that moved from one posh party to another. They reported how much my mother paid her cleaning service, for God's sake."

"What did they say about you?" Paul asked, taking her hand. Gently, he removed the piece of chicken and wiped the grease from her fingers.

Allison sighed heavily. "They reported that I made top grades and left the implication that I'd probably cheated to get them. Like father, like daughter. They even dug up my grandfather's past." When Paul raised his eyebrows, she sighed again. "My grandfather was a carny grifter back in the twenties."

"What on earth is a carny grifter?"

"He traveled with the carnivals that moved around the country in those days. Sometimes he worked as a shill for the carny games, all of which were rigged. And sometimes he identified suckers by brushing a chalk mark on their backs. Sometimes he ran the games or one of the sideshows."

"Sounds like an interesting fellow," Paul said, smiling.

"He lived his whole life conning people," Allison snapped. And she had adored that old man with his sly, twinkling eyes and his big lap and the smell of cherry tobacco that clung to his hair and hands. She had loved his robust laugh and his stories about the carnival days and the way he could pull dimes out of her ears. She couldn't believe it when he died; she had been positive it was only an old carny trick and he would jump up, grinning and telling her not to act like a sucker.

It was only later, when the tabloids were finished with Grandpa Ames, that she realized he had never done an honest day's work, that he was merely a small-time con man who made his living by fleecing the gullible. And she had felt ashamed of him.

Shame was the primary emotion of those terrible years. Shame for her family. Grandpa Ames had conned folks out of nickels and dimes; her father had profited to the tune of millions.

That was why she had turned to the security business. In some small way, she felt as if she were atoning for the past sins of two generations. She could not undo what her father and grandfather had done, but she could help make her clients a little safer from others like them.

And she could live her own life under rules of strict honesty.

"I never really understood it," she said, speaking more to herself than to Paul. "It wasn't the money...my father's yearly income ranged in the high six figures, sometimes more. I drove myself crazy wondering why he broke the law to earn yet more money."

"But now you understand, don't you?" Paul asked quietly.

She stared at him. "I've never understood."

"Maybe he did it because he could. Because he was good at it."

"He wasn't *that* good. He got caught," Allison said bitterly. "And because of what he did, my mother became a recluse, ashamed to go out. She was dropped by previous friends. She's fifty-three now, but she looks and acts years older. She's never recovered from the humiliation."

"You said your father died in prison...." A combination of sympathy and curiosity was reflected in Paul's steady gaze.

"He paid an enormous fine—millions of dollars. He was barred from ever working in securities again, and he served three years in prison." Her shoulders heaved in an unconscious sigh. "When he was released, he didn't know what to do with himself. Eventually, he did the only thing he loved and knew how to do... he went back to securities under an assumed name." She shrugged and spread her hands in a helpless gesture. "He was caught, of course, and sent back to prison. Last year, he died there of a heart attack." She glared at Paul. "I don't know why I'm telling you all this."

"Did you make peace with him before he died?"

"What are you talking about?" she snapped.

He stroked her hand and wouldn't let her pull it away. "You loved him because he was your father, but you hated him for destroying a nice safe life and for bringing attention and embarrassment on you and your mother."

She stared. That's exactly how it had been.

"Did you work out those feelings before he died?"

For some reason, she thought again of Jeffrey De-Wilde. She'd met Jeffrey while she was struggling with her feelings about her father's death. Jeffrey was about the

same age as her father had been, he wore the same alluring aura of power and success. . . .

"Good heavens. I was looking for a man like my father
should have been. Honest, steady, with no whiff of scandal about him. Someone I could be proud of."

"I beg your pardon?" Paul frowned, a puzzled look on
his face.

She blinked, then her gaze cleared. She pulled her hand
away and waved it in the air. "Nothing. Never mind, I was
just . . . thinking about something else."

"Someone, I forget who, once said that all family relationships are adversarial. Sometimes I think that's true to
one degree or another."

"Really? I thought you said you loved your brothers."

"I do. I also envy their success and feel competitive with
them. At family gatherings, I wish my father looked at me
with the same pride that he looks at Peter and Eric with. I
wish I could tell him that I'm successful, too, that I'm not
the wastrel he thinks I am." A frown furrowed his brow.
"Hell, maybe I am a wastrel."

Sitting side by side, they watched a family of tourists
open a picnic basket in the shadow of the castle. Allison
was the first to break a brooding, introspective silence.

"We've taken a lovely sunshiny day and a terrific mood
and wrecked it." When she turned to face him, her mouth
was only inches from his. "Now do you see why I don't
like to talk about myself or my background?"

"Family isn't my favorite topic, either," he said, staring into her eyes. "But discussions like this are how trust
begins."

Her gaze slid to his lips. "It's a painful process."

"I know. And we aren't through yet."

"I know. And I hate that."

They grinned at each other.

"Come on," he said, picking up their plates. "I'll race you down the cliff."

"No, let's walk down to the car. We'll take the path and jog off lunch. A brisk walk will do us both good."

"You do me good," he said softly, pulling her to her feet. They stood close enough that Allison could feel the strong warmth of his muscular body. His breath smelled like roast chicken and white wine. "I've never been able to talk about what I do. Do you have any idea how good it feels to be able to talk about all of my life instead of just part of it?" He gazed deeply into her eyes. "Yes," he said softly, answering his own question, "of course you understand."

"I feel," she said slowly, leaning her palms against his chest, "as if I've been to confession." She gave him a weak smile. "To my great surprise, the sky didn't fall and the world didn't end because I told you about my father and grandfather."

He kissed her lightly, chastely on the lips, then grinned down at her. "You bring powerful credentials to this partnership, *mademoiselle*. I just hope you take after your grandfather, who didn't get caught, rather than after your father, who did." He tapped her lightly on the nose, then turned away to finish packing the debris from their picnic.

Allison stood where he had left her, staring into space.

Paul hadn't pulled away after learning about her family. He had asked sensitive and caring questions. Suddenly, she experienced a terrible sinking feeling that she was striding headlong into the worst trouble of her life, and that trouble was spelled with a capital *P.*

CHAPTER FIVE

WITHOUT REALLY DISCUSSING a course of action, they fell into the habit of meeting every day. They met for breakfast or for lunch if they'd been out late the night before. They drove to Grasse to explore the perfume shops, wandered around a perched village one lazy day, went to Italy to Imperia and sampled the steamed mussels Paul had raved about, attended a theater performance above the Casino, and took the yacht out for some swimming and diving.

"Well, let's see—where are we?" Paul said, rising on an elbow to look down at the sunlight gleaming on Allison's body. She was sunning herself on the deck of his yacht in a stunning black swimsuit that plunged low on top and rose high at the thighs. He couldn't take his eyes off her golden skin and perfect figure. *Lovely* didn't begin to describe her.

"We're a few miles out of the bay," she murmured, smiling without opening her eyes. "Behaving like decadent jet-setters with nothing to do but soak up the sun and ask the crew to bring us more champagne."

"What should we be doing?" he asked, drawing a finger down one of her shoulders. Her suntan oil smelled like a piña colada, a mixture of coconut and pineapple. He decided this was possibly the most erotic scent he had ever inhaled. "Have I mentioned lately that you have fabulous legs?"

She opened her eyes and pushed up her dark glasses. "Only about one hundred times." She laughed, flashing perfect white teeth before she winked at him. "You look pretty good in a swimsuit yourself."

"Thanks. Now that you've noticed, I can stop holding my breath and sucking in my stomach."

The sound of her low, throaty laughter made his thighs tighten with desire. "Right," she said. "Like you need to hold in your stomach."

"Ah, I love compliments!" He lay back down beside her, their shoulders touching. He kept telling himself that the better he knew her, and once the mystery had dissipated, he wouldn't be so fascinated by everything about her. But it wasn't happening that way. And he was beginning to suspect that it wouldn't; the better he knew her, the harder he seemed to be falling for her.

"Your yacht is fantastic, your crew well trained and discreet, lunch was wonderful. And I'm grateful for the balmy day you arranged. Are those enough compliments to hold you for a while?" Her oiled body glistened in the sun. "Or should I also mention that you swim as well as you climb, and that I lust for your diving equipment?"

"I'd rather that you lusted for me," he murmured, taking her hand and holding it on top of the towel between them.

She hesitated a beat, then murmured, "Slow down, cowboy."

The hesitation was an encouraging sign. Every day he had managed to steal at least one kiss, trying to take her by surprise. So far, he'd kept it light, teasing, and had held his passion in check. But seeing her in that swimsuit was wreaking havoc with his senses and his good intentions.

"I was talking about where we are in relation to us," he said, squeezing her hand.

"I know," she murmured, her voice sun-drowsy. "About trust and getting to know each other. So, in your exalted opinion, where are we?"

"We're a few miles out from the bay."

Lifting their clasped hands, she smacked him on the hip and smiled. "Fun-ny."

"All right, in the few hours you've allowed us to get away from a hectic schedule of doing and seeing—"

She lifted her sunglasses, opened one eye, and glared at his grin.

"I've done what I can to check you out on my computer," he finished.

"And?" she demanded.

"And you seem to be exactly who you claim to be."

She sat up. "Did you think I was inventing a background? Making that up about my father and grandfather?"

"Now, don't get testy, you've checked me out, too. You probably know where I ranked in my class..."

"Tenth in Munich, thirty-first at Oxford."

"And when I took my first step."

"You were ten months old. Rather late, if you ask me."

He sat up as she lay back on her towels. "Really?" He stared down at her cleavage. "I took my first step at ten months?"

"I have no idea. I was teasing you," she said with a smug smile. "Don't act like a sucker."

"In the immortal words of Grandpa Ames, that wise old man."

"Right. Now, as you were saying?"

"There are still some loose ends I want to look into, but by and large, you check out."

She made a face before she pulled her dark glasses down over her eyes. "By and large, huh?"

"Except for items like music, art, literature and things we've discussed in recent days, your personal life is still largely a mystery...."

"And I'd prefer to keep it that way. Hand me my bag, will you?"

He gave her a black-and-yellow bag and watched her remove a pair of binoculars, then idly scan the coastline as if she were casually passing time. Except this woman didn't do anything idly.

"See anything interesting?"

"I was hoping to catch a glimpse of a royal," she said with a shrug.

"You'd have a better chance if you'd direct the binoculars at the palace."

She lowered the glasses and looked at him. "You don't miss anything, do you?" she asked softly. He flattered himself that he heard a note of admiration mixed with the hint of irritation.

The admiration nudged him to show off a little. "You're interested in the yellow villa near the top of the hill."

She studied him with a speculative expression as if trying to decide whether to admit her interest or deny it.

"I had a life before you appeared," she said after a minute, still studying him. "Plans..."

She had eyes a man could drown in; he felt his thoughts floating away from the villa on the hillside. "In this life you had before I appeared . . . was there a man in it?"

"There used to be. There isn't now." Her gaze dropped to his lips and lingered there. "Is there a woman in yours?"

"There used to be. There isn't now."

The speculation deepened in her eyes and, he suspected, in his. They had maintained the fiction that their interest in each other was mainly professional, but now the

door had opened to personal considerations and they both
became aware of subtle changes.

"I look at you and I forget what we're talking about,"
he said in a husky voice. Her hair had dried in a sleek,
wheat-colored cap, curling at the tips on her shoulders.
Their earlier swim had left her face glowing and free of
makeup. Today this chameleon woman looked ten years
younger than he knew she was, and she entranced him in
all her various guises.

Leaning forward, gazing into her eyes, he kissed her. By
effort of will, he kept the kiss light and nondemanding. He
let his mouth linger and tease, but he tried not to react to
the lightning that sizzled through his system when he
touched her. She hadn't objected to his daily kisses, but she
hadn't encouraged anything more, either.

He was very much aware that Allison controlled the
progression of whatever relationship they would have; she
permitted him to go so far, but no further. During the days
they had spent together, he had glimpsed her discipline and
a self-control to rival his own. Based on this observation,
and her assurance and cool self-confidence, he sensed that
she was capable of walking away without a backward
glance if he moved too fast or if he offended her.

Suddenly, it was important to him that she didn't walk
away. It was also important that any partnership, either
professional or personal, be equal. While he was willing to
let her set the pace of their developing personal relationship, he was not willing to surrender control on a professional level. They had to join in equal trust and equal
confidence in each other, or a partnership would not be
successful.

"So, what are you planning, partner?" he murmured
against her lips, sliding his hands up her shoulders to frame
her face.

She opened her eyes and gazed at him from beneath a sweep of lashes.

"What I'm planning has nothing to do with us," she replied huskily. "In fact, there is no 'us.' I haven't yet made a decision about a partnership."

He kissed her tanned shoulder, letting his tongue sample the piña colada taste of her. "If you can't trust me enough to tell me what you're planning..."

Her eyes closed again and her head tilted backward, offering her throat to his lips. "I thought you said I checked out...."

The feel of her skin against his bare chest drove him crazy. Gently, he eased her body away from his and smoothed a tendril of sun blond hair behind her ear before he kissed it.

"Your background is what you say it is...."

"But?" The word came from deep in her throat as her arms circled his neck. The embrace was loose, but not casual. This was the most encouragement she had given him so far.

For an instant Paul couldn't think. Her fingers on the nape of his neck were electric, sending pulses that his body recognized and reacted strongly to. He had to put some space between them before he could recall what they were talking about. Trying to control his breathing, he moved backward a few inches.

"It occurs to me that I have only your word that you stole the Waldheims' Rubens...."

"What?" Her eyelids flew open and she gazed at him with sudden amusement dancing in eyes that today were the deep blue of a cloudless sky.

With regret, he released her and settled back on his towel. Amusement was not conducive to the desire permeating his mind and body. He drew a steadying breath and focused his thoughts.

"Think about it, Just Allison." He watched her shake back her hair and send a smile toward the sunshine. "I left before you actually removed the painting from the wall, and there was no public mention of a theft ever having occurred."

"So you've decided that I didn't steal the Rubens?" she asked. Twinkling eyes laughed back at him.

"It's possible," he said stubbornly.

"I did steal it." She leaned back on her elbows. "I can't prove that and I'm not going to try. You'll just have to take my word for it."

"You'll have to do better than that if we're going to be partners," he said, keeping his voice light and trying to hold his gaze on her face and not on her spectacular cleavage.

"Oh? What would you suggest?"

When she gave him that slow, speculative glance, his heart rolled over in his chest. It was the same look a woman gave a man when she was trying to imagine him in her bed.

"It would go a long way toward establishing trust if you'd tell me what's so interesting about the yellow villa on the hill." Reaching across her body, he picked up the binoculars and scanned a sprawl of red rooftops, yellow stucco and stone balconies.

"Nikos Trazakis," she said after a lengthy pause. "Greek. Shipping. Owns more oil tankers than he can count."

Interested, Paul ran the binoculars slowly across the villa's facade. "Trazakis. I may have met him a few years ago. What are we after?"

"*We* aren't after anything," she corrected him sternly. "This one is all mine. I've been planning it for a while. I started researching Trazakis before I knew you existed."

"Isn't this a little soon after the Waldheims?" he asked, glancing at her frown. "Another big hit right now would be like taunting the Monaco police, wouldn't it?"

She shook her head. "I don't believe the Waldheims reported the Rubens. If they had, I would have heard something."

He considered her statement. It suggested that she was plugged in to police information. She had an inside source. His professional admiration rose another degree.

"I think you're too savvy, too careful to focus unwanted attention on yourself," he said, thinking out loud. "So I'll take your word that it isn't too soon." He gave her a steady look. "But it should be obvious that joining forces is the best course. Acting alone, we'd certainly draw attention. There would be too many incidents. Some of them would get reported."

"Very likely," she said, looking away from him.

"What's the target?" He didn't go in without knowing exactly what he was after, and he guessed that she didn't, either. Neither of them was the type to leave details to chance.

She answered after a pause and with obvious reluctance. "Madame Trazakis owns a priceless collection of antique ivory figurines. Most are delicate and fragile. Chinese. They're over a thousand years old and irreplaceable."

"An interesting challenge." Raising the binoculars, he studied the villa carefully. "How do you plan to get them out without breakage?"

"Professional secret," she said, grinning.

Laughing, he returned the binoculars. "And when does this hit take place?"

The grin faded to a cool stare. "None of your business, cowboy. This doesn't concern you."

"Ah, it's another of those take-your-word-for-it incidents."

"Yes."

"Will it also be another theft that isn't reported to the police, do you think?"

"I'm counting on it, as a matter of fact." Rising to her feet, she stretched, making him catch a breath, then she glanced at her watch. "I hate to end this lovely lazy day, but I have a dinner engagement. Perhaps we should be heading back."

"A dinner engagement?" A surge of jealousy brought him within a heartbeat of inquiring if she was meeting a man. But he sensed it would anger her if he asked, since she had told him there was no special man in her life right now.

Here was another trust-me incident, he thought sourly. He didn't like it. So far he had no reason not to trust her, but he didn't have any proof that he could trust her, either.

"In fact, I'll be engaged every evening for the rest of the week," she announced, pulling on a yellow cotton shirt and stepping into black shorts.

At once he understood what she was saying and what she was doing. She would hit Trazakis this week, but she didn't want him to guess which night it would be.

He watched her button the yellow shirt, thinking it odd that she was sexier getting dressed than most women were getting undressed. Standing, he signaled to Enzio, the yacht's captain, to take them back to the harbor, then he joined Allison at the rail, standing with his back to shore so he could study her face.

"Where are you and I going, Allison? What's happening here?"

A brief look of helplessness flashed in her eyes, and her gaze dropped to his mouth. "I don't know," she said finally, her voice almost a whisper.

"This man, the one who used to be in your life but isn't anymore . . . was he important to you?"

"If you're asking if it's really over, believe me, it's definitely over. It was his choice to end it," she added with brutal honesty.

But that wasn't what he had asked. He'd noticed that she had a way of evading questions she didn't care to answer. Examining her expression, he saw anger deep in her eyes. Whoever the man was, he had hurt her and left a residue of pain. He had been a fool to leave. A woman like this didn't appear but once in a lifetime.

"You must know that I'm very attracted to you." He brushed his knuckles lightly across her cheek. "I don't know if that's good or if it's a complication."

For a fleeting moment she leaned her cheek against his fingers, then turned to face the approaching coastline. "It's more of a complication than you could possibly imagine."

"I think you're also attracted to me."

She gave him a shrug and a smile, feigning an indifference that wasn't believable. "That would complicate things even more."

They leaned on the railing, shoulders touching, holding hands. Paul watched with regret as the harbor approached. He didn't want this moment of closeness to end.

For the first time it entered his mind that a thief had only the present. The future was denied to those who lived on the wrong side of the law. Happy tomorrows existed only for those who could promise they would be there to enjoy their future. He thought about Allison's father and conceded that no thief could make that promise. The specter of capture and prison loomed in his thoughts.

It was odd that he hadn't previously considered the lack of a future. Perhaps he hadn't wanted to take a hard look at uncertain eventualities. But meeting Allison was causing a reevaluation of possibilities he had taken lightly before. The realization that he had no future profoundly disturbed him. Especially when he looked at the beautiful, alluring woman standing beside him.

ALLISON SPOTTED her secretary, Monique, at the sidewalk café where they had agreed to meet for lunch. She slid into a chair, then placed her briefcase beneath the table. It was identical to Monique's briefcase and they would switch the cases before Allison departed.

Monique touched a wineglass to Allison's, sipped, then lifted an eyebrow. "Mind telling me what this cloak and dagger stuff is all about? And why we're making such a secret about your office mail, memos and notes?"

"In case someone is following me, I don't want to lead him to Alliance," Allison answered.

Startled, Monique looked around, studying the people passing on the sidewalk. "Is someone following you?"

Allison smiled. "If so, you won't spot him." She chose a light lunch from the menu, then sampled the stuffed mushrooms that Monique had already ordered. "I don't know if I'm being followed, but it's possible. That's why I changed my mind about going to the office once a week. It's better to meet like this, like two friends having lunch."

"I suppose you're right," Monique said uncertainly, still watching passersby with suspicious eyes. She looked back at Allison. "Is something going on that I should know? Are you in some kind of trouble?"

Allison paused. She was in trouble, all right. She was infatuated with a man who was so right in so many ways, but so wrong overall. If only he weren't a thief... and if wishes were horses, then beggars would ride, she thought, recalling an old saying of Grandpa Ames's.

"It's nothing I can't handle," she said to Monique, hoping she was telling the truth.

"How are things going with Paul Courtwald?" Monique asked archly, believing she was changing the subject.

Allison pushed back a lock of hair. "I thought I'd lose interest after I knew more about him." She sighed. "But we like the same music, the same books... in the areas where we don't agree, the discussion is spirited and stimulating." She frowned up at the fronds of a palm tree. "He's wonderful," she said softly.

"I'm glad," Monique said, affection in her dark eyes. "Shall I start looking for a dress to wear to the wedding?"

Allison stared, then laughed even though she suddenly felt like weeping. "It isn't going to work, Monique. Our differences are profound. They cancel any similarities." Dropping her gaze, she toyed with the salad the waiter had delivered. "I should stop seeing him, I know that. It's just... I'm just..."

She didn't know what she was doing, which was unusual for her. But she knew she could not have a relationship with Paul. No future was possible. If she aligned herself with him, then her business became a farce. To be with Paul, it would be necessary to leave the security field, and she would have to abandon deeply held principals of honesty, everything she stood for and believed.

She couldn't do that. Wouldn't do that.

So why didn't she just walk away from him? And there was no rule that said she absolutely had to turn him in to Monsieur DeVault. Just this once, she could compromise her code of ethics and shut her eyes. She could leave Monsieur DeVault to do his own work, and hope that Paul left Monaco.

Her chest tightened at the thought of never seeing him again.

"It's just a physical attraction," she said, trying to explain herself, making it sound as though a physical attraction were a small thing and not the cataclysmic event it actually was.

She couldn't be near Paul without feeling as if a volcano were bubbling inside her. Every time he touched her or accidentally brushed against her, it was as if hot lava shot through her system, building toward an eruption.

And when he kissed her, as he managed to do whenever they were together, his kiss rocked her like a thousand-volt jolt of electricity. His kisses set her aflame, and it was all she could do not to respond like the wanton his mouth made of her.

Curiosity sparkled in Monique's eyes, and a dozen questions that she didn't ask. She and Allison were friends, but Allison was also her employer.

"Are you ready to test the Trazakis systems?" Monique inquired, instead of asking more about Paul Courtwald.

Allison nodded absently. "Late tomorrow morning the phone system will go out in the villa. The housekeeper will undoubtedly phone for repair service and I'll be with the repair crew. It's all arranged."

"Do the phone people know who you are?"

Allison's smile didn't reach her eyes. "No. My contact at the repair service is a man named Jean. Jean thinks I'm a college student who's longing for a peek inside one of the large estates. He also thinks I lust for his body." She shrugged. "Everything to date is in the file in my briefcase. If anything is unclear, we'll straighten it out when I call you with my final report."

"Then you don't think your phone is bugged?" Monique asked, teasing now.

Allison considered the question seriously before she answered. "No, that would be an unforgivable breach." She knew her answer would seem peculiar to Monique, but she didn't explain further.

Paul was aware of her home address by now. And she knew that he leased a small villa not far from the Waldheims'. She knew he loved Italian food but didn't care much for Greek dishes, preferences she shared. She knew what CDs would be stacked beside his stereo system and what book was on his bedside table.

She knew he laughed at the same things she did, and could predict what would incense or outrage him. She knew he tugged his earlobe when deep in thought, and was slow to anger and slow to calm once he did get angry.

She knew so much about him—and had yet to discover something she didn't like. A small voice deep inside whispered that this was a man she might have loved until the end of time.

Except he was one of the most sought after thieves in the world.

THERE WERE TELEPHONES in every room in the lavish Trazakis villa, and half of them were not working. The housekeeper inspected the uniforms Allison and the two other telephone repairmen wore. Then she and the other servants went about their tasks and left the phone crew to wander from room to room testing telephones.

Allison had told Paul the truth when she mentioned that she had been planning this for a long time. It had required a month to learn how to create a sophisticated problem on the phone lines. What she wanted, and what she had achieved, was called an Ingleman split, an adjustment that disabled some phones in the villa but not others. The Ingleman split made it appear the problem was in the phone units, a ploy that directed the repairmen to check the telephones first before they tracked the lines coming into the building.

But she had to act swiftly, as it wouldn't take Jean and his companion long to ascertain that the problem was not with the actual telephones.

"Wow," she said softly, her eyes rounding. "This is a fantastic place." She placed her fingers on Jean's sleeve. "Is it okay to wander around a little and have a look?"

Jean winked at her and flexed his shoulders. "Sure, honey, but make it fast. Luis and I think the problem is probably in the line, so we won't be here long. Don't touch anything."

"I won't," she promised, beaming a smile at him.

In less than five minutes she had found Mrs. Trazakis's private sitting room and the collection of tiny ivory figurines. Working quickly but carefully, she wrapped each in shredded newspaper, then set them in compartments inside two egg cartons. She taped completely around the cartons to make certain the lids wouldn't pop open, then placed them inside the small empty toolbox Jean had provided her for authenticity.

After making a swift survey of the interior security systems and noting they were disabled, she returned to the front of the villa in time to hear Jean and Luis explain to the housekeeper that the problem didn't seem to be with the telephones themselves, so they were leaving to check the outside wires.

Allison departed with the phone crew, gushing thanks for letting her accompany them and at the same time scanning outside cameras and alarms. The cameras tracked movement, but the housekeeper had switched off the alarms to accommodate the telephone repairmen. Allison waited while Jean and Luis searched and finally discovered the problem. They cursed as they repaired the malfunction Allison had so meticulously created. Two hours later, arguing about the Ingleman split, which neither repairman had seen before, Jean, Luis and Allison climbed into the phone company truck and drove away from the Trazakis estate.

Allison sighed, feeling her usual mixture of elation at a successful operation and depression that almost anyone was vulnerable to a clever and determined thief.

Jean stopped the truck beside Allison's car, which was parked a few blocks from the building housing the phone company. "Thanks," she said brightly, hopping out of the truck. "I'll launder the uniform and get it back to you."

Jean leaned out the window and leered at her. "See you tonight at Mauro's café?"

"Sure." She gave him a big smile, then pulled her fingers through the dark wig she wore, watching the truck pull away. Eventually Jean would realize that he didn't have a phone number for her and didn't know her address. Marcie O'Brien, the American coed, would disappear from his life as suddenly as she had come into it. In fact, Allison could have gone to Mauro's and sat next to Jean with no fear that he would recognize her as the college student he thought he knew.

Carrying the toolbox close to her side, praying Jean wouldn't suddenly ask to take it with him, she walked briskly toward her car and unlocked the door.

Before she could slide inside, a hand clamped down on her shoulder and a deep voice spoke behind her.

"You're under arrest."

CHAPTER SIX

ALLISON WHIRLED OUT from under the hand on her shoulder and spun to face a grinning Paul Courtwald.

"That was not funny!" she snapped.

"Sorry," he apologized, his smile instantly vanishing. "I was certain you saw me waiting for you."

It shocked her that she hadn't. He wore tailored slacks and a maroon T-shirt; he'd made no effort to disguise himself. She glared at the sunlight teasing reddish highlights from his dark hair, then sighed deeply.

"What are you doing here?" Abruptly she realized that he must have followed her this morning when she left her house. Maybe he had watched her enter the phone company building. One thing was certain, this was not an accidental meeting.

"How long have you been here?" she demanded angrily, her eyes narrowed. Had he also followed her to the Trazakis villa?

"The wait wasn't unpleasant. There's a café nearby." He ran an amused glance over the gray-and-green phone service uniform she had borrowed from Jean, ending his examination by smiling at her brown curly wig. "It appears you've taken a day job," he commented evenly. An inquisitive glance lingered on the toolbox clutched in her hand.

"Get in the car," Allison said sharply. She jerked open the door on the driver's side and slid inside.

Actually, her anger was directed more at herself than at
Paul. She had expected something like this. That's why she
had mentioned fictitious appointments every night this
week, to make it difficult for him to guess when she intended to strike the Trazakis villa. The implication that she
would enter at night was deliberate.

Allison hadn't anticipated that he would recognize her
smoke screen for what it was and follow her in the morn-
ings. That she could err so badly shocked her to her toes.
Hastily, she ran a mental check of where she had gone and
what she had done every morning this week. Other than
today, following her would not have proved very enlight-
ening.

"You told me that you were busy all day today," she
said in a level voice that contained only a hint of accusation.

Paul draped himself across the car seat, a study in casual elegance, and smiled. "One would almost think I was
trying to force your hand," he suggested. Sucking in his
cheeks, he inspected the roof of Allison's Renault. "One
could almost suspect that I was hoping to encourage you
to make the hit within a time frame that I could antici-
pate."

Her stare lengthened, then she burst into laughter, unable to remain angry when he looked so happy and pleased
with himself.

"I'm sorry," she said finally, "but today's incident was
planned well in advance of your sudden announcement
that you had to run errands." She smiled. "I would have
made some excuse not to see you today, regardless."

"Are you going to show me the figurines?" he inquired, nudging the toolbox that Allison had placed on the
floor of the passenger side next to his loafers.

"Here? Within sight of the sidewalk?" She pushed the key into the ignition. "I don't think so." Easing the car into the street, she made a turn, then zipped along avenue de Monte Carlo until she reached avenue Princess Alice, where she slowed for town traffic. The route she took would pass near the DeWilde store.

"Allison? Are the figurines in this toolbox?"

His tone made her look at him. "You really aren't sure, are you?" she asked softly, raising an eyebrow. "You still think I might be trying to trap you. If I were a policewoman, don't you think I would have arrested you before now?"

"I don't know," he said thoughtfully, examining her expression. "I've considered that possibility."

"And what did you conclude?"

"As of this minute, neither of us can do more than speculate about the other. If you are the law, you really don't have anything on me except supposition." He paused, watching her. "And I don't know if you're really who I think you are." He tapped the toolbox with the edge of his shoe. "There's an easy way to discover if you're who you claim to be. We can put that question to rest here and now."

Allison gripped the wheel and stared through the windshield. They could end it here and walk away from each other. She could tell him to get out of her car and he would. He'd assume that for reasons known to herself, she had misled him; there were no figurines. He would disappear into the crowds and she would never see him again.

Her life would resume as if Paul Courtwald had not entered it like a whirlwind. She would return to working twelve hours a day, bitterly scanning the newspapers for mention of Jeffrey's name, occasionally attending social events with old friends for whom she felt no romantic interest. Living alone. Being lonely. Missing Paul and his teasing, his competitiveness, playfulness, his vibrancy and his high-voltage sexuality.

Even now, half angry and uncertain, she was aware of him sitting beside her in a way that she hadn't been aware of a man since Jeffrey. His after-shave scented every breath; she sensed the solid warmth of his body and knew when he looked at her.

She wasn't ready to end whatever was building between them, even if it meant trouble and possible danger. For some reason, Paul had very quickly become important to her. He made her feel as if she were awakening from a long slumber; because of him, the painful world she had escaped in sleep was bright and good again.

Soon, she promised herself, she would quit playing with fire. Soon...but not yet.

"Open the toolbox," she said between her teeth, not looking at him. What he found inside would confirm his impression of her as a thief and dig her in a little deeper. The choices were to mislead him and cement his trust, or watch him walk away.

She sensed his speculative gaze on her profile as they waited for the stoplight to click to green. As Allison drove through the intersection, he bent to the toolbox and lifted it onto his lap. After easing open the lid, he frowned at the taped egg cartons. "Where did you get these?"

"My mother sent them from the States."

"Egg cartons?"

"I don't know what she thought of the request. Maybe she assumes I'm doing arts and crafts that involve using egg cartons." She shrugged, glancing at the corner of the DeWilde store as she passed on a side street.

"If this is packing for what I think it is, then I'd agree you found an artsy use for them."

Carefully, he peeled the tape off one carton, then raised the lid. After pushing aside a nest of paper, he lifted one of the tiny ivory figurines in his palm and drew a sharp breath.

"Exquisite!"

"Are you satisfied now?" Allison asked, unable to prevent a touch of sarcasm.

"Completely." He returned the figurine to its compartment in the egg carton and replaced the toolbox on the floor of the car. "Even at ten percent of actual value, this collection is worth a fortune. You'll net enough to keep you in Chanel and Dior for years." His smile lit the interior of the car.

"Have we settled the issue of trust?"

"A lot of issues were settled the minute you offered permission to look in the toolbox." He glanced out the window. "Where are we going, by the way?"

"To my house. I'm eager to get out of this wig and these clothes."

Stretching an arm across the backs of the car seats, he studied her with a thoughtful expression. "You must have used the Ingleman split, that's how I figure it. Right?"

She nodded. "Speaking of by-the-ways, I don't want you to follow me again, understood?" She took her eyes off the road long enough to glare at him. "I should have spotted you, and I would have if it had occurred to me that you'd do such a thing. But since we're attempting to establish trust, it didn't enter my mind that you'd sink to such a sneaky level." Every time she thought about him following her—and her not noticing—she felt a fresh surge of irritation.

"I think we've reached a point where we can trust each other as long as we're honest."

Allison's head turned sharply. "I am *always* honest! Always. It's who I am, it's what's important to me."

"You weren't exactly straightforward about the present operation." One dark eyebrow rose. "And how does your philosophy about honesty square with being a very accomplished thief?"

Color flooded her face. Damn it, she kept forgetting their entire dangerous relationship had begun with a misconception. She chewed her lip and frowned at the road, struggling to align her vision of herself with a relationship based on a lie. Well, not a lie, exactly. It was more like a series of omissions and false impressions. This rationalization made her feel a little better, but not much.

"Aside from that," she said lamely. "I may steal things out of people's houses, but..." This was the most illogical position she had ever tried to defend. "But I'm honest about it." She drew a deep breath and paid attention to the narrow road twisting up to her house. "And yes, I used the Ingleman split. The repairmen suspected the lines had been tampered with, but they didn't recognize the split."

He laughed. "That's the most ludicrous explanation I ever heard. But all right, I'll let you change the subject and wiggle off the hook. Obviously you had a contact on the repair crew?"

She nodded. "Everything went according to plan."

"Your home is charming," Paul mentioned as she turned through stone gates into a short driveway that led to the house she had purchased almost five years ago. It had belonged to her mother's cousin, who had sold it at a price Allison could afford, largely as a favor to her mother.

"Thank you."

From the first moment she saw the house, she had loved it. Tall windows looked toward the sea, French doors opened onto a garden balcony. The design was simple but made the most of the steep site and abundance of natural stone. She stopped the car in front of the garage and slid out, once again in possession of the toolbox containing the figurines.

Paul stood on the stone path that led to her front door. "The vines and flowers make the house appear as if it's growing out of the hillside, as if it's been here for a century. Did you do the landscaping?"

"Me?" She laughed. "I don't know a weed from an herb. And the house is old, actually. I believe it was built in the mid-1800s. Since then, it's been renovated, of course."

"The size surprises me," he commented, falling into step beside her. "Considering your income—" he nodded at the toolbox "—I expected something more lavish, a sprawling villa, at least."

"Like yours?"

"Mine's rented, but yes. More like that."

She gave him the toolbox to hold while she unlocked the front door. "I prefer to keep a low profile," she answered truthfully. "Besides, a villa is expensive to maintain. Compared to your family, mine are paupers. We don't own sprawling villas."

He gave her a curious look. "What on earth are you doing with your money? I'd think you could live as luxuriously as you pleased. Or have Rubens and rare figurines sunk to dime store prices?"

Allison straightened and blinked. The road she trod with Paul was strewn with land mines. If she truly were a successful high-ticket thief, of course she would be wealthy in her own right. Her mind raced.

"I invest my money," she said when her voice was under control. "For the future." She sounded stiff and knew it.

"Ah, preparing for the moment of decision—to retire or get caught. Do you really think you can retire, Allison? Wouldn't you miss the challenge? The thrill of it?"

"Yes," she admitted. The challenge and the thrill were part of the reason she'd chosen her profession.

"What kinds of things do you invest in?"

"Actually, I don't discuss money with casual acquaintances." This was a strange conversation to be having on the doorstep.

Paul's hands closed over her shoulders and he gazed deeply into her eyes. "Are we merely *casual* acquaintances, Just Allison?" he asked softly. "I've never felt like this about a casual acquaintance before...."

She looked into the desire darkening his gray eyes and felt her senses reel out of control. What was it about this man that made her melt inside as soon as he touched her? When he looked deeply into her eyes, her heart rolled over in her chest and she felt her breath quicken. Her lips parted and her gaze dropped to his mouth.

"How long have you been watching my house, spying on me?" she whispered. His mouth was perfectly shaped for kissing, for murmuring words of love.

His hands moved upward and he removed her brown wig. He let the wig fall to the slate porch and gently pulled the pins out of her hair. "Long enough that I know you jog for forty-five minutes every morning. When you return, you cool down beside that chestnut tree, then watch the sun on the sea while you drink a glass of orange juice." He tilted her face up to his and brushed his thumb across her mouth, then he kissed her.

Allison's eyes closed and she sagged against his body as if his kiss drained her of resistance and the energy to stand upright. "What else?" she whispered, her voice husky.

He kissed her deeply then, exploring the taste of her, the shape of her lips, the feel of her body pressed next to his. "You don't seem to have servants," he murmured. "But a man came to trim the gardens the day before yesterday. As the terraces are well maintained, I assume he comes once a week."

They kissed again, this time with growing heat and urgency. "He does," Allison conceded, her reply no louder than a moan.

Paul's hands slipped to her hips and he fit her body against his, letting her feel the heat and hardness of his arousal. A tremor shot through her limbs.

"I've always heard that uniforms turn women on, but I didn't know it worked in reverse," she murmured. "Or do you get this passionate about all phone company employees?"

When Allison opened her eyes, she found him looking down at her. There was no mistaking the deepening desire that smoldered in his gaze. When she'd told him to open the toolbox and when he'd found Madame Trazakis's figurines within, they had entered a new phase. Paul trusted her now, and his trust allowed him to go forward personally as well as professionally. He had wanted her from the beginning, she knew that. Now he was free to pursue his desires.

But what about her?

A look of confusion clouded her eyes. "I don't know why I'm doing this," she said softly. "What is it about you that's made me throw aside good sense and everything I believe in?" Right now, with his arms around her and his lips nuzzling her throat, she doubted she could remember the principles she claimed to hold dear.

"Whatever it is," he said hoarsely, speaking against her breasts, "the same thing has happened to me. You're kissing a man on your porch, and I'm proposing a professional partnership. Neither of us is acting in character.''

He thought her comment about tossing aside her beliefs referred to a public display of affection. Guilt stung her. And when he kissed her again, her guilt deepened. But she didn't want his kisses to end.

"Are you going to invite me inside?" he whispered against her earlobe.

She gazed into his eyes for a long, long moment, during which the course of the immediate future was decided.

There were stop points along every road, Allison realized, places where it was still possible to turn around and go back before one drove full speed off the edge of a cliff. She had experienced two of them today, one in the car when she knew he expected her to show him the contents of the toolbox and prove she had stolen the figurines, and the one that was occurring this instant.

They both knew if she invited him into her house, they would make love. From the moment she had met him, Allison had sensed that Paul would be a skilled and exciting lover. The way his hands moved on her body made her feel wild inside; he seemed to know exactly what she wanted. But making love to him would complicate everything she was feeling by a thousandfold.

She could not do this. Making love to a man like Paul Courtwald, a thief, would violate everything she believed she stood for or believed about herself.

Helplessly, she watched in dismay as her hands rose to the shirt of her phone company uniform and her fingers played with the row of buttons. She heard Paul suck in a breath, and he stared as she opened the top two buttons and a wedge of tanned skin widened at her collar.

He wrenched his gaze to her eyes and murmured in a hoarse voice thick with arousal, ''I'm not interested in a casual fling, Allison, not with you. So be very certain what you want before we go any further.''

The desire in his eyes matched her own, and she could not have turned away from him even if she had wanted to. Never in her life had she wanted a man as she wanted Paul. Since meeting him, she had thought of little else but having his arms around her and kissing him and . . .

''Come inside,'' she whispered hoarsely. Trembling, she opened the door and set the toolbox in the foyer.

Having passed the stop point, they sped ahead with all urgency. Hungry for each other, they stepped into the foyer and kissed deeply, hands racing over shoulders, waists, hips. There was nothing gentle or leisurely about their kisses now. They had teased each other every day for nearly two weeks, and their desire had reached fever pitch.

''Which way?'' Paul's voice was a groan of anticipation.

Allison broke from his lips long enough to take his hand and lead him to her bedroom. There he spun her into his arms and kissed her passionately until they were both breathless and tearing at their clothing.

Too hungry to wait, Paul crushed her against his body, taking her mouth with hard heat, pressing her against his bared chest. His fingers teased up her back and opened her bra with an artful movement. She pushed down his pants and in a moment, between deep, hot kisses, they threw off the rest of their clothes.

Paul held her at arm's length and stared. ''You are exquisite! Absolutely beautiful.'' He turned her in a bar of sunshine, and drew in a hard breath. ''You're a goddess.''

She laughed, suddenly shy beneath his inspection. Then she, too, swallowed. ''I love the look of you,'' she said softly.

Paul was tanned to a golden hue, pale where the sun had not touched. His taut skin stretched over muscle and tendon, firm and smooth. She stared at him with appreciation and a quickened breath of anticipation.

Allison had always thought that most men were sexier and more attractive when dressed, but in Paul's case he was sexy and attractive dressed or undressed. She gazed at him and felt her heartbeat accelerate and her nerves tense. He was a gorgeous man. And the sensations he aroused in her were powerful, exciting and new.

Trembling, she stood naked before his inspection, almost paralyzed with a desire unlike anything she had ever experienced.

"Beautiful Allison," he whispered, stepping forward to take her into his arms. When their naked bodies touched, they both drew a sharp, involuntary breath. "You can't guess how many times I've imagined this moment."

But she could. She had dreamed of him at night, fantasized about him during their days of sightseeing and on the yacht. Something deep inside recognized they had been destined for this moment from the first.

Standing beside Allison's bed, they kissed and let their fingers and tongues explore. They began almost as strangers, tentatively, a question in their fingertips. But as their kisses deepened with feverish desire, their hands grew bolder and more confident, seeming to know where to stroke, where to caress, how to enhance the passion that left them breathless.

Lost in kisses and caresses that swept all thought from her mind, Allison wasn't aware when they tumbled onto the bed. It seemed to her that one minute she was standing, the next she was lying on the bed, her head thrashing across the pillow, her body arching toward his.

"Paul!" The word was a groan, a plea. Her hands pulled at his shoulders, and she wrapped her long golden legs around his hips.

"Slowly," he murmured in her ear.

"No...I..."

Then he was fluttering his tongue across her nipple and doing wonderful things with his hands. She gasped and forgot what she had been about to say. Wave after wave of hot sensation surged through her body. His hands and teasing tongue coaxed feelings from her skin and nerve endings that she hadn't known existed.

"Paul! If you don't...I'm about to..."

He brought her to orgasm with his tongue and hands and the husky murmur of his voice. Before she could catch her breath, he kissed her again and again, and she felt a new flood of heat rise in the trail of his fingertips.

He teased her to the brink of a second explosion before he entered her, moving slowly at first, then with greater force and thrust, as if he knew exactly what she wanted and needed. They moved together as if they had been part of each other always, as if they communicated with no need for speech other than gasps and breathless murmurs of pleasure.

Afterward, sated and drenched in sweat, they lay in each other's arms and waited quietly for their heartbeats to resume a normal cadence.

Allison pressed her head to his chest, listening to the strong, steady beat of his heart. His fingers played in her tangled curls, and she raked her nails through the hair on his chest.

"I'm falling in love with you," Paul admitted quietly. He kissed the top of her head. "I can't stop thinking about you, and I want to be with you every minute of every day."

Allison's hand stopped moving on his chest. She closed her eyes and bit her lips. "You don't know anything about me," she whispered.

"I know the things that are important," he answered, tilting her face so he could look into her eyes. "You're bright and beautiful, daring and bold. You're adventurous and competitive. You're fire one minute, ice the next, and I suspect there will always be a hint of mystery about you no matter how well I think I know you." He smiled and kissed her tenderly on the lips. "One of the best things about you, Just Allison, is that with you, I can be myself. For so long an entire area of my life has been closed to other people. Finding you has been like finding the last piece of a puzzle, the piece that makes the picture whole."

"Paul—"

"I can't recall the last time I genuinely trusted someone, but it's been a very long time." He stroked a damp curl back from her cheek. "As I'm sure you know, it's impossible to have an intimate relationship when you can reveal only portions of your life. With you, I don't have to censor everything I say. I don't have to worry about giving myself away. I can be totally honest for the first time in years." His smile turned into a grin. "That should please you, since honesty means so much to you."

Guilt slammed into Allison's chest. He was falling in love with her; he trusted her. She, who wrestled daily with her conscience and thoughts of turning him in to Monsieur DeVault.

She pressed her forehead against his shoulder. For Paul, their relationship meant he could be totally honest. For her, this was the most dishonest relationship she ever had entered into. His entire impression of her finances, her profession, her character was false. And she'd done nothing, *could* do nothing, to correct that impression.

Easing away from him, she pulled the sheet up to cover her nakedness, then gazed at the ceiling.

Paul propped himself up on an elbow and frowned down at her. "I've upset you." When she didn't answer, he spoke again. "I know this seems fast, but it really isn't. I've been waiting for you all of my life."

"I don't know what to say," Allison whispered.

"I'd love to hear you say that you could love me, too. Could you, Allison?"

She turned her head to look into his steady gaze. "Yes," she whispered. "I could love you."

The lines disappeared between his eyebrows and he smiled, then leaned to place a light kiss on her lips. "That's good enough for now."

"Paul...don't ask me to explain, but I don't think this— you and me—can go anywhere. There's something..." She felt like weeping. "I don't want to mislead you, so...please don't expect anything from me."

The frown returned to his eyes. "Is it the man you were involved with before me? Do you still care for him?"

"I hate him!" she said forcefully, the vehemence in her voice surprising even her. She drew a breath and covered her eyes with her hand. "Hate is too strong a word."

"He hurt you badly."

She nodded, then lowered her hand and stared at the ceiling. "I want—I don't know, I want him to pay for what he did to me, for the shoddy way he ended a relationship that I thought was important."

"No one is good at ending a relationship. I don't want to sound like I'm defending this guy, but maybe he didn't realize that what he did would be so hurtful to you."

"I don't care if he knew! All I care about is evening the score!" Heat flooded her cheeks and she clenched her hands at her sides.

Paul was silent for a long moment, watching his fingers caress her arm. "Revenge hurts the perpetrator more than the victim," he said finally. "Let it go, Allison. Move on with your life."

"I wish I could," she said at length, swinging her legs over the side of the bed. Before she stood, she studied a spot on the carpet. "I want to forget him and move on. But it feels like closing a book without reading the last chapter." She frowned at Paul over her shoulder. "It won't be finished until..." She spread her hands. "I don't know. But something more has to happen. I know revenge is ugly, but..."

"I'm sorry."

They gazed at each other in the fading afternoon light. "So am I," Allison said softly. She shook her head and a stubborn glint iced her gaze. "He has to realize what he did. And he has to pay somehow. It won't be over for me until that happens."

"If it's all the same to you, I'd rather not talk about the bastard who hurt you." Paul ran a finger down the curve of her spine and Allison shivered with pleasure. Moving up behind her, he kissed the nape of her neck. "Come back to bed, Just Allison," he said in a thick voice. "I'm going to make you love me. I'm going to make you forget any other man."

TWO HOURS LATER, they made dinner together, then ate in the garden facing a twilight sea. They talked about the play they had seen earlier in the week, compared impressions of London, Rome and Manhattan and argued the merits of the Cannes Film Festival. Paul complimented Allison's choice of wine; she complimented him on a perfect filet mignon. They laughed, flirted with each other, and lazily rode a wave of fresh desire, knowing they would make love again and knowing it would be fabulous.

"Well, is my plan working?" he asked, refilling her wineglass. "I've fed you, plied you with wine...do you love me yet?" A deep, smoldering flame appeared at the back of his eyes. "Or do I have to make love to you again?"

Allison laughed. She hadn't known it was possible to enjoy a man's company this much. She suspected Paul was a man whose humor and vision of the world would always be fresh and interesting no matter how old he became or how life treated him.

She looked into his eyes and felt her smile fade, replaced by a thrill of excitement. "I think you'll have to make love to me again," she murmured in a throaty voice.

Taking her by the hand, he drew her to her feet and folded her in an embrace.

When his lips found hers in a possessive, demanding kiss, Allison felt the deepening night swirl around them. He was succeeding in half of his objective. Helplessly, she realized she was indeed falling in love with him.

But not even Paul's kisses could make her forget Jeffrey DeWilde. Or her vow to get even.

CHAPTER SEVEN

IN THE MORNING they jogged together, both competitive enough that jogging turned to running and then into a race. They laughed at themselves over orange juice on Allison's terrace overlooking the sea.

"But I like it that we can disagree—that you don't defer to me," Paul said, rolling the frosty glass of orange juice across his forehead.

"Do most women defer to you?" Allison inquired, a look of amusement sparkling in her clear gaze.

He pretended amazement at the question and they both laughed. Everything made Paul laugh this morning. It was a glorious day, the air soft and scented with the fragrance of spruce and orange trees. He felt wonderful, he was with a woman who fascinated him, and he was in love.

There had been other women throughout his life, but none like Allison Ames, and none whom he had let himself love. In the past when he had felt his emotions begin to engage, he had pulled away from the relationship.

He had done this for two reasons. First, a thief had nothing to offer a woman except anxiety, worry and the fear of eventual loss. Second, none of his relationships had been founded on honesty. They couldn't be. The women he had known believed he lived an idle life, enjoying family money with no greater aspiration than to romp through the world's playgrounds. He hadn't trusted any of them enough to reveal himself, and without trust there could be no enduring relationship. Without honesty, a man and woman lacked the cornerstone for any future.

Now, for the first time, he had met a woman like himself, a woman with whom he could be completely truthful about his background, his life, his profession. Knowing he could tell Allison anything was an intoxicating experience. He couldn't get enough of it.

Long into the night they had discussed previous experiences, exchanged anecdotes and laughter. The stories poured out of him, a part of his life he had never before been able to share with anyone.

Toward morning, as Allison slept in his arms, Paul recognized that he was happy, and pondered what it would be like to feel this wonderful always, to be with her forever. At first he visualized them working together, two quick, bright minds planning daring escapades, confounding authorities on three continents. He suspected a partnership between them could result in exploits that would become legendary.

But as dawn lightened the sky, his vision of a brilliant professional union faded with the shadows. To his surprise, he realized that his imagination had sketched a future he didn't really want, not with Allison. He didn't want a life of worrying that she might be apprehended and taken from him; he didn't want to lose his edge by fearing his own possible capture or dreading that he might put her through what she had suffered when her father was arrested and imprisoned.

Watching dawn tint the sky, he accepted that his career as The Ghost was nearing an end. The thought was sobering. He enjoyed his work; he liked the mental and physical challenge, the thrill of it. But unless he and Allison both retired, a future together was impossible. He had to make a choice.

Now, sitting on her terrace, he felt a faint smile curve his lips. His friends would be astonished that he hovered on the brink of making a commitment to a woman. His playboy existence was winding down.

"A penny for your thoughts..." Allison said, jarring him from his reverie.

"I'm sorry, what?"

"You look so pensive. You're not usually this quiet."

He studied her face, admiring her chameleon beauty. She hadn't yet put on makeup, and he was glad. Of all her many faces, this was the one he liked best, unadorned and free of artifice. Sunshine glowed on smooth golden skin and bright hair, and slanted across her eyes, turning them as translucent as blue crystal. "I was thinking about trust," he said softly, "and caring for someone and the future and making changes."

"All that?" she asked, teasing him.

"All that." Drawing a breath, he did something he had never done before. He placed his safety squarely in her hands. "I'm flying to Munich tomorrow. Alinor Von Basch has a stamp collection...."

Her expression told him that she understood he was offering her the greatest gift he had to give, his trust. At once the twinkle disappeared from her eyes. Leaning forward, she refilled their glasses from the pitcher of orange juice in the center of the terrace table. She didn't speak immediately, which puzzled him, and he couldn't guess what she was thinking.

"As a matter of professional interest, how do you plan to get inside?" she finally asked. "If I recall correctly, Frau Von Basch lives in a fortress."

"Do you know her?"

"Last year I attended a charity ball at her home."

Paul wasn't superstitious, but this impressed him as a good sign, another example of their compatibility. "At this time of year, Frau Von Basch vacations in the south of Spain. Security will be lax in her absence." As he confided his plans, he watched her face subtly reflect a variety of expressions, not all of which he understood. Her reaction surprised him. He'd expected pleasure; instead, she seemed almost dismayed. "I've learned that the servants invite friends over every Friday night while Frau Von Basch is on holiday." He shrugged and grinned. "The alarm system is relatively simple to disable, and the house is stone, which, as you know, is the next best thing to a ladder."

"Sounds simple enough that you could do it in your sleep," she commented lightly, turning her head to look at the morning sunlight glistening on the waters of the Mediterranean.

He laughed. They both knew stealing was not simple. A lot of planning was required, and the possibility always existed that something could go very wrong.

"How long will you be gone?" she asked.

"I figure eight days. Tomorrow night I'll enter the estate and check my information, confirm that the servants party on Fridays. The following Friday I'll go in." Leaning forward, he caught her hands and gazed into her eyes. "Come with me, Allison. We'll make a holiday of it, visit Ludwig's castles, go to the theater, take a moonlight cruise down the Danube...."

"I'd like to, but—" she looked aside "—I'm planning something here."

"Oh?"

She withdrew her hands. "It's too soon to discuss—it's still in the surveillance stage. There are several things I need to check out."

Standing, he pulled her to her feet and into his arms. He locked his hands around her waist and kissed her until his head spun. "Will you miss me?"

"Yes," she whispered.

"You don't need to sound so irritated about it," he said, laughing, enjoying her. He loved it that she could surprise him. "I want you to miss me." But when he examined the strange expression on her face, his smile faded. "Allison . . . what's wrong?"

"Oh, Paul." For a moment she didn't seem able to say anything else. She shook her head and closed her eyes. "A relationship isn't going to work for us."

He stared at her in surprise and sudden bewilderment. Minutes ago, she had been laughing and teasing, but now she looked upset. Thinking back, he tried to recall when the change had occurred.

"I understand," he said gently, tilting her face to his. Her mood had altered after he mentioned Alinor Von Basch. "Don't worry, I'll be careful. I'm not going to get caught." When he kissed her, he decided she had the softest, most yielding mouth in the world. "I won't put you through what you experienced with your father."

"Oh, Paul."

He couldn't interpret what he saw in her eyes and expression. Sadness? Resignation? Helplessness?

"And I don't want you to put me through that," he added, stroking her cheek. Now the color of her eyes reminded him of a stormy sky. "I don't want you to get caught, either. I couldn't stand losing you now that I've finally found you." He folded her against his body and gazed at the sea over her head. "This is something we're going to have to talk about, Just Allison. Soon, I think."

A low moan issued from her throat, and she pressed against him. "How did this happen?" A fist formed on his chest. "I told myself I wasn't going to get involved again."

Smiling, he kissed the top of her head, then her forehead. "I'm taking that statement as encouragement, *chérie*. As a sign of progress. You're going to love me."

Letting her head fall back, she gazed up at him. "I don't want to love you," she whispered. "It would be a disaster."

"It doesn't have to be. We can make changes...."

There was almost a desperate feel to the way she suddenly kissed him, and he didn't understand it. But part of her mystery was her complexity. In time he would know her better, but he doubted he would ever comprehend her fully or take her for granted. She would always challenge him.

"Paul, make love to me."

There was nothing he wanted more.

"THEY JUST CALLED your flight," Allison said tersely.

"You're in a strange mood today," Paul commented, touching her cheek.

"I'm sorry. I just...I have a lot of things on my mind."

"May I hope that I'm one of those things?" he asked, smiling down at her.

Allison felt her heart soar. For a moment the hustle and bustle of the Nice airport faded and she was aware only of his eyes and smiling mouth. He wore a tan jacket over chocolate-colored slacks, and a tie striped in muted tones. This morning he'd had his hair cut, and it was shorter than she'd seen it before. She liked it.

In fact, she admitted with a sinking sensation, she liked everything about him, his quick smile, the confident way he moved, the manner in which he met life head on. At the moment, there was a tension about him that she understood and found exciting. It was always like this at the beginning of a new job. By this time next Friday, Paul would fairly vibrate with suppressed excitement, adrenaline flooding his body, preparing him to handle whatever problems might arise.

He glanced toward the flow of people moving to board the Munich flight, then he leaned forward and placed a lingering kiss on her lips. "I'll be thinking about you every minute."

When he released her, Allison gripped his arm. "Paul...what if this is the time—" She glanced at the people around them and rephrased her question to make it more discrete. "What if this is the time that you don't come back?" Her eyes searched his face, memorizing his features. In the back of her mind, she saw him surrounded by police, his hands cuffed behind his back.

"You're so pale." He brushed a gentle thumb across her lips. "I'm prepared for the worst," he assured her quietly. "But it isn't going to happen."

"But if it did..." She bit her lips and had to exercise great willpower not to twist her hands together. He looked so flattered and pleased by her concern that it raised a lump of guilt to her throat.

"Darling, nothing bad is going to happen." Clasping her shoulders, he peered into her eyes. "I have to go. I love you. I'll call you."

He kissed her quickly, deeply, then dashed for the plane.

Allison watched him go, then she sank into the nearest chair and covered her face in her hands.

He had promised that nothing bad would occur, but Allison knew differently. Because she was going to make it happen.

She could not know about a crime in advance and do nothing to halt it. She *had* to phone Monsieur DeVault and inform him that The Ghost intended to steal Frau Von Basch's immensely valuable stamp collection a week from tonight. She no longer had a choice.

Lifting her head, she stared at a point in space, remembering a night of blissful lovemaking, the most exciting lovemaking she had ever experienced.

He loved her. He trusted her.

Turning him in to Monsieur DeVault was going to be the hardest thing she would ever do.

MONIQUE LOOKED UP from her desk as Allison strode past, her smile turning to concern. "Allison? Have you been crying?" Astonishment widened her eyes, and she half rose from her chair.

Allison waved a hand. "Give me a few minutes, then bring me the Von Basch file."

Shutting the door to her office, she leaned against it and closed her eyes. The drive from Nice to Monte Carlo had blurred in her mind. All she recalled was that she had driven too fast, taking the mountain curves at a furiously dangerous speed.

Pacing in front of her desk, she asked the same question over and over, as she had been doing since leaving Paul at the Nice airport.

How could she betray a man with whom she had made love only hours before? How could she do that to a man she knew she could love if she would only allow herself?

But the alternative was unthinkable. She absolutely could not let Paul steal Alinor's stamp collection.

"Allison?" Monique looked around Allison's office door. "I brought you the Von Basch file. What's up?"

"I'm too tense to sit or to concentrate." Allison pointed to a chair and urged Monique to take it. "Look through the file and see if we received the follow-up information we requested. Did Alinor take our recommendations? Did she update her systems?"

While Monique reviewed the Von Basch file, Allison stepped to the window and frowned down at the pedestrian traffic below. It had always amused her to think that she could identify Frenchwomen by their chic dresses and clever accessories, and Americans by their jeans and trendy tops and sandals. In her opinion, Italians generally wore bright primary colors, while Germans preferred pastels and prints. The international mix, as viewed from her window, usually gave her a sense of pleasure and reminded her why she had chosen to establish her base in Monaco.

There were rumors that Monaco was losing its luster, that *le patron,* as the locals referred to Prince Rainier, was preparing to abdicate in favor of his son. Since Princess Grace's death, tragedy and scandal had rocked the little principality. Some claimed the fairy tale had gone sour.

But to Allison, this was still the most sophisticated spot on earth, the richest, the most beautiful, the most exciting. She had lost count of the celebrities she'd met here and those she had added as clients.

She loved the weather, the shops, the people, the scent of the sea and the foliage. She loved her house on the hillside, the *pâtisserie* around the corner from her office, her view of *le patron*'s palace. But today, right now, she felt like running away.

"Frau Von Basch only took a few of our suggestions," Monique said, frowning as she studied the opened file. "I don't understand why some people pay large fees to have their systems reviewed, then don't take our advice. Such a waste."

"Did she update the alarm system on the house?"

Monique ran a red fingernail down a page. "No."

Allison nodded slowly. No wonder Paul had said it was a simple alarm, easily disabled. She had thought so, too, when she'd tested it ten months ago.

Her heart sank. He would do it. He would slip past Alinor's mediocre security systems, and he would steal the famed Von Basch stamp collection. He'd do it without breaking a sweat.

If she let him.

"What on earth made you think of the Von Basch file?" Monique inquired curiously, watching Allison resume pacing. "Allison?"

She flung herself into her desk chair and stared at Monique. "Men drive women crazy."

Monique laughed. "Wait. You're changing subjects too fast for me to follow. Do I take it from this that the romance with Paul Courtwald has struck a rocky patch?"

"We've hit a granite boulder."

"Does this boulder have a name?"

"Philosophical differences, I guess you could say." Allison turned a brooding expression toward the window and away from the phone on her polished desk. Monsieur DeVault's number rang in her head. She had to make that call; there was no alternative.

Monique responded with a classic French shrug. "You must find a compromise."

"There is no compromise in this instance."

Or was there? She sat a little straighter and stared at the Picasso sketch brightening the wall across from her, her thoughts racing.

"Monique . . . do we have a phone number for Alinor's vacation house on the Costa del Sol?"

"I can get it," Monique said, frowning. "You're jumping from subject to subject so rapidly I can't keep up with you."

"Good!" Perhaps there was a compromise. Leaning back in her chair, Allison relaxed for the first time that day. "Is there anything going on in the office that I should know about?"

Monique updated her on current assignments, then moved to more personal items. "Gina received an engagement ring last week."

"Lovely." Allison smiled. "It's Frederico, of course."

Monique nodded. "They're planning a big wedding. Gina already has an appointment at DeWilde's to look at gowns and accessories."

Instantly, Allison's smile faded and she stared down at her hands.

"Forget him," Monique softly advised.

"If only I could. But every time I turn around there's the DeWilde name."

Allison was unaware of how long she drifted in reverie, but during that time Monique must have gone and come again, because Alinor Von Basch's number in Spain lay before her on the desk.

Sighing heavily, she reached for the telephone. After a dozen rings, a breathless voice answered. *"Hola."*

"Alinor? It's Allison Ames, in Monaco."

"Allison! How lovely to hear from you. Give me a second to catch my breath, I just ran upstairs from the shore."

"I don't wish to distress you, but my sources believe your stamp collection may be the target for an upcoming theft by a very skilled international cat burglar." Closing her eyes, she listened to Alinor's gasp. "If my information is correct, you have a couple of days before The Ghost makes his move. I'd like to give you some numbers to call, and I'll help in any way I can, of course. But I strongly urge you to replace your current systems with security that's tougher to crack, and I believe you need to do it at once."

"Of course! I just never got around to it...I've been so busy that... what are those numbers?"

After three hours of tense international phone calls between Monaco, Spain and Germany, Allison stood from her desk and stretched her back against her hands. Bending slightly forward, she rolled the tension out of her shoulders.

She felt reasonably confident that the Von Basch servants' Friday-night parties had come to a halt, that dozens of workmen and local security experts were converging on the Von Basch estate to install state-of-the-art surveillance equipment, and that Paul Courtwald, aka The Ghost, was not going to walk away with the Von Basch stamp collection.

She had not found a real solution to her dilemma with Paul, but she'd found a compromise that meant she did not have to turn him in to Monsieur DeVault, at least not yet. She had bought them a little more time together.

She wished her obsession with Jeffrey DeWilde could be solved as easily.

"HELLO, *CHÉRIE*. Did I wake you?"

"No, I was reading. Did you go sightseeing today? Tour Crazy Ludwig's castles?"

Paul leaned back on mounded pillows and crossed his stockinged feet on the bedspread. The Munich Hilton, near the English Gardens, was reassuringly similar to Hilton hotels all over the world. At one time or another, he'd stayed in all of them. He'd been living in hotels most of his adult life. Until this week, he hadn't given his living arrangements much thought. But during the last two days, it had occurred to him that his infatuation with room service menus and for fluffy white towels undoubtedly stemmed from hotel living.

"I've been thinking it might be pleasant to own a home of my own for a change."

Allison laughed, the sound full and throaty in his ear. "The castles must have made a big impression on you."

"Actually, I was thinking about something more of a cross between your house and the villa I'm renting in Monte Carlo."

"What brought this on?"

He gazed at the darkness pressing against his hotel window, unsure how to explain new yearnings that he didn't fully understand himself. "I'm not sure. Since meeting you, I've been having strange thoughts. Do you do that to every man you meet?"

"I'd like to think so, but I doubt it," she said, laughing again.

"It's time to get down to business, *chérie*. So...the first item on the agenda— Do you love me yet?"

"That's business?" Her voice teased, but a suggestion of wariness had entered her tone.

"We *are* considering a partnership...."

"Professionally," she interjected. The amusement was fading from her voice by the second.

"And personally, unless I imagined a certain black silk nightgown and the gorgeous woman inside it. And aren't you the lady who insists she doesn't do anything halfway?"

A silence ensued, followed by a sigh. "I used to be that lady. Lately I seem to do everything in half measures."

"*Chérie*, is your phone scrambler turned on?"

"Of course," she answered promptly.

"Now, don't get feisty, it's better to be safe than sorry."

"Ah, platitudes. How about, An ounce of prevention is worth a pound of cure?"

He made a sound of amusement and annoyance. "You can't guess how apropos that particular platitude is." Frowning, he leaned forward and pulled off his socks, tossing them toward a chair. "It appears Frau Von Basch has chosen this particular week to install an ounce of prevention."

"I beg your pardon?"

"Friday night, everything was quiet and exactly as expected. But I drove past the estate late this afternoon and discovered a bevy of workmen crawling all over the place. You wouldn't believe what's going on there."

"Tell me."

"If you thought the Von Basch mansion resembled a fortress before, you should see what's happening to it now." He told her about the new guardhouse going up beside heavy gates and abetted by video surveillance on a cross grid that swept the driveway and the grounds. He ended a recitation of the improved security by adding, "And my stone ladder? The mansion is getting a face-lift that includes smooth stucco all around the base and as high as a story and a half."

"Can you still get in?" Her anxiety pleased him.

"Yes, but it won't be as easy as it would have been last week. It appears guards are living on the premises while the renovations are in progress. And the new systems are going to be formidable."

"Perhaps it would be wiser to postpone the project."

A sigh of frustration lifted his chest. "I'm considering it. Certainly I'm not going to attempt anything until I know a lot more about the new systems."

His disappointment was acute. He could be reckless, but not when planning a job. Then, patience and caution emerged. He'd put weeks of research into the Von Basch hit and had spent thousands of dollars buying information, only to find it wasted. A frown wrinkled his brow.

He wanted a success to impress Allison. In the month that he had known her, she had scored a Rubens and the Trazakis collection of ivory figurines. He had netted exactly nothing. No wonder she was slow to commit to a partnership.

He was tempted to try for the Von Basch stamp collection in spite of the guards and improved security, just to salvage his pride and her opinion of him.

"Don't do it," she stated flatly.

He laughed, loving her for knowing him so well in so short a time. "How did you know what I was thinking?"

"Would it influence your decision if I told you that I'm going to the casino tomorrow night with some friends? And that Didi Robillard has a man she wants me to meet?"

He sat straight up. "Is this a ploy to make me jealous?"

"Absolutely. Is it working?"

He hesitated. A discreet buyer was eagerly awaiting the stamp collection, and the agreed price was much higher than he had initially expected. Getting into the Von Basch estate would be about twenty times more difficult now, but not impossible. Ordinarily he welcomed an interesting challenge. And he wanted Allison to see him as successful.

On the other hand . . .

"I'll be on the first plane out in the morning," he said gruffly.

They talked for another twenty minutes, then he hung up the telephone and leaned back against the headboard, folding his arms across his chest.

What the hell was he doing?

He was walking away from something he had planned for two months. He was going to abandon the Von Basch stamps, and not because he feared the new security systems but because he couldn't stand the thought of Allison Ames on the arm of some suave bastard that Didi Robillard knew. Didi was a friend of Paul's mother, and he'd often heard his mother refer to Didi as a woman who fancied herself a matchmaker. Her choice for Allison would offer real competition.

Scowling, he moved around the hotel room, throwing things into his suitcase.

Damn it, this incident proved what his instinct had always told him. A thief either gave up the idea of a relationship or found another line of work. There was no middle ground. The minute you fell in love, you lost your edge. And that was dangerous.

Feeling moody and frustrated, he opened the minibar and then mixed a Scotch and soda. Allison had proved herself to him; he had to prove himself to her.

Afterward, he vowed to retire The Ghost and settle into a more predictable life. Part of him would miss the excitement and the adrenaline highs. But the larger part of his mind had turned to thoughts of owning a home, and to thoughts of a certain chameleon beauty who filled a black silk nightgown to perfection.

Somewhere deep inside he supposed he had always known this day would come.

Now all he had to do was make Allison admit that she loved him, make her forget her obsession for revenge against the man who had hurt her, and find out if she was also willing to retire.

"Nothing to it," he muttered, downing his Scotch and soda.

Then he laughed aloud.

CHAPTER EIGHT

"YOU *CAN'T* BEG OFF! I won't let you!"

Allison laughed. Holding the phone to her ear, she bent over her knees and applied deep rose polish to her toenails. "Didi, I already have plans for this evening."

Overnight rain had cooled the air, but the morning sun flooding the hillside warmed the terrace stones. Allison sat on an oversized towel, soaking up sunshine, painting her nails and trying to decide what she would wear to meet Paul's plane from Munich.

"We aren't going to the Casino after all," Didi said. "Too many in the party are Monaco residents and can't gamble there. Instead, Prince Fahed has invited everyone to his yacht for an evening cruise. Don't tell me you aren't tempted . . . lobster and caviar on moonlit waters, a lovely view of Cannes at night, and a man I promise is just perfect for you!"

Allison shook her head and smiled. "You think any two people who are single are perfect for each other. Remember the last man you insisted was perfect for me? The Greek Toad?"

Didi Robillard laughed. "All right, the Toad wasn't one of my better efforts. But *this* man is one I'd chase after myself if I weren't married."

"Didi, you're sixty-two. This man can't be right for both of us."

Now was the moment to confide about Paul, and she wanted to talk about him, but she didn't. If she told Didi or any of her friends about Paul, they would insist on meeting him, which Allison couldn't allow. She couldn't risk that a friend might inquire about her business in front of Paul. That would be a disaster.

No matter which way she looked at it, she had to accept that her relationship with Paul would necessarily be brief. It couldn't be otherwise. If she'd had any sense, she would have ended it before now. But somehow, she couldn't envision a future without him. The dilemma revolved hopelessly in her mind, keeping her awake nights searching for a solution she knew did not exist.

"This paragon is in his early fifties," Didi continued. "A tiny bit young for me, a tiny bit old for you. But otherwise perfect." She stubbornly persisted over Allison's laughter. "He's very rich, the CEO of an international corporation, handsome, crème de la crème socially, charming and lonely."

"Which means that he's recently divorced, right? Didi, that's the worst kind of man. Newly divorced men aren't looking for a relationship, they're looking to recapture their fraternity days. They want a series of flings with show-girl types."

"Not this man," Didi insisted confidently. "This is definitely good husband material. This man was married for thirty plus years, he liked being married, and I predict he won't remain single long. You like intelligent, analytical men, Allison, I guarantee you'll fall in love with him overnight! So, okay, he isn't into all that physical stuff you're so wild about. I've never known him to climb a mountain or jump out of a plane, but believe me, this man is going to knock your socks off!"

Suddenly Allison straightened and the polish wand dropped from her trembling fingers. She felt the color drain from her face.

"Didi. What is his name?"

"Sweetie, if you play your cards right—" Didi paused for dramatic effect "—you could be the next Mrs. De-Wilde! Now that I think about it, you look enough like a young Grace DeWilde that the two of you could be related."

The air rushed out of Allison's lungs. "Jeffrey. He's here? In Monaco?"

"Do you know him?"

"Oh, yes," Allison answered softly, closing her eyes. And it had been exactly as Didi predicted. She had fallen in love with Jeffrey almost overnight. "Actually, I've even done some work for DeWilde's. I met Jeffrey about a year ago, in Paris. I went for a late-night jog and was nearly struck by a car. I sprained my ankle. Jeffrey was out walking, witnessed what happened and helped me to his hotel. He had the hotel doctor wrap my ankle, then called for a limo to take me back to the friends with whom I was staying."

"There you are. Concerned, caring and heroic. And now he's available. Rumor has it that he and Grace will divorce soon." Didi's voice dropped to a purr. "Come with us to Prince Fahed's yacht and you can thank Jeffrey properly for his gallantry."

That, she had already done. She had phoned Jeffrey the next day and invited him to dinner as a gesture of gratitude. She'd persisted until he finally agreed. He'd been so charming, so attentive, that she'd phoned again a few days later and wheedled him into an evening at the theater, and the following night she had persuaded him to accompany her to the ballet. A day later, as she had hoped, Jeffrey phoned her. And their affair began.

She couldn't remember the beginning without leaping ahead to their painful ending. Shifting on the towel, she scanned the red rooftops below, wondering where he was staying. At a hotel? With friends?

"How long has Jeffrey been in Monte Carlo?" she asked, struggling to keep her voice light.

"I believe he arrived last weekend," Didi replied. "This is the only night he has free before he returns to London."

Shock bled the color from Allison's gaze. Jeffrey had been in the principality for a week and she hadn't known it.

Didi continued speaking, but Allison wasn't really listening. "Grace's departure rocked the DeWilde empire, you know. Things are beginning to steady out now, but there's been a lot of speculation, and I mean a *lot,* about how badly the corporation was hurt when Grace left. She was a major force in marketing, and there's no one in the company who can really replace her. Naturally, everyone at DeWilde's is trying to keep this quiet. They don't want investors or the public to know how badly Grace's defection hurt them. Even so, I understand the stock is wobbly, especially now that Grace has her own store in the States."

Allison stared at the yachts bobbing in the harbor. What would she have done if she'd known earlier that Jeffrey was close at hand? Would she have confronted him? Would she have found a way to hurt him as he had hurt her?

"No one knows why the DeWilde marriage broke up," Didi continued, prattling along in a gossipy tone. "If there was one marriage on earth that everyone thought would last forever, it was Jeffrey and Grace's. Someone said they'd heard Jeffrey had a fling with a bimbo in Paris—"

Allison doubled over as if she'd received a blow to the abdomen. Squeezing her eyes shut, she covered her face with her free hand. *A bimbo.* God. She couldn't bear this.

"But Jeffrey just isn't the type for a hit-and-run fling. He adored Grace. And she adored him. Well, never mind, what's done is done. The good news is that Jeffrey is free as a bird, or will be soon, and he's the catch of the season. Best of all, you have a chance to renew his acquaintance and dangle your gorgeous self in front of his eyes. Say you'll come."

"I told you," Allison whispered, "I already have plans. I'm seeing someone else."

"Whoever he is, he isn't as rich, as available, as interesting as Jeffrey DeWilde!"

"Believe it or not, he is."

"Give, darling, tell me everything."

"I'd love to, but I'm running behind schedule. I need to check in at the office, and I have a dress fitting in two hours, a tennis match this afternoon, then it's back to the office to catch up on the mail and paperwork. I'll tell you all about him next time we talk."

"Promise?"

"If I'm still seeing him then...."

After she hung up the phone, Allison dropped back on her towel and stared at the sky with damp eyes. Her stomach hurt. The word *bimbo* echoed in her mind. Jeffrey had used her. He had hurt her deeply, he had made a fool of her, and he had left her vulnerable to gossip.

But he was emerging as the catch of the season. As good husband material. As a man who had "adored" his wife and had been "adored" by her. Jeffrey was rich, interesting and available, damn him.

And what was Allison? She'd been rejected, her affection paid for with a box of jewelry, and, to those who heard the whiff of gossip, denigrated as a bimbo. How long would it be before someone identified her as Jeffrey's former lover?

She couldn't stand it.

Somehow, some way, Jeffrey had to pay for treating her like this. He couldn't continue to go unscathed through his perfect world. Justice demanded retribution.

PAUL SPOTTED ALLISON the minute he entered the gate area. Dressed in a lemon-colored silk slack suit trimmed in apple green, she stood out like a bright flower. By far, she was the most beautiful woman present, the most exciting woman he had ever known. Pride swelled his chest when he noticed several envious glances as she ran into his arms.

He forgot the people around them when he realized she was trembling against him. Gently, he eased her away and studied her face. "I'd love to think I make you quiver, but I suspect this is something more. Allison? What's happened? What's wrong?"

He'd hoped for an enthusiastic greeting, and she'd given it to him, but something painful glistened in her eyes. Something was hurting her.

"I'm so glad to see you," she whispered, touching his cheek.

"I'm glad you're glad." He kissed her, and was surprised when she turned the kiss from one of light greeting into something deeper. Her mouth was like a damp flame, her body a slender, urgent promise against his. "God, I missed you," he said gruffly, speaking against a fragrant cloud of blond hair.

Leaning back in the circle of his arms, she gazed up at him as if she were searching for something in his face.

"You and I are so much alike. We're both athletes, we like strenuous sports, we like physical challenges. We're about the same age. We're both bright and ambitious."

Paul laughed. One of the things he loved about her was her ability to surprise him. She was never predictable. "We're both masters of disguise, good chess players, we like crossword puzzles and puzzles of all kinds," he answered, following her lead. "We like Italian food and fast cars, we can be honest with each other, and would you mind telling me what this is all about?"

"It's about you and me." She frowned into his eyes. "It's about a perfect fit versus an imagined fit. It's about a man who understands women versus a man who doesn't. It's about being happy that you're back safely, and that we...we..."

He kissed her, telling her with his mouth and embrace that he didn't really care why she felt it necessary to list some of the reasons they were so right for each other. He was just happy that she'd allowed herself to reveal her deepening emotions.

Once on the road from Nice to Monaco, he shifted on the car seat and watched her drive. Allison drove as he did, fast and with total concentration. Because he didn't like to be interrupted by conversation when he was driving, he assumed she didn't, either, and contented himself with admiring her profile and the bright ribbons of hair that tossed in the breeze flowing through the window.

It was going to work out between them. They had been destined for each other. He'd never felt more sure of anything in his life.

He believed Allison knew it, too, and would have sworn to it when she drove directly to his rented villa and followed him inside without a word, as eager as he to reaffirm their deep feelings by making love.

He led her to his sunwashed bedroom, where they tore their clothing off without looking away from each other, hurrying, hungry for each other. Kissing, stroking, they tumbled onto the king-size bed and came together with fierce, explosive need. Never in Paul's life had he wanted a woman this passionately, this urgently. And never before had lovemaking been so exciting, so concentrated and satisfying.

Afterward, the sense of urgency appeased, they made love again, infinitely more slowly this time, with the tenderness of two lovers desiring to please each other, wanting to savor each lovely, delicious moment and make the experience last.

"I've been thinking about you—and an afternoon like this—every day since I've been gone," Paul confided drowsily, cradling her head on his shoulder. They had been wild in their lovemaking, and then tender. Urgent with passion, then urgent with the desire to please each other. She was as surprising and wonderful in bed as she was in conversation.

"So have I." The admission clearly took her off guard, but her voice also revealed that she murmured the truth. He smiled against her hair.

"What time are we supposed to meet your friends at the Casino?"

She hesitated. "Their plans changed and they're taking a yacht to Cannes. I didn't feel like going so I declined on our behalf. Do you mind?"

"Mind? A night of having you all to myself?" His arms tightened around her and he stroked his fingertips lightly across her silky skin. "I spent the entire flight fantasizing about punching the guy Didi wanted you to meet."

He expected her to laugh and offer some teasing remark, but she remained silent.

"We'll go to the Casino ourselves and I'll break the bank for you."

"If you like," she said quietly.

Gently, he eased her up on the pillow beside him, then gazed into her eyes. "Allison...something's different. What's wrong?"

To his astonishment, tears brimmed beneath her lashes. "Nothing...and everything," she whispered.

"I love you," he said, kissing her eyelids. "If you weren't so stubborn and would only admit it, you love me, too." Still she didn't smile. "Allison, listen to me. You and I were made for each other. You'll never find another man who will love you more than I do."

She gazed searchingly into his eyes, her own swimming in tears that left him feeling bewildered. "I'm beginning to believe you," she whispered.

"Excellent. That makes me happy."

But it didn't seem to make her happy.

"I WISH I HAD MY OWN CAR here," Paul commented, giving the keys of his rented Porsche to the valet. He eyed a line of Ferraris and Maseratis parked before the Casino. "I own the sweetest, hottest Ferrari you ever saw. Unfortunately, it's in Rome."

"I always wanted a Ferrari," Allison mentioned absently. Lifting the hem of her gown, she placed one glittering slipper on the stone steps leading to the Casino's entrance.

"Why don't you buy one?" Paul asked, taking her arm.

"I...someday I will," she said, frowning. He'd never believe her if she told her the truth, which was that she couldn't afford a Ferrari.

"Have I told you how fabulous you look tonight?" Paul said, leaning close to her ear. "And you're wearing that perfume I like so much. Mmm. Wonderful!"

"You look pretty fabulous yourself."

A tuxedo made him look older than his actual years, more cosmopolitan and worldly. Allison had thought he looked born to wear climbing gear. And then tennis shorts. Or a diving tank. Now she ran an appreciative gaze over his impeccably tailored jacket and slacks and decided Paul Courtwald wore formal clothing as if it were a second skin. He liked to tease her about being a chameleon, but he was equally adaptable, equally at home in a variety of milieus.

For herself, Allison had chosen a cream-colored Dior that enhanced the golden tones of her tan. Cream colored silk hugged her bosom, nipped at her waist, then flowed in a thousand cunning pleats to silver evening sandals. Because Paul was so tall, she could wear her hair gathered into a cluster of shining curls on top of her head, a style that was particularly becoming. She had chosen diamond studs for her ears, knowing hers would be the simplest jewelry she would see tonight, but she had left her throat bare. Habit dictated her choices. She knew she looked attractive, but she also knew she would fade next to the brilliant gowns and bejeweled bodies of the women they were likely to encounter within the Casino. That was exactly how she wished it to be.

It was a risk accompanying Paul to the Casino, but a calculated risk. Residents of Monaco were prohibited from gaming there, but, like Allison, it was possible that someone she knew had accompanied an out-of-town guest. And it was possible that someone from outside Monaco might recognize her; she had an international clientele. If she spotted anyone who might let it slip that she owned and operated a securities business, she intended to plead a severe headache and persuade Paul to leave at once.

Her preference was to spend a short evening on the main marble-columned floor where the tourists usually gambled. But Paul was no neophyte. He led her along a colonnade toward the private gaming rooms in back. An entire second, more opulent casino existed that few tourists knew about. Here Europe's elite could be found. Here were the designer gowns moving from table to table like bright petals on a revolving flower, the Bond Street tuxedos, the thousand-dollar markers that changed hands with a shrug and a casual call for more chips.

Paul slid into place at a roulette table and patted the stool beside him. Allison shook her head, scanning the gilt-and-mirrored room for familiar faces.

He blinked, then snapped his fingers and frowned. "I owe you an apology. I only now remembered that you can't play." Turning to the croupier, who had overheard, he said in a low, suggestive voice, "Unless..."

But the croupier cast an admiring glance at Allison, then gave Paul a reluctant shake of his head. "I'm sorry, *monsieur*. It is impossible."

Allison placed a hand on Paul's shoulder when he started to rise. "Enjoy yourself. I'll just have a look around. See if I spot anyone I know."

"We could go to the casinos in Cannes or Nice."

Such a plan would only compound her chances of encountering a client or someone else who might make mention of her business. "I'm not much of a gambler," she murmured.

He laughed. "You're very much a gambler," he said, smiling at her.

She returned his smile, loving the way his eyes crinkled and the lines deepened along his cheeks when he smiled. "Perhaps you're right. But not this kind of gambling."

Leaving Paul to enjoy himself at roulette, Allison moved around the fringes of the casino, studying other players. She spotted a few faces she recognized, but none familiar enough to pose a risk of her identity being revealed.

Minutes later Paul startled her by appearing at her side and slipping a hand around her waist. "I'm not lucky without you by my side. Is this the job you're considering?" he inquired, smiling at their lavish surroundings. A pointed glance swept the paintings on the wall, the stacks of markers and chips piled on the tables.

Allison laughed. "Only a lunatic would attempt such a thing." A guarded look shielded her eyes, and she studied him thoughtfully. "I have something else in mind."

One dark eyebrow rose. "'Oh?' he asked the beautiful and mysterious woman, leaving an expectant pause."

"'Yes indeed,' the woman answered, warning the handsome and dashing man that this was not the place to discuss such matters."

They grinned at each other, and Paul offered his arm. "Then I suggest we go someplace terribly expensive and very private where we *can* discuss such matters. We'll have dinner and we'll speak of cabbages and kings, of love and lovemaking, of partnerships and fortunes. Agreed?"

"It sounds lovely."

"I'm sorry the casino part of the evening didn't work out," he remarked as the valet brought their car to the entrance. "But I'm looking forward to the rest of the evening. And very curious to learn what you're suggesting."

"DeWilde's," Allison said softly. The word slipped out of her mouth as if she had intended to say it, as if what she was about to suggest didn't horrify her. "And a priceless tiara that once belonged to Empress Catherine the Great of Russia.''

Paul stared at her and whistled softly. He helped her inside the car, then drove two blocks to the row of designer shops. Half in shock, Allison held her breath as they slowly cruised past DeWilde's, examining the peach-and-navy facade. A mannequin wearing a stunning bridal gown stood in the lighted display window, flanked by two bridesmaids smiling eternal happiness.

''It's a corner location, well lit on two sides,'' Paul murmured, thinking aloud. ''One side abuts Henri & Co....we can't be sure what's at the back side. Looks like an attic or storage space above the second floor.''

Allison stared at the building in sick fascination as they drove past. Maybe Jeffrey was inside. No, he would have left by now to join the guests on Prince Fahed's yacht. But undoubtedly he had been here earlier.

What they'd shared together had meant so little to him that he'd probably forgotten all about Allison Ames, the ''bimbo.'' Didi's word made her cringe. Knowing that's all she'd been to Jeffrey was as much a slap in the face as the jewelry box had been.

Paul took her to Pinon's, a very small, very exclusive and very private restaurant. One had to know its location on an obscure side street to find it. ''I had no idea this place existed,'' Allison murmured, sliding into a candle-lit booth. ''How ever did you find it?''

She *did* recognize a former client as they approached their table, but, thankfully, Pinon's was not a place for table-hopping. The restaurant was designed for privacy, a place to firm multimillion dollar deals and decide the fate of empires, and for romance. It didn't surprise Allison to recognize international celebrities. They could dine here and discuss matters of a private nature without fear of interruption or eavesdropping.

Once drinks had been served, and the wine and menu decided upon, Paul leaned back on the banquette and gazed at her. "Your eyes shine like sapphires in the candlelight," he said softly. "You look different every time I see you, depending on what you're wearing and the light and your mood."

"I like you best when you're wearing nothing at all," she teased in a low, throaty voice. Their lovemaking was spectacular, an event of such passion and tenderness that she ached even to think about it.

"That's exactly what I plan to wear later this evening. I hope you'll join me." His gray eyes caught the candlelight and danced with flickers of love.

"I'd like that," Allison said, smiling. She melted inside at the look of him, so handsome and self-assured.

They touched the rim of their glasses and gazed into each other's eyes. "To our partnership," Paul proposed in a husky voice.

"To us," Allison answered after a brief hesitation.

Taking her hand, Paul idly ran his thumb over her ring finger. "About this current project . . . how long have you been considering it?"

"For several months." To Allison's astonishment, the minute she said the words, she suspected they were true. She wanted to hit Jeffrey back, and this was one way to do it. The only way she could think of.

And of course it was crazy and unthinkable. She had to stop this before Paul began to believe she was serious. But the part of her brain that kept repeating "bimbo" was not getting the message. "I ran across an interesting piece of information. Not all of the famed DeWilde family jewels are insured."

She spoke quietly, with an undertone of anger, but also with dismay at each word that took her forward. There was something dangerously exciting, too, something sickly satisfying about striking back at Jeffrey. A tug of conflicting emotions pulled her toward reason one instant, then spun her toward an abyss the next.

Paul frowned. "How do you know this?"

She drew a deep breath. "An accidental remark, followed by some deep digging on my part. Two insurance companies insure the DeWilde collection." This was pillow talk information. The rest she had learned on her own, prompted by professional curiosity. "When one of the DeWildes inspects either of the policies, he or she probably assumes the unlisted pieces are insured by the other company. And most are. But not the pieces displayed in the stores."

She had planned to point out this disastrous oversight to Jeffrey on the night he broke off their affair. It now seemed fortuitous that she hadn't gotten the chance.

"Hmm. No insurance..."

It wasn't necessary to mention that since the pieces displayed in the DeWilde stores were not insured, they were therefore not protected by the strict rules, restrictions or security requirements of any insurance company. The security obviously was handled through private arrangements.

"This could be very good," Paul mused.

"Maybe. But the stores probably used insurance requirements as a guideline for their systems."

"Possible," he agreed, nodding. "I think we should assume, given the nature of the pieces, that security is excellent." He studied her face. "More realistically, it probably isn't as excellent as it ought to be."

"That's my guess," Allison agreed, frowning down at her drink. What in the hell was she doing? Had she lost her mind? She had to stop this discussion before things went too far. She had to.

"Have you checked out the security?"

"I haven't been inside DeWilde's Monte Carlo for several months," she said, speaking slowly. Part of her mind listened in amazement to the words falling out of her mouth. "When I was there last, the tiara was inside a glass case. It appears the case is resting a fraction of an inch above a pressure-sensitive base with the tiara itself actually on the base. It looks like a weight-responsive pad."

Paul's eyes gleamed. "Very nice. If the case is broken, a single piece of shattered glass falling on the base will be enough to trigger an alarm. Conversely, lifting the tiara will also trigger the alarm."

"That's how I see it. It's an interesting challenge."

"How is the glass case mounted? Suspension?"

"No. It sits on a metal frame. There isn't enough room beneath it to insert fingers for lifting, assuming the sheer weight *could* be lifted. There's no chain above or anything like that. To clean the tiara or the inside glass, the alarm would have to be disabled." She drew a breath. "The only way to get past the case is to tinker with the alarm or break the glass."

"Which then shatters onto the pad and triggers the alarm."

"That's my guess."

"A nice problem," he said. Allison could see it was the kind of problem he most enjoyed. His eyes danced in anticipation of the puzzle waiting to be solved. Not a shadow of doubt darkened his expression; he was certain they *would* solve it.

And suddenly Allison understood why she liked her job so much and why she was good at it. If she hadn't chosen security, she might have chosen to be exactly like Paul, a thief. She too liked the challenge of stealing a presumably unstealable object. She thrived on the danger and excitement. She liked outwitting the systems. Fortunately, given her passion for honesty, she could indulge herself on the right side of the law. But it could easily have gone the other way. How easily shocked and frightened her a little and acted as a cold dose of reality.

She had to stop this conversation now, right now.

But after dangling an interesting challenge in front of Paul, she knew this was exactly the wrong moment to back away. Yet to appease a screaming conscience, she had to try.

"You know, after talking about it, I don't think we should go any further with this," she said after the waiter delivered squab in orange and almond sauce. "I'm sorry I mentioned it. Really, we should just forget it."

Instantly Paul tensed, and he pushed aside his plate. "Why? Because you're not sure of me?"

Allison lifted her eyebrows in surprise. "Why would you say that?"

"Because I abandoned the Von Basch project," he stated bluntly. "In fact, Allison, you don't know what I can or cannot do. And you have only my word—" he glanced at the entrance to their private booth "—that I'm who I claim to be."

"Not exactly," she said after a minute. "I've checked your movements against those of, uh, who you claim to be, and I don't doubt that you're telling the truth. Besides, you've pulled off some spectacular hits. The one in Morocco was amazing."

Frowning, he drummed his fingertips on the tablecloth. "I should have stayed in Munich. I wanted to prove myself to you. I should have."

"That would have been very foolish," she snapped. Then her voice softened. "Paul, you don't have to prove anything. Remember how we met, cowboy? You've proven yourself to anyone's satisfaction."

For a long moment he didn't say anything, then he released a breath. "This is what I wanted—a partnership." He contemplated her in the flicker of candlelight. "Why doesn't it feel right?"

"If it doesn't feel right, then we shouldn't proceed," Allison answered promptly. "Please, just forget I mentioned anything about DeWilde's. It was a foolish idea."

Relief poured through her body like a rush of warm cognac. She felt dizzy with it. For a few nerve-racking minutes she had lapsed into some kind of lunacy. She, who had not knowingly broken the law in her entire life, had actually suggested that she and Paul commit an illegal act.

Shocked by what she had done, Allison sagged against the leather upholstery of the banquette and rubbed moist palms against her napkin. She could not believe how close she had come to doing something totally against everything she believed in and stood for.

Sobered by the close call, she now found it ludicrous that for even one minute she had considered involving herself in an actual theft. Or that some rash, wild part of her mind had suffered a momentary delusion that stealing a piece of the DeWilde collection would somehow punish Jeffrey.

"No," Paul said, studying her face, "the challenge is too interesting to pass up. We'll do it. This will be our partnership venture. It's perfect." He raised his glass in a toast. "To you and me and success!" He gazed into her wide eyes and spoke in a voice as soft and exciting as a caress. "First,

I'm going to prove myself to you. And then I am going to place the Empress Catherine's tiara on your head.''

"Oh, Paul," Allison whispered. She felt sick inside.

What had she set in motion?

And more important, how could she stop it?

CHAPTER NINE

THEY WALKED OFF Paul's tennis court, both perspiring heavily, and climbed a set of stone steps to the terrace, where a buffet breakfast waited.

"Thank you, Signora Cruzi." By now, Allison was familiar with Paul's cook and his part-time staff. Signora Cruzi beamed, then discreetly withdrew into the interior of the villa, murmuring fondly about *amore.*

Smiling, Allison mopped her face and throat with a towel, then shook her hair free of the ponytail she'd worn to the tennis court. Slamming the ball across the net had released some of the tension that was steadily increasing as the days passed, but she would continue to feel edgy until she resumed control of her life. She wished she knew exactly how to do that.

Paul poured two frosty tumblers of orange juice. "You were in killer mode this morning, *chérie.*" A rueful smile crossed his flushed face. "I demand a rematch. Tomorrow morning, same time, same place."

"Sorry, I have an early appointment tomorrow morning." After filling a plate from Signora Cruzi's buffet, Allison took a seat at the umbrella table, then studied Paul's expression. Soft sunlight played through his hair. The rosy warmth of exertion had begun to fade from his face. He looked fabulous in tennis whites.

Good-natured annoyance lingered in his expression at having lost at tennis. Otherwise he appeared as relaxed as

Allison was tense. Perhaps this was the moment she had been seeking.

Ever since the night she had proposed the DeWilde project, she had searched for an opportunity to put a halt to it. But it was like trying to stop a speeding train; there was no convenient moment to make the attempt. By the time she recognized an opening, momentum had already swept them beyond it.

Earlier this morning, she had finally conceded that the perfect moment to stop the DeWilde project would not arrive. But the target date would. She and Paul had spent the past three weeks in exhaustive research and preparation, and then, last night, Paul had announced they were ready and had settled on a week from tonight as the target date. There would be no moon that night. A regatta, the opening of a new play at the theater and a ball at the palace would draw tourists, and consequently the police would have their hands full dealing with traffic and the sheer number of people in town. The timing was ideal.

Unless Allison could stop them, she and Paul would steal Catherine the Great's tiara a week from tonight. She could no longer wait for the perfect opening, because it wasn't going to arrive. She had to speak out, regardless.

"An appointment?" Paul sat at the table across from her, his plate heaped with Signora Cruzi's fluffy scrambled eggs. Curiosity lightened his eyes as he buttered a croissant. "Where do you go on these mysterious appointments?"

The question cut through Allison's anxiety and focused her thoughts on the present. Paul believed he knew her so well. Yet the most defining aspect of her life was completely unknown to him. How had she allowed this to happen? Helplessness flickered in her gaze. They were so right for each other, so perfectly matched in every way but one simple, fundamental thing—honesty.

"I have an interest in a business," she said carefully, watching his eyebrows curve in surprise.

Her heart constricted painfully and moisture appeared on her palms. He would ask what kind of business, she would answer, and their relationship would end. He would leap to the conclusion that the entire DeWilde project was a setup, an entrapment. The assumption would be that she was working hand in glove with Monsieur DeVault. And if The Ghost had been anyone but Paul, that's how it might well have played out.

"What kind of business?" he asked, interested. Then he laughed. "Darling, you never fail to surprise me." Desire, admiration and amusement blended in his gaze. "You can't possibly guess how much I love you." Leaning over the table, he kissed her, long and deep. When he drew back, his expression was serious. "Now that I've found you, Allison, I'm never going to let you go. You know that, don't you? Rely on it."

She gazed longingly at him, her heart in her eyes. She loved him too. There was no point in continuing to deny it. Soon enough she would experience the pain of loving and losing... and so would he.

"Oh, Paul." Hopelessness flooded her whisper. "I've made such a mess of things."

He lowered his croissant and frowned. "Allison, talk to me. What's going on with you?" Concern roughened his voice. "You've been wound tighter than a clock ever since I returned from Munich. Is it us? The DeWilde project? Something going on with this business you have an interest in... and which you haven't yet explained?"

"All of the above," she answered in a barely audible voice. "I'm not sure how it happened, but somewhere along the line I've lost control." She pushed a hand through her hair. "That isn't like me. I just...I don't know how this...I guess I thought..."

Paul grinned. "You know what you're describing, don't you?" Coming around the table, he knelt beside her chair and took her hands in his. His voice sank to a deeper register. "Love is about losing control, about letting things happen. Don't fight it, *chérie*. Let yourself go." He reached to touch his fingertips to her lips. "I know that loss of control can be frightening to people like you and me. But it can be exhilarating too, and exciting and liberating."

"I love you."

The instant she blurted the words, she regretted saying them. Admitting she loved him only complicated matters a thousandfold.

The joy that brightened his eyes was like a dagger of guilt straight into Allison's heart. Jumping up, Paul pulled her to her feet and crushed her against his body in a fierce embrace. "I knew I'd wear you down," he murmured gruffly.

It amazed Allison that she could laugh in the midst of feeling miserable. Then he kissed her, a long, deliberate kiss of breathtaking tenderness that told her so much of what he was feeling. He saw them as soul mates, as two halves of a whole, coming together in a union that was destined to be. When Allison was with him, when he held her in his arms, she too felt these incredible emotions. But she knew they weren't true. Destiny only toyed with them, dangling might-have-beens in front of their hearts. When he released her, tears glistened in her eyes.

"Are you finished eating?" he asked, mistaking her tears for the deep emotion of happiness.

"Yes. I..."

She had to tell him everything, she had to. But not now. Please, not after having admitted her love for him. Would it be so wrong to seize a few minutes of warmth and happiness for herself? Was that so terrible?

Later she would tell him about Alliance de Securité Internationale. And she would tell him about Jeffrey De-Wilde and how wanting to punish Jeffrey had led to the crazy suggestion that they steal the Empress Catherine tiara. Once Paul knew about her company and how strongly she felt about not letting clients be victimized by people like him, he would understand that they could not possibly proceed with the DeWilde project. That problem would be resolved.

And the problem of broken hearts would begin.

He would think she had lied to him. She hadn't, she thought defensively. She had merely omitted mentioning certain things. She had allowed him to believe a misconception. But that wasn't an outright lie. She had never lied to him, not exactly, she told herself uneasily.

"Come with me." Taking her by the hand, Paul led her to the balcony railing, then turned to her beside a stone urn overflowing with crimson roses. Placing his hands on her shoulders, he smiled into her eyes, loving her. "There's something I've been thinking about for several weeks. These thoughts came together while I was in Munich and I've been refining them since I returned to Monaco. I promised myself I wouldn't say anything to you unless..." He grinned and kissed the tip of her nose. "Make that *until* you said you loved me. Say it again."

"I love you," Allison whispered, trembling beneath his hands. She felt as if she had stepped onto the runaway train she had set in motion and now was speeding toward a collision.

"I want to spend the rest of my life with you, waking up with you beside me, being surprised by you, loving you." He peered into her eyes. "Is that what you want too?"

"Oh, Paul." Her heart soared then crashed to her toes. "I wish that were possible. I wish we could."

Her answer didn't seem to surprise him. He sat on a wrought-iron bench facing the blue-green sparkle of the Mediterranean and pulled her down beside him, keeping her hand tightly in his.

"I know what you're thinking because I've been thinking the same things. You're thinking that two thieves can't have a successful future. Working as a team would increase the odds of getting caught. With that possibility hanging over us, we couldn't establish a permanent home, couldn't make real plans, couldn't risk starting a family."

Allison raised a hand to cover her eyes. He wanted to marry her, he wanted them to be together always. She should have been happy, but she'd never felt more miserable. Frantically, her mind sought a way in which she could tell him everything and still hold on to him. But she knew that such a solution didn't exist.

"The obvious answer is the best solution."

"What?" She felt panicked, thinking for an instant that he had read her mind.

Paul took her other hand and held them both in his lap. "We retire." Looking into her eyes, he studied her reaction. "Before you reject the idea out of hand, hear me out. I don't want to expose you to humiliating headlines or ever have to ask you to wait for me. And I don't want to risk losing you to a prison sentence. You're thinking we're too young to retire, that we'll miss the excitement and the challenges. And you're right. But we'll find something as a replacement, something well within the law." He smiled at her. "How does this sound so far?"

Hope leapt in her eyes. "You're suggesting we abandon the DeWilde project?"

"No." His smile widened into an apologetic grin. "That's planned, and planned well, and I need to prove myself and show you what The Ghost can do." When she started to protest, he raised her hands and kissed her palms. "The DeWilde job will be a career capper, our joint swan song, our goodbye to a way of life. It seems fitting that we end one life together before we begin a new life together." Lifting his head, he gazed into her eyes. "The DeWilde project is important to me, Allison. I want this for us." He paused. "After that, we retire. We begin fresh."

The light dimmed in her eyes and she dropped her head. For a fleeting moment she had hoped there might be a way to jump off the speeding train. But even if they had decided not to proceed with the DeWilde heist, their difficulties would not have been solved.

Paul cupped her chin and raised her face to look into her eyes. "Can you agree to this plan?" When she didn't answer, he chewed the corner of his lip and frowned. "I know how addicting thievery can be, *chérie*," he said. "The thrill, the danger, followed by the enormous high of success. But you must have thought about quitting. You must have realized you couldn't be successful forever." Tenderly, he caressed her cheek. "We can't have a future together unless we both retire. Allison? It's time."

"It isn't that," she murmured. She kept hearing cracking sounds inside her. A heart breaking.

"Are you worried about money?" His laughter rang across the terrace. "You must have several fortunes invested by now." A gray light twinkled in his eyes. "And there's this mysterious business of yours. Or are you merely an investor?"

"I really don't have a lot of money," she murmured, hedging. "I'm comfortable, but by no means rich."

"Rich is a state of mind, the dollar definition differs for everyone. In my opinion, I'm not rich, either. I have a comfortable income from trusts set up by my grandparents, and a few negligible investments, but no real money."

This caught her attention and her eyes widened. "But The Ghost—"

Embarrassment warmed his face. "The Ghost disposes of his ill-gotten gains through anonymous donations to his victims' favorite charities." The red deepened at his throat. "If I'd stolen the Rubens instead of you, the Opéra Monaco would have received an enormous benefit."

Allison stared. "Paul Courtwald, you're a fraud." She burst into laughter, not speaking again until she caught her breath. "I can't get over it. The Ghost is the greatest boon to charity since Robin Hood!"

Frowning, he straightened his shoulders defensively. "I don't do it for the money. Money was never part of it. Most of the people I steal from are friends or acquaintances. Some are business associates of my family. It wouldn't be right to profit personally from friends or acquaintances without their knowledge."

Allison shook her head helplessly. "My Grandfather Ames used an expression—the morality of thieves. I never understood it until now."

"Are you sure you aren't thinking of that other famous Grandfather Ames saying about suckers?"

She leaned forward and kissed him, loving him. "I'm thinking about your yacht, and this villa, and the life you've led. The trusts your grandparents established must provide generously."

Pulling her onto his lap, he kissed her soundly and slid his hands up her waist to her breasts. Allison drew a breath

and groaned softly. "Do you agree? We hang up our burglary tools and go straight?"

She couldn't think when his hands were on her body. All
she could do was surrender to the waves of sensation that
rose in the wake of his skilled fingers.

"Stop that," she protested weakly, kissing his eyelids.
"Signora Cruzi could reappear at any minute."

"We'll find a mansion with a white picket fence," he
said huskily, nibbling her earlobe. "Stop laughing. There
must be a mansion out there somewhere with a picket fence
around it. If not, we'll build one. Where would you like to
live? Italy? England? France? If you promise never to
force me to eat American french fries, I'd even consider
the States."

For a moment Allison forgot the obstacles and gave in
to sheer happiness and the shudders of pleasure his kisses
evoked, the delicious sensations he aroused by trailing his
fingers along her bare thigh to the hem of her tennis skirt.

"There's only one question left to settle," he said in a
thick voice.

"And that is?" Sliding her hand inside his white shirt,
she flattened her palm against the steadily accelerating beat
of his heart. The touch of his bare skin thrilled her and she
wanted to freeze time, wanted to capture this moment and
hold it forever.

"Do you know what the DeWilde family's favorite
charity is?"

The question washed over her fevered mind like a bucket
of ice water, and she stiffened in his arms.

"Paul, listen to me a minute." Framing his face between shaking hands, she gazed at him with pleading eyes.
"Let's forget about the DeWilde project. Let's just . . . we
could just walk away. We could go somewhere and begin
our new life now, immediately."

Her mind spun, painting wild, impossible visions. She could sell her business, and she wouldn't have to tell him about it. They could go someplace where she would never encounter anyone who had known her before, where there was no possibility of anyone ever mentioning that she had once owned a business that tested security systems. Paul could continue to think she was exactly like him, his soul mate.

The fairy tale vanished as swiftly as hope had imagined it.

He brushed a thumb across her trembling lips. "Stop worrying. We've planned this down to a gnat's eyebrow. We aren't going to get caught." Kissing her, stroking her, he murmured against her arched throat. "Darling, this is the job we'll remember in our old age. We'll sit in front of our fireplace and reminisce about the project we pulled off together."

Dimly, Allison was aware that he lifted her and carried her inside the villa and down the corridor to his bedroom. But her mind remained fixed on one thought only.

The runaway train had sped out of control. There was no stopping it.

They were going to steal the fabled tiara that had once belonged to Catherine the Great, Empress of Russia.

THE ONLY WAY ALLISON got through the next few days was by concentrating on Jeffrey DeWilde. She wrote the word "bimbo" on a slip of paper and tucked it inside her purse, where she could look at it whenever her mind recoiled in shock at what she had agreed to do.

In Jeffrey's eyes, she'd been no better than a bimbo. That's how he had seen her; that's how he had treated her in the end. He had refused to acknowledge that she genuinely believed she was in love with him. He had turned away from the pain he must have known his rejection would cause her.

She fanned the flames of an old hurt until it ignited into fury and burned away the shock and revulsion, dismay and guilt at compromising everything she believed in.

Jeffrey deserved to lose the Empress Catherine tiara. He had offered her a piece of jewelry, hadn't he? Well, she'd changed her mind. She'd take his jewelry offering, but she'd choose the piece herself, and it wasn't going to be a bracelet or a pair of earrings, it would be a priceless tiara.

She hoped the theft created international headlines and that all the DeWilde stores suddenly saw their piece of the family collection as vulnerable and in danger. She hoped panic spread through Jeffrey's safe empire; she hoped the tiara was the most valuable of the DeWilde jewels. She hoped the theft would be viewed as a new disaster and DeWilde stock would plummet through the floor. If justice were served, Jeffrey would suffer anxiety and self-doubt exactly as Allison had done.

Spinning her chair away from the window, she placed her elbows on her desktop and dropped her head into her hands.

What was she doing? What was happening to her?

Monique rapped lightly at her office door, then stepped inside. Instantly Allison dropped her hands, then shook back her hair.

"Yes?" she snapped. "What is it?"

Monique's eyebrows rose like soft, feathery wings. "Here are the reports you requested." She placed a stack of file folders on Allison's desk, then turned to go.

"Wait." Allison drew a deep breath, then let her shoulders collapse. "I'm sorry." Standing, she positioned herself beside the window and frowned down at the tourists crowding the sidewalks. "I shouldn't have come into the office today."

Monique glanced at the closed door, then sat lightly on the edge of Allison's desk. "I hope you'll take this in the spirit it's offered, which is one of friendship. But when I suggested you take a vacation, I didn't realize it would last this long." She watched Allison's back stiffen. "We've managed through phone calls and an occasional catch-up session here at the office, but this is a hands-on business, and it's *your* business."

"Go on," Allison said tersely. "Say it all, get it out of your system."

"We've missed you," Monique said carefully. "There are decisions only you can make. And no one manages the clients or the operatives like you do. When Dominique ran into trouble on her assignment, we followed your instructions and we didn't try to phone you or contact you, we handled the problem, but it put everyone here under tremendous strain, and we could have made the wrong decisions with disastrous consequences."

"You didn't. You handled the situation exactly as I would have done."

"Allison, we've been friends a long time. We've worked together since the inception of the business. Maybe I'm imposing on that friendship, but...I've never seen you like this. Not long ago, I would have sworn it would be absolutely impossible for you to virtually vanish for almost two months. I would have said you are the most open, up-front woman I know, the most driven and the most dedicated. I would have sworn you were always in control, always cool, deliberate and emotionally level."

Allison turned her head, smiling weakly. "Not all of those qualities are flattering."

"But they're honest, and I thought they were you." Monique spread her hands and returned Allison's steady gaze. "I'm worried to death about you. Suddenly you're mysterious and withdrawn. You don't seem interested in a business you've worked so hard to build. And, Allison, my dear friend, you seem very unhappy, and that worries me most of all. Is it Paul?"

Allison turned back to the window. "It isn't going to work out between us." To her embarrassment, her voice cracked. "After tonight..." *Careful,* her mind warned. *Don't involve Monique by so much as a hint.* "Well, when you come in on Monday, I'll be here at my desk."

Grief trembled in her voice. The world outside her window appeared flat and colorless. *Get used to it,* she told herself. *This is the world without Paul.*

It was a good thing that she had focused so heavily on the element of revenge in tonight's business because that was the only success she would have, the only good thing that would result from so much planning or from the brief joining of talents and skills that seemed to mean so much to Paul. She would have the cool satisfaction of knowing she had struck back at Jeffrey.

But Paul. Her heart broke every time she thought of him.

"I'm sorry," Monique said finally, breaking a tense silence. She ran her palm over the stack of files. "We need you here, Allison. I'm glad you're coming back. The others will be relieved, also." She raised her dark head. "But I'm sorry for your pain and sorry about whatever is causing it. If you wanted the relationship with Paul to endure, then I wish that's how it had worked out."

"I do, too," Allison whispered, blinking back a rush of tears. It appalled her to go teary in front of Monique, mortified her to cry in front of *anyone.* If she had needed additional proof that life had spiraled out of control, the hot sting in her eyes provided ample confirmation. "I've never been more confused in my life," she said, swallowing hard.

Behind her, she heard the rustle of Monique's skirt as she stood from the desk. Instantly, Allison's shoulders stiffened with pride, erecting a barrier between them. If Monique attempted to comfort her, she sensed she would fall apart and end by telling her everything. Then Monique would have to phone Monsieur DeVault and warn that thieves would strike DeWilde's tonight, or else her silence and loyalty would make her a conspirator and as culpable as Allison. She couldn't place a friend in that position.

"Please," she whispered. "I can't talk about Paul, not yet. Maybe someday..."

She sensed Monique's hesitation and her need to reach out. But they knew each other well, and Monique turned away. She paused beside the door. "This is worse than ending it with Jeffrey, isn't it?" she asked softly.

"A thousand times worse."

She managed to hold herself together until Monique quietly shut the door behind her. Then Allison dropped into her chair and pressed the heels of her palms against her eyelids and pretended that she wasn't crying.

ARM IN ARM, Paul and Allison strolled through the balmy evening. A light breeze off the sea stirred palm fronds overhead. The streets were thronged with cars and the sidewalks crowded with tourists who bemoaned the frustrations of trying to locate an unoccupied taxi. In the span of ten minutes, they walked past conversations conducted in five different languages, at the same time carrying on a benign discussion between themselves in flawless German.

They wore walking shorts and a common brand of tennis shoes sold all over Europe. Paul's T-shirt advertised EuroDisney; Allison's brandished an ecology slogan. They each wore oversized, heavily scuffed backpacks that created the illusion that they were shorter than they were. They looked like two students on a walking tour, but neither looked like themselves.

A nondescript baseball cap covered most of Paul's hair. The street lamps washed the color from what hair could be seen. He wore a pair of glasses with flipped-up dark lenses. If anyone had peered into his eyes, they would have seen dark green contact lens. A three-day growth shadowed his chin and cheeks.

Allison wore a short brown wig beneath a crushed beret. She had penciled heavy dark eyebrows, which drew the eye away from her features and created an illusion that her face was thinner than it was. An absence of additional makeup further concentrated attention on her eyebrows. Her contact lenses were dark brown.

No one paid them a minute's attention.

They wandered down designer's row, pausing here and there in front of shop windows, nibbling cones of Italian *gelato*. When they reached DeWilde's, they stood for several minutes looking at the mannequin in the display window.

Allison's gaze fastened hungrily on the bridal gown, a confection of satin, lace and tiny seed pearls. Fate being a trickster, her mother had promised years ago that Allison would have a DeWilde gown for her wedding. Staring at the mannequin, she reached for Paul's hand and clasped it. Her mother would be disappointed, but there would be no DeWilde's bridal gown in her future.

But there would be a piece of DeWilde jewelry.

"Ready?" Paul asked, glancing at her from the corners of his eyes.

"As ready as I'll ever be."

"Take a deep breath. Clear your mind."

"I'm a professional," she snapped, suddenly angry. "I don't need coaching!"

His brow furrowed. "Sorry. But you're trembling."

She knew it, and the small tremors embarrassed the hell out of her. "Stage fright," she explained in a softer voice. "It always happens. I'll be fine once we actually begin." Paul hesitated, then nodded.

But stage fright was not the entire explanation. This job was different. She wasn't testing a system tonight. Tomorrow she wouldn't be returning the stolen item. If she were caught, the embarrassment wouldn't be cleared away by a few words of verification from smug clients.

This time it was real. For the first time in her life, Allison was about to steal something for personal gain. She was about to violate everything she believed in.

A wave of shock and nausea gripped her and she felt sick inside.

Paul pressed her hand then released it as he scanned the crowds on the sidewalks. Excitement danced in his eyes.

"Let's do it," he said softly.

Allison swallowed hard, then fell into step beside him.

CHAPTER TEN

THE ALLEYWAY WAS DARK and less than six feet wide. Deep shadows swallowed them the instant they ducked into the corridor. Paul faced into the darkness, letting his eyes adjust, while Allison peered back toward the street.

"If anyone watched us turn into the alley, they aren't curious enough to investigate," she reported.

Paul touched her hand. He would lead her around garbage cans and any litter until her eyes adjusted to the shadows. They would walk the entire length of the alleyway to assure that no one else lurked here. Monte Carlo was not noted for derelicts, but the principality did attract low-budget drifters who might have made an alley nest near the shop's back stoops.

Once they were certain they had the alley to themselves, they returned to within one hundred feet of the entrance, halting alongside the barred back door of Henri & Co. Ideally, it would have been preferable to enter DeWilde's directly. However, as DeWilde's occupied the corner site, this would have meant making entry within thirty feet of the alley opening. That was not a comfortable safety margin; there was too much danger of attracting attention. For this reason, they had decided to go in through the building housing Henri & Co.

Working quickly and efficiently, with a smoothness born of experience, they stripped off their backpacks and removed simple climbing gear.

"I'll take the lead," Allison announced tersely.

"No," Paul said sharply, gripping her arm. "We don't alter the plan."

He was right. "Sorry," she said between her teeth.

The pressure increased on her arm. "If you aren't comfortable, *chérie*...we don't go."

She could feel him waiting in the darkness and sensed the tension and excitement resonating in his fingertips. If she pulled out now, he would expect and be entitled to a reasonable explanation. And she didn't have one.

"I'm not accustomed to working with a partner, that's all."

"Take a minute," he suggested next to her ear. His warm breath flowed across her cheek. "Relax. Focus your thoughts."

This time Allison didn't object to his advice. Bending, she performed a quick loosening-up routine, flexing muscles, trying to empty her mind.

Imagining a Grecian urn filled with mental turmoil, she drew a deep breath then poured out all thoughts concerning the committing of an actual theft. This was an assignment like any other, she told herself firmly. There was nothing unusual about it. She poured out the image of the bridal gown in the front window. She poured out the aching emotions she felt whenever she thought about an empty future without Paul. She poured out the shock of what she was doing. Anxiety flowed from her mental urn and drained away until all that remained was three words, which assumed the calming cadence of a mantra: *Jeffrey, bimbo, revenge.*

"Go," she said in a low tone. Her voice sounded cool and crisp, in control.

If her senses had not been operating on full alert she would have missed Paul's brief hesitation. Finally, he

nodded. She heard him release a breath. Then he was on
the wall, moving as if he climbed a ladder instead of a
smoothly faced stone facade.

Allison followed, concentrating intently. The climb was
short but difficult. It would have been interesting in daylight; in full darkness, the challenge presented dangerous
possibilities. Finger- and toeholds existed, but the width of
each tiny ledge was less than an inch.

Above her, she heard a muffled curse and immediately
pressed herself flat against the building stones, frozen in
place and waiting, listening to her heart race.

"Careful. There's a row with worn faces. No holds."
Paul's whisper floated down to her.

She inhaled the musty tang of mildew and old mortar,
then nodded, although he couldn't see her, and continued
upward.

When she felt a slight tug on the light rope that con-
nected them, she knew Paul had reached the three-story
mark and had begun to move sideways toward the red tiles
capping the DeWilde rooftop. Allison climbed another
four rows of stones, then began her own angled approach.

When the tether again rose straight above her, she
pressed herself in place and waited. Unaccustomed to
working with a partner, she found the waiting almost as
difficult as not being able to watch him unscrew the
wrought-iron grill covering the narrow window above her.

A minute passed, then another. From Allison's per-
spective, clinging to tiny ledges two stories above the alley
floor, the wait seemed interminable. She told herself that
Paul would know that. He was working as swiftly as he
safely could. She closed her eyes and released a low breath
when he eased the grill down and it nudged her shoulder.

He had removed it from the window and secured it to a dangling rope.

Another two minutes passed, ticking away like years. Allison tried not to think of the strain on her fingertips and toes, tried not to allow negative thoughts.

"The window is painted shut," Paul called in a low voice. "I'll have to break it."

She didn't answer. They had discussed this possibility and whether or not Henri & Co.'s second-story window would be on an alarm. The probability, considering the grill, was that it was not secured by additional measures. They would know in a few minutes.

The tinkle of breaking glass sent a surge of adrenaline shooting through her body. There was no audible alarm, but one could be ringing somewhere else.

Less than a minute later, she felt a tug on the rope, the signal that Paul was inside the building. Fighting an instinct to hurry, she cautiously inched up the wall, feeling for the window ledge, grinning when she found it.

Mindful of broken glass, she lifted herself to the ledge and accepted Paul's help inside, then stepped aside as he examined the window frame.

"No alarm."

Allison accepted his word for it and looked around in the darkness. They were in a tiny office that also served as a ministoreroom. Boxes marked Buttons were stacked against one wall. Scarves filled the cartons near the doorway.

Although the broken window faced the blank brick wall of the building across the alley, Paul was careful to position himself between the window and the thin beam of light he held in his hand. He skimmed the flash across the floor and desk and held it for an instant on a stack of mail.

"Madame Effrond will thank us for opening her stuck window," he murmured, smiling.

Allison's professional integrity was shocked by the ease with which they had gained entry. Frowning, she glared at the shards of broken glass littering the floor. "Complacency is a thief's best friend." She shook her head and made a sound of disgust. In her opinion, Henri & Co. was all but begging to be burglarized. "Come on, cowboy, time's wasting."

Madame Effrond's office door was locked but so easy to open that a novice could have managed it. They stepped into a short, narrow corridor. Moving to the right, Allison opened a door and played her pencil light beyond the jamb. Here the client dressing rooms opened off a lavishly appointed hallway. After listening to the deep silence, she closed the door. Security in that part of the building would surely be better than in the employees' area.

She returned to the end of the narrow corridor where Paul knelt beside his backpack. "How does it look?" she whispered.

"About like we figured from the building prints," he said in a normal voice, then grinned when she twitched. "*Chérie,* we are going to knock a hole in the wall shared by the two buildings. That will make more noise than the sound of two voices." He smiled as he removed a short-handled sledgehammer from his backpack.

This was the part of the plan that Allison most disliked, even though she knew the chance of being overheard was minuscule. "I'll return to the window," she said in a low voice.

Leaving him to do the muscle work, she went back to Madame Effrond's tiny office and knelt beside the window. From this angle she could not see into the street at the end of the alley, but she could hear the sounds of honking traffic and the low buzz of pedestrians, occasionally punctuated by a peal of laughter or a shout for a taxi. Like the steady thump of a heartbeat, she heard the muffled sounds of Paul hammering at the wall between the two stores. The floor vibrated slightly beneath her feet with the impact of Paul's blows.

By now she was positive that there had been no silent alarm on the broken window. And if she could hardly hear Paul battering at the wall, no one would hear him on the street. So far, so good, she told herself.

Playing lookout in the darkness was a new role for Allison, but the feelings evoked by being in a place where she shouldn't be, by the challenge she faced and the anticipation of success . . . those feelings were thrillingly familiar.

She loved doing this.

How pallid life would be if she had to live it within conventional rules, if she had lacked the opportunity to jumpstart her nerves with a dose of danger and excitement. How pale and dull life would seem if all she had to look forward to every day was eight hours of sitting behind a desk.

Was that how her father had felt? The question came out of the darkness and startled her. It was easier, less confusing, not to think about her father and the pain and humiliation he had caused her mother and her. When she did remember him, it was usually with a conflicting spin of love and fury. How could he have broken the law? How could he have risked his reputation, his freedom and the well-being of himself and his wife and daughter? How could he have done what he did?

Sitting alone in the warm darkness, Allison truly glimpsed her father for the first time. She stared into the night and saw him sitting at his desk high above Wall Street. Day after day after day.

And then one afternoon, perhaps motivated by nothing more than boredom and a desire for something more exciting in his life, he had acted on inside information and had risked a buy order on that information.

Allison stared at the blank brick wall across from her and wondered if her father's heart had beat faster as he waited to learn if he'd been discovered. And she followed in her mind as he felt the thrill of success, of knowing he had played with fire and emerged unscorched.

He had done it again, she knew that. He had refined his methods and his network and had increased the risks and the payoff.

Why? She had asked herself that question a hundred times without really examining the answer, an answer she now realized she had known for years.

Her father had broken the law and traded on inside information because he could. Because he was good at it, exactly as Paul had suggested. Because danger made a pastel world more vivid and exciting. Because playing with fire was addictive, and succeeding had made him feel ten feet tall, smarter, bigger, better than anything his ordinary life could offer him.

Just like Allison would feel when she and Paul walked out with Empress Catherine's tiara. Just like she felt every time she successfully slipped into a client's house and stole a target item.

Dropping her head, she closed her eyes and rubbed her temples.

She was like her father, like her Grandfather Ames. They had operated on the far side of the law, but otherwise, there was not an iota of difference. The feelings were the same. Perhaps the motivations were the same, also.

"Forgive me," Allison whispered. "I didn't understand." She had conceived Alliance de Securité Internationale in the belief that she started the business as a form of personal atonement for the crimes of her father and grandfather. But maybe her motivation had been more complex. Maybe she needed risk and danger in her life. Maybe she needed to balance on a razor's edge to appreciate and live her life to the fullest.

If Allison hadn't developed the idea for a security firm, she might very well have followed in the family footsteps. With a flash of insight, she imagined herself drawn into a life similar to Paul's. She had simply been lucky enough to find a lawful means of injecting the excitement she thrived on into her work.

"Sorry for the delay," Paul said from the doorway. Leaning on the jamb, he mopped sweat from his face and throat. "I hit a brick wall not shown on the building plans. I've almost got a hole big enough to squirm through." When she didn't react, he frowned and called her name.

Allison looked up at him. "This is the strangest thing," she murmured in a wondering voice. "I just forgave my father. All these years I've blamed him for betraying my love and trust. I've never attempted to analyze what he did from his viewpoint, only from my own. I can never condone what he did, but now...I think I finally understand what it might have been like for him."

Paul's laugh was low and wonderful. "*Chérie,* there will never be another like you." Crossing the tiny office, he pulled her to her feet, then kissed her so deeply that Allison went limp and breathless against him. "I'm happy that you've enjoyed a personal epiphany, and I'd like to hear more about it. But right now we're running behind schedule, and we have a tiara to steal."

Leaning against his body, Allison pressed her forehead to his chest. She could hear his heart pounding from exertion, and she inhaled the erotic scent of male sweat. It was an utterly inappropriate moment to be having sexy thoughts, but she couldn't stop herself. Sex had never been as fabulous as it was with Paul. "Perhaps I understand you better, too."

"Which delights me no end. It would delight me even more if you would hustle your tantalizing butt and wriggle through the hole I've made. We need to know where we're coming out on the DeWilde side."

"The thing is, I truly didn't accept how much alike you and I are," she continued, flattening her hands against his chest. His heartbeat thudded against her palms, quick and hard, as it did when they made love. "I thought we were worlds apart philosophically. And all the time ... we're so much the same."

"Which I've tried to tell you a hundred times, my darling. Now, about the hole that I've gone to great effort to make ..."

She threw her arms around his neck and kissed him with a quiet desperation. "No matter what happens, remember that I love you. And I love what we're doing, except that I wish we weren't doing it. I wish ... I know that doesn't make sense, but ..."

"Allison, darling, *chérie*, my love ... sweetheart. We can't retire right this instant, not after I've spent nearly an hour smashing a hole between two buildings. Wishing we could retire at once is a wonderful thought. Wasting time and ignoring my hole in the wall is not so wonderful. It could even be dangerous. Much as I'd love to continue standing here kissing and holding you, I can't help thinking that every minute we stand here increases our risk."

"What happened to that reckless joie de vivre I recall from our encounter in a similar circumstance?" she asked in a teasing voice. Lightly, her fingers ran over his face, his shoulders, his chest. She loved the solid feel of his body, loved the scent of him and the sound of his voice.

"No recklessness tonight," he answered in a voice suddenly serious. Catching her hands, he held them to his heart and looked down at her. "Now I have too much to lose. I have you."

"Then move it, cowboy," she said, ducking under his arm and gliding to the door. A surge of excitement flooded her system with adrenaline. "Let's get that tiara and get out of here."

"That's my girl."

The hole between the buildings was just large enough for Allison to wriggle through. As soon as she crawled out on the DeWilde side, she scrambled to her feet and scanned her pencil light around her. She stood in an air-conditioned room filled with racks and racks of gleaming white gowns. Her light caught the opalescent glow of pearls and net, shimmering satin and silk. The room smelled faintly of roses and lily of the valley.

Foolishly, she found herself hoping the dust from the shattered wall had not settled on the gowns. Giving her head a shake, she hastily moved through the racks to a locked door that any experienced thief could have opened as swiftly as she did.

Before looking to see what lay beyond the door, she ran her beam over the jamb. If the door was on an alarm, she would find a tiny magnet embedded somewhere on the jamb and a matching magnet on the ledge of the door. When closed, the magnets would align; when the contact was broken, an alarm would sound somewhere.

She and Paul had made the assumption that interior doors would be trusted to locks and not protected by alarms. Having inspected the jamb thoroughly, Allison concluded their speculation had been correct. She hurried back to the hole in the wall.

"It's a storeroom," she said, speaking past hanging bricks. "No interior door alarms."

After fifteen minutes of concentrated hammering, Paul had enlarged the hole enough to gain passage himself. They moved past the bridal gowns and stepped into a model's dressing room. Their flashlights cast beams that bounced off a wall of mirrors above multiple vanities.

"All right," Paul murmured, and Allison wasn't sure if he spoke to her or to himself. "Visualize the building plan, place where you are."

Allison's gaze strayed to their reflection in the mirrors and the two dusty students portrayed there. Her eyes met Paul's in the glass.

"It will be hard to give this up," he said quietly, excitement sparkling in his gaze.

She looked at him for a long moment, then moved past him. "I know where we are. Follow me." She had trusted him to this point, now it was his turn to trust.

He followed without question, only a step behind as Allison moved to a carpeted landing and paused to listen and look down the staircase.

It was her turn to mutter to herself. "Assume the usual entry would be from below. What are the most valuable items on the ground floor? The jewelry counters and the tiara. You'd install a system to prevent a thief from reaching the jewelry, but most especially you'd protect the tiara."

They'd had this conversation before. "Let's go," Paul said behind her.

"No recklessness, remember? This one's for real. Switch off your flash."

"They're all for real," he answered, amusement in his voice. But he cut his flashlight at once and they waited without moving, letting their eyes adjust to the dim light seeping into the ground floor from the leaded glass flanking the entrance and the display windows.

Allison moved to the first step of the staircase leading down, concentrating on the risers. When she spotted no break in the darkness, she placed one foot on the step, then repeated the process for the next step and the next, Paul right behind her. Two steps from the bottom, she halted and reached back to stop him.

"There. See it?"

Motion sensors had been recessed in the risers. The faint red glow showing the system was armed was so dim that unless one knew what to watch for, it would have been missed.

"I don't see anything," Paul said. A difference of one step made the faint glow invisible.

"They did protect the gowns, after all." A beam ran parallel to the step. If it were interrupted by a shoe or anything else, the broken contact would trigger an alarm. "It's only two steps."

"Not a problem, we can step over them. Or..." Grinning with inspiration, Paul hopped onto the banister and took a short ride to the marble floor.

Frowning, Allison remained where she was. She swung her backpack around and rummaged inside, then cursed between her teeth. "Something doesn't feel right. Paul? Did you bring your goggles?"

"You didn't?"

"We agreed DeWilde's would have state-of-the-art security. But they don't." She had already scanned the ceilings and corners and noticed the cameras and motion detectors were not armed. A frown wrinkled her brow. "I can hardly believe this, but I think the cameras and detectors are fake, merely for show. I'm getting the impression that DeWilde's security system is wildly inadequate, and what there is is as old-fashioned as a floor safe. At least at this store.''

Paul dug in his backpack, then pulled a pair of goggles over his head and adjusted them. He emitted a low whistle. ''Trip beams,'' he reported in an amazed voice. ''I haven't seen trip beams in at least six years. You're dead right about old-fashioned and inadequate.''

''You could have landed on one of them,'' Allison said tartly.

The main-floor showroom opened before them, aisles of skillfully arranged display cases and countertops, arches leading to private showing rooms, columned entries to the in-store boutiques, a locked grille protecting the section with the jewelry cases. Thick carpets of DeWilde blue cushioned the areas with clothing racks. The walls were upholstered in blue-and-peach-colored silk. Enough light filtered through the front windows to reveal an ambience of elegance and luxury and an array of treasures designed to gladden the heart of any bride.

Allison studied the layout. What Paul would see through his goggles would be a checkerboard grid of glowing green beams invisible to the naked eye.

She hadn't brought her own goggles because she would have bet everything she owned that DeWilde's security systems would be top of the line. But the only A-line system she noticed was focused on the jewelry section of the store. It made her uneasy that the tiara had been left shockingly vulnerable, and also that DeWilde's overall systems were old-fashioned and open to penetration. The laxity stunned her.

"The grid is large," Paul said, interrupting her uncomfortable speculation. The goggles made him look as if he were preparing for a dive. "It won't be a problem. And the other systems are about as threatening as an invitation."

"I know we agreed not to alter the plan, but it might be wise to locate the central alarm panel—my guess is it's in the manager's office—and double-check if those cameras are really fakes." She was having difficulty believing it would be this easy.

Paul moved forward, lifting a leg and stepping over a beam that was invisible to Allison. After turning in a full circle, he lifted the goggles and peered at her on the staircase. "We don't know how the central alarm is configured. If it's as archaic as what we're seeing here, I'd guess it would be relatively easy to disarm. But if I'm wrong, if we screw it up, then we've blown it. Why take the risk? Actually, I don't think we need to mess with the central controls. This is going to be a piece of cake. I can walk you through it easily."

Allison frowned. "Something is not right here. It shouldn't be this simple. If you had a tiara worth at least six million dollars, not counting the historical value, wouldn't you train a motion sensor on it? Or at least a camera? Why put the high-tech stuff on the jewel cases and not on the tiara?"

Paul shrugged. "An oversight? Complacency? Who knows?"

Lifting her head, Allison inhaled and flexed her fingers. "Okay. If I jump the last two stairs, what do I land on?"

"The nearest trip beam is three feet away." He watched her hop the steps and land on a marble tile. "Don't move. Your jump was shallow. Your left ankle is about three inches from the cross beam. The squares are about four feet wide. If you'll step one pace to your right, you'll be almost dead center."

Allison positioned herself as directed. "I should have brought my goggles, damn it!"

"No harm done," Paul said absently, studying the grid. "At least not yet. I'll walk you through."

It occurred to Allison that she had to trust him. For a moment her heart wobbled in her chest. She had trusted her father and her father had destroyed the family reputation and life as Allison and her mother had known it. She had trusted Jeffrey DeWilde enough to fall in love and he had tossed her away. If she was wrong about Paul, she could end up in prison.

As if he'd read her mind, Paul gazed at her. "I'm not your father," he said quietly. "And I'm not the man who hurt you. Trust me, *chérie*. I will never let you down. I love you."

"I know." Swallowing hard, she smiled at him. "But I'll still feel better when we're out of here."

No matter how hard she tried to pretend this job was no different from any other, it was. Her nerves wound a little tighter with each passing minute. And when she allowed herself to remember that she was actually going to steal something, her mind went numb with shock. She wanted it over with.

They both turned toward the center of the store. During business hours, a beam of dazzling light fell from the ceiling through a glass case onto the Empress Catherine tiara, which was displayed on a blue velvet cushion. The entire case slowly revolved, causing light to flash and sparkle off the seven hundred rubies, forty diamonds and fourteen emeralds encrusting the gold circlet. The large shell-cut emerald alone was worth more than a million dollars. At present the case was stationary, and no light shone down from above.

"The grid narrows near the case," Paul commented, frowning. "At the base of the pedestal, the space between the beams is less than a foot."

"You can see better than I can. Describe the situation."

"The top of the glass case is about chest-high. Maybe two feet square." He high-stepped it closer and studied the grid. "The beams narrow too tightly for me to approach the pedestal." Lifting his head, he gazed back at her. "You're going to have to do this, Allison. I'll guide you as close as I can, then you take the goggles."

Allison swore softly. As long as she didn't lift the tiara out of the case, she could tell herself that she wasn't really part of stealing it. This tiny distinction had soothed her conscience somewhat. Now she was left with the stark shame of actual theft.

"Damn it!" Knots rose along Paul's jawline. "I wanted to show off for you. I wanted this one to be mostly mine."

"Shall we call it off?" Allison asked, keeping her voice level.

"We're here, and we're adaptable," Paul answered. He was a pro, he could set aside his personal disappointment. The challenge of a new problem tightened the muscles along his shoulders.

Allison ground her teeth. "Jeffrey," she whispered as she stiffened her spine. It really *was* a challenge. It really *was* exciting. She felt the same dangerous thrill that she knew Paul was experiencing. "All right, cowboy. Guide me in."

Paul directed her by inches to the first trip beam. "It comes across at midcalf on you." He watched her lift her leg. "A little higher. That's it. Good. Now, step over and move one pace forward." Allison exhaled slowly. "Excellent," Paul said. He moved easily across the grid and came up to the square beside her. "Okay, move forward—slowly—and we'll take the next one."

With painstaking care and what seemed agonizing slowness, they progressed until they stood within six feet of the tiara case.

"Stop," Paul said sharply. "You are standing in the center of a square that has narrowed to about two feet wide. You have about six inches on either side of your legs. Cough hard, and you'll set off alarms all over the principality."

"Not to worry, I've got iron lungs and nerves of steel." She smiled without humor then turned to study the glass case around the tiara.

"It's your baby, *chérie*," Paul said. "Sorry, but there's no way I can approach any nearer without tripping an alarm." Peeling off the goggles, he handed them to her.

Allison adjusted the goggles over her eyes. Immediately she saw the green beams criss-crossing the floor and aisles. They narrowed drastically near the tiara case. It was going to be tricky, the kind of challenge that sent her nerves into overdrive and made her feel tinglingly alive.

And somewhere deep inside she had always known that she would be the one who actually stole the tiara. That's how it had to be. "Bimbo," she whispered between her teeth, staring at the case. "Jeffrey."

"What?"

"Nothing." She drew a deep breath. "I can do this. But you should have stayed over by the staircase."

"No way," he objected cheerfully. "I'm here to inspire you."

"I'll need some inspiration," Allison said lightly. Her heartbeat accelerated and she was aware of a light film of moisture beneath her arms as she reviewed each step in her mind. Opening the case should have been a two-person operation. Doing it alone was risky. She'd need split-second timing. And a bit of luck. "Jeffrey," she whispered. It didn't occur to her to walk away, not now. Jeffrey had to pay for what he had done.

"Do you trust me to do this alone?" she asked Paul.

In answer, he handed her the router, which she would now wield instead of him. "I'd trust you with my life," he said simply.

That's exactly what he was doing. If Allison tripped the alarm, they would both spend the rest of their lives in prison.

After inhaling deeply, she carefully placed one foot into the next light square and then the next, moving more slowly as the size of the grid diminished. She had almost reached the case when a loud crash sounded.

Allison froze, one foot in two different grids. The squares were small enough now that an involuntary twitch could trigger the alarm. Heart slamming in her chest, hardly daring to breathe, she waited.

"A car crash. Right in front of the store," Paul explained. Without the goggles, he couldn't move to investigate. Outside, angry voices erupted.

This was the kind of situation in which Allison thrived. A coolness flowed down her spine and she calmly moved up to the case and peered through the glass at the tiara resting on the velvet cushion. The rubies appeared lusterless, the gems curiously dull without the benefit of the bright light focusing down on them.

She concentrated her thoughts, shutting out the fracas outside the store. Since the public touched the glass case, she correctly assumed it was not wired in any way. After settling her weight equally between two small squares of light and testing her balance, she placed the router on top

of the case, then carefully, slowly, opened her backpack
and removed the suction cup. A single act of carelessness
could be disastrous. If she dropped a pin through the light
grid, the alarms would sound.

A sizzle of electricity tightened her nerves. God, she
loved this. Absolutely loved it. Every fiber of her body was
wildly alive. The only thing better was sex with Paul.

The rise and fall of a police siren broke her concentration. A quick glance toward the front of the store revealed furious shadows pacing and gesturing in front of
the windows.

"We're fine," Paul assured her in a steady voice. He too
appeared calm, controlling the exhilaration aroused by
danger and excitement. "The police are coming to attend
to the car accident. They don't know we're here. Do you
know how beautiful you are? I can't wait to get you home.
Oh, what I'm going to do to you!" he promised in a low,
husky voice.

Allison laughed softly. She shared the surge of sexuality and knew what he was feeling, knew the hot excitement that bubbled in his veins. Already, she had forgotten
the accident outside the front door. "Whatever you're
planning, it isn't half as wild as what *I'm* planning!"

"Hold that thought," he said with a grin, then added,
"I won't talk again unless you do."

Allison nodded, then filled her lungs with a deep breath.
Concentrating, she positioned the suction cup in the center of the top of the glass case, gently pressing it flat. With
her thumb, she pumped the button beside the handle to
inflate the cup. After testing for a secure bond, she ut-
tered a low sound of satisfaction and reached for the
router.

"I need half an hour," she said softly. "And there's
going to be noise."

In movies, the crooks ran a glass-cutting blade around a suction cup, then lifted out a cut circle of glass. It was silent and appeared as easy as cutting through butter.

In real life it didn't work that way. The blade would not cut entirely through the glass, nor was it designed to. Moreover, the glass would have to be tapped hard from the inside before the cut circle could be lifted out.

In this instance the glass could not be tapped from the inside nor would such an action be desirable, since a broken piece could fall and trigger the pressure pad on which the tiara rested.

The only tool that would accomplish what Hollywood did so easily and falsely was a diamond-studded router bit. Allison lifted the router.

"I checked the batteries before we left," Paul said, guessing her thoughts. "We didn't expect people right in front of the shop, but they're focused on the accident. They won't be paying attention to anything in here."

"We hope," Allison murmured. Outside the wail of the police car reached a crescendo, then died away at the curb. The sound of shouting voices increased.

She flexed her shoulders, then began cutting around the suction cup. The noise of the router sounded like a buzz saw to her ears. A light film of glass powder sprayed over her hands and filtered down on top of the tiara and cushion.

At the fifteen-minute mark, Paul murmured admiringly, "You're doing fine. Talk about nerves of steel . . ."

Allison paused to wipe perspiration from her forehead. She blinked hard several times before she returned to work. At the twenty-five-minute mark the router seemed to falter and her heart lurched. She waited a minute, studying the last two inches of uncut glass.

This was where she needed Paul. Once she completed the full cut, the suction cup and circle of glass would drop into the case on top of the tiara. An alarm would sound. If she tried to break off the last bit of glass holding the circle, the entire top could shatter and fall inside, triggering disaster.

When she lifted her head, Paul was watching her. "It's your choice," he said softly. "You might be able to hold the suction cup while you complete the cut. Or...if you break the last section of glass, it might be a clean break. You decide."

She read the trust in his eyes and loved him for it. "I'll go for a combination," she said finally. "I'll hold the cup and cut to about an inch. Then I'll break it."

She waited for him to say, "Justify." But he didn't. He accepted her decision. Again, the noise of the router sounded like a jet engine to her and she felt weak with relief when she finally withdrew the diamond bit. That part was finished.

The suction cup wobbled in her hand as she tried to hold it in place as she set down the router.

Carefully, aware of the perspiration on her brow, she gripped the suction cup with both hands, paused for a beat, then gave it a sharp tug upward, sliding a hand beneath at the same moment. The last inch of glass broke and a small piece fell into her gloved hand.

For an instant she didn't move, thinking of might-have-beens. Then she cautiously set the broken piece on top of what remained of the glass case. Finally she lifted her head and watched the tension easing from Paul's expression.

"Good job. Nice catch," he said. "You are one fabulous woman."

"What's happening outside?"

"Just about everyone has gone."

"Give me ten more minutes."

"Take as long as you need."

She gave him a grateful glance. In a way, his job was harder than hers. Waiting was never easy. And the noise must have sounded as loud to him as it had to her, yet he hadn't so much as twitched, hadn't urged her to haste, hadn't exhibited a hint of nerves. If a genuine partnership had been possible, Allison could not have chosen better than Paul Courtwald.

No, she thought with a frown, battling an onslaught of emotion, she couldn't think about what would happen next between them. Not now. Right now she had to remove the tiara from the pressure-sensitive pad. Fortunately, doing so was child's play. She had experimented and practiced with pressure-sensitive pads until she could have made the switch in her sleep.

In less than five minutes, she had the tiara in her hands. When the manager of DeWilde's opened the store tomorrow morning, he or she would find a recipe book weighing slightly more than one pound resting on the blue velvet cushion.

After padding the tiara with foam and placing it and the router in her backpack, Allison stepped over the green trip beams, forcing her excitement down to manageable levels, forcing herself to move slowly and with exquisite care. When she reached the spot where Paul stood, her lips curved in a wide, exultant grin and they slapped hands above the trip beam before she guided him back to the staircase.

Moving swiftly, they exited the way they had come. Once they dropped to the alley floor, they fell against the building wall and gulped deep breaths of air in the darkness before they grinned at each other, then strolled out of the alley, gripping each other's hand.

Within minutes they reached the rental car and wound a random route back to Allison's house, not speaking, both watching in the rear and side mirrors to see if they were being followed.

"We did it," Allison breathed as Paul cut the engine in front of her house. The knot of tension deep inside her began to unwind. "My God. We actually did it!"

He grabbed her in a crushing embrace. "We're a hell of a team!" His mouth claimed hers in a wild, passionate kiss that bubbled through Allison's system like hot lava, dissolving her bones.

Her hands tore at him, ripping his shirt, pulling at his belt. She needed him now—*now!*—wanted him inside her, wanted the tensions of the night to explode in wild lovemaking. Just as his mouth and racing hands told her that he did, too.

Laughing, grabbing at each other, they ran to the front door, leaving a trail of clothing behind them. Hungry for each other, feverish with need, they left the front door wide open and didn't remember it for hours. All they could think of was their overpowering desire for each other.

Sometime before dawn, Paul placed the tiara on Allison's head, then stepped back in awe. Wearing nothing but the tiara that had graced the head of Catherine the Great, she turned slowly in front of him.

"You are so beautiful," he whispered, staring at the curve of breast and waist and hip. "I love you so much!"

When Allison caught sight of herself in the mirror above her vanity, she stopped and gazed at the tiara. Light from the bedside lamp sparkled and flashed from the shell-cut emerald surrounded by diamonds and rubies.

"We stole this," she whispered.

Paul grinned. "That we did, *chérie.*"

This was possibly the worst moment of her life.

CHAPTER ELEVEN

"ALLISON? WHAT'S the matter?" Paul put down his morning newspaper and gazed at her across the terrace table.

Immediately following the theft of the ivory figurines she had been exhilarated, flying high, then later relaxed, basking in her success. But something had drastically altered her mood after he placed the tiara on her head the night they stole it. The reality of the tiara on her head seemed to upset her badly. For the past two days, she had been a bundle of nerves. Her mounting anxiety puzzled him and created a strain.

"I just don't understand this," Allison said sharply, pushing aside her morning coffee. She tossed her own newspaper onto the tabletop. "It's been two days. We should have heard *something.*"

Not a word about the theft of the Empress Catherine tiara had appeared in the newspapers or on radio or television news.

Paul nodded, studying the lines of stress pinching her forehead. "As this isn't a private theft, I tend to agree. DeWilde's manager would have discovered the loss, the hole in the wall between DeWilde's and Henri & Co.... He or she would have called the police." He spoke in a light voice. "It's curious. Why didn't the store manager notify the police?"

"I don't know." She thrust a hand through her hair, then stood and paced the length of the terrace. "It's not possible to cover this up. DeWilde's is a public corporation. The theft should have made the news."

"As I understand it, the tiara is part of the DeWilde family's private collection," Paul pointed out in a mild tone.

"But it was stolen from a store owned and operated by the DeWilde Corporation! Don't the shareholders have a right to know when something worth millions of dollars is stolen from their store? Isn't that news? Plus, the tiara has been a tourist attraction ever since DeWilde's Monte Carlo opened!" She paused in her pacing and jerked at the belt of her terry robe. "So, what are they telling people to explain the missing tiara?"

Catching her hand, Paul gently pulled her onto his lap. "Calm down, *chérie*." He kissed the tip of her nose, then smoothed an errant tendril behind her ear. "This was a strange job," he said, watching the edge of her robe part to reveal a stunning length of tanned leg. He would never get enough of this woman, he thought. Not if they lived to be a hundred years old. He'd made love to her only an hour ago, but he wanted her again.

"Stealing the tiara was too easy," Allison agreed, chewing her bottom lip. "I don't understand it. The security was outdated, as if there were nothing valuable inside the store."

"Except for the jewelry cases. That section was heavily protected. If we'd checked more closely, I have a feeling we'd have discovered that stealing an engagement ring would have proved more challenging than stealing the Empress Catherine's favorite tiara." He nibbled her earlobe and nuzzled her throat.

"Which doesn't make sense!" she said, pulling back to scowl at him.

He sighed, then agreed. He didn't understand the DeWilde security arrangements any more than he understood Allison's growing distress. Something had changed the instant he placed the tiara on her head. She had recoiled from her image in the mirror and had stared at the tiara with horrified eyes, as if she could not believe they had stolen it. The incident continued to baffle and nag at him, a mystery she refused to discuss.

During the ensuing two days she had become increasingly jumpy and on edge. And he didn't know why.

"Chérie," he said gently, "when are you going to tell me what's troubling you so greatly?"

She went very still against him, so still that he could hear her heartbeat accelerate against his chest.

"What do you plan to do with the tiara?" she asked finally. The strain in her voice was as painfully obvious as it was puzzling.

He shrugged. "The piece is instantly recognizable," he said, stating the obvious. "The only way to safely dispose of it will be to break out the stones. Then, unless you disagree, we'll make an anonymous donation to one of the DeWildes' favorite charities. I compiled a list of organizations from newspaper articles."

A deep shudder trembled down her spine before she climbed off his lap. "We can't destroy the tiara," she announced quietly but firmly. Beneath her golden tan, her face was white. "Paul, this is a historical piece. It would be criminal to break it up."

Her words took him by surprise. "It's too dangerous to keep the tiara intact. I thought you understood that."

Of course she understood. The tremor in her fingers had nothing to do with the tiara. Suddenly he realized that whatever was going on inside her, it was serious. And the strain and tension that she struggled to contain had been building from the moment they first discussed stealing the tiara. He studied her and was amazed to realize that this cool, controlled woman hovered on the verge of exploding.

"Allison? What's happening here? If I didn't know better, I'd say you *want* this theft to make headlines."

She'd been glued to the local radio station and had pored over newspapers, drinking enough coffee to float a yacht. She had practically worn a path in the terrace stones while pacing throughout the last two days. To his astonishment, the nervy, self-controlled woman who had helped him steal the tiara was swiftly unraveling in the calm aftermath.

"I just...damn it, I don't understand why DeWilde's didn't report the theft! I was certain they would!"

Confusion puckered his brow. Her reaction didn't make sense. "Look," he said finally, standing. "If it will make you feel better, let's visit the store. Maybe we'll pick up some information and settle whatever is bothering you."

"Yes!" Gratitude returned a rush of color to her face. "I'll be dressed in fifteen minutes."

While he waited, Paul poured another cup of coffee and thought about the tension that had been building during the last two days. He understood tension *prior* to the job— he'd been tense, too. But now? He simply couldn't comprehend Allison's mounting distress.

Stealing the tiara had been far easier than either had anticipated. There had been one or two interesting moments, but by and large, the job had been completed without undue excitement and with a minimum of risk. They had worked smoothly together, they had left behind no incriminating evidence. They should have been celebrating.

Instead, Allison was uncharacteristically on edge. Whenever he tried to discuss retirement and their freedom to pursue a future together, moisture leapt into her eyes, which was so unlike her that it astonished him. One moment she was perusing the newspapers with a cool eye, the next instant tears brimmed behind her lashes. In a move that bewildered him, she had concealed the tiara in a hatbox on her highest closet shelf and refused to look at it.

His calm and collected partner had dissolved into weepy confusion, and he didn't understand it at all. Allison Ames was disintegrating before his eyes and he didn't know how to help her.

"I'm ready," she called, sticking her head through the French doors. Impatient, she jingled her car keys in her hand.

They didn't speak during the ride into Monte Carlo. Paul wasn't sure she was even aware of him beside her. She drove with her mind clearly on other things, and what they might be, he couldn't guess. But days ago he had recognized a tiny kernel of alarm deep in his chest, and he felt it growing by leaps and bounds.

Something was occurring that he didn't understand. He almost felt as if he didn't know her anymore. And that alarmed him more than anything else could have.

After they parked the car, they walked hand in hand to the DeWilde store, passing it once. From the outside, nothing seemed amiss. Tourists and prospective brides passed in and out of the leaded glass doors, chatting happily. It appeared to be business as usual.

Frowning, they glanced at each other. "Let's go inside," Allison said tersely. Propelled by curiosity, Paul agreed.

He opened the door for her and they stepped into the elegant gilt splendor that was DeWilde's. By daylight the display counters gleamed, highlighting artfully arranged items chosen to delight a bride's heart. The heavy iron grilles were pushed back from the entrance to the jewelry section, and cases of exquisite gems sparkled and beckoned from nests of blue velvet. Sample racks of clothing suitable for honeymoons in any clime were arrayed across the main floor. Boutiques featuring headdresses, lingerie, footwear and all else required for the perfect wedding opened seductively off the main floor. A hint of vanilla and lavender perfumed the air.

Like Allison, Paul had eyes only for the mahogany pedestal occupying the center of the store. Irresistibly drawn, they moved forward, walking toward a guard who stood a few feet from the pedestal. As they knew from their research, the guard's duties ended when the store closed at the end of the business day.

"I don't believe it," Allison whispered, the color draining from her face and neck.

Bright light shone down from above on the Empress Catherine tiara, which rested undisturbed on a blue velvet cushion. As the pedestal slowly revolved, light glittered and flashed from instantly recognizable rubies, diamonds and emeralds.

"It has to be a replica," Paul muttered under his breath. And a damned good one. This tiara looked exactly like the tiara they had stolen. If the two had been placed side by side, he wouldn't have been able to tell them apart without a loupe. Something about this thought disturbed him, but he couldn't pinpoint what it was. Instead, he focused intently on practical matters.

The glass case had been replaced, and when he looked up, he noticed two workmen, one on a ladder, back near the private showrooms. DeWilde's Monte Carlo had lost no time in installing an updated security system. He gently nudged Allison to draw her attention to the workmen's activities, but she stood frozen, staring at the tiara revolving beneath the bright overhead spotlight.

"It was all for nothing," she whispered, looking sick. "We did it for nothing!"

He glanced quickly at the guard, then gripped her elbow. "Darling," he said for the guard's benefit, "we're late. We'll return when we have more time." Tugging gently at her arm and frowning, he led her toward the entrance of the store.

She moved like a sleepwalker in the throes of a bad dream. When he released her arm to push open the door, she walked straight into a chicly dressed woman carrying a Cartier box.

"Allison!" the woman exclaimed with obvious pleasure. "I was going to phone you!" She glanced at Paul, smiled, then turned back to Allison, who stared at her with dulled eyes. "We almost had a burglary last week at our place in Paris, but the system you recommended stopped the bastard from getting inside. He got onto the grounds, but not into the house, thanks to you." She beamed up at Paul. "If you're looking for someone to test the security in your home, you won't find anyone better than Allison Ames. Her company is the best there is! Jewel thieves beware!"

The woman babbled on about burglars and security systems, thanking Allison again and again. Shock prevented Paul from following everything she said. He turned in disbelief to stare at Allison's sick expression, seeing a dozen emotions flickering in the depths of her imploring gaze. Apology, resignation, helplessness.

Without breaking eye contact with her, he directed a question to the woman. "Allison owns a security company?" he asked in a voice that was steadier than his hands.

"Alliance de Securité Internationale. She hasn't told you about it?"

He stared into Allison's eyes. "It seems our Allison is adept at keeping secrets."

The woman laughed. "In her business she needs to keep secrets. If you're looking for someone to update your security systems, you won't find anyone better." Although Paul didn't look at her, he felt the woman's beaming smile. "No one knows how to thwart the bad guys like Allison Ames."

Anger slammed into his gut. She had deceived him from the first. She'd been hired to steal the Rubens and the ivory figurines. Allison Ames, the woman he had waited for all of his life, was not the woman he had believed she was. She wasn't anywhere close.

Abruptly he released her arm and strode outside, sensing that she followed. Oblivious to the crowds thronging the sidewalk, he turned and stared down at her. "Where?" The harshness in his tone revealed the betrayal slicing his insides like strands of barbed wire.

"It doesn't matter," she answered, her own voice expressionless. Only a trembling at the corner of her lips betrayed the emotion hinted at in her eyes.

A small park opened at the foot of the street and he led her there. Leafy chestnut trees shaded pebbled paths that wound through beds of red and yellow blossoms; the scent of fresh popcorn floated on a light sea breeze. Paul chose a park bench backing a stone wall that afforded a clear view of anyone who might approach. He would have preferred greater privacy, but his anger demanded immediate answers.

He seated himself on the bench but he was too enraged to look at her. Every instinct urged him to simply walk away, warning him that he didn't want to hear the answers to the questions he had to ask.

But he loved her. With a sick feeling, he recognized that no matter how she answered him, he would still love her. And because he loved her, he prayed she could explain Alliance de Securité Internationale in a way that wouldn't threaten him. Against all logic, he hoped she could erase what her former client had said.

"Where do you want to begin?" he asked tightly, trying to control the tension in his voice and in his stomach.

"Paul..."

He raised a hand. "Before we start, I want you to understand that I love you. Whatever you have to say, and I suspect you have a lot to tell me, my loving you isn't going to change. I'm going to try very hard to understand and to believe what you have to say."

He had to trust there was an explanation that wouldn't destroy how he felt about her.

A shaft of sunshine filtered through the overhead leaves and illuminated her hair like a halo. "Whatever you think about me after we've talked...please remember that I love you, too," she whispered. "I didn't intend to love you, I didn't want it to happen. But it did. I love you."

The quaver in her voice made his chest tighten. He drew a breath and stiffened his spine. "You own a company that tests security systems. You recommend improvements."

She shifted on the bench beside him, then she lifted her chin and turned her head away from him toward the harbor. "Yes."

"You're paid to steal items to test a client's existing system. You don't steal for personal gain."

"That's correct." Her eyes closed, forming a dark crescent of silky lashes against her cheeks. The breath seemed to leave her body.

Anger exploded against his rib cage. "This isn't a game of charades, damn it! Talk to me!" Standing abruptly, he shoved a hand through his hair. This perfect woman, their perfect relationship, everything he had believed she was and they were... it was going to come apart. He was foolish to hope otherwise.

"Until two days ago, I didn't understand why my father threw his life away and destroyed our family. I thought I had to do something to atone for what he had done." She spoke in a low, strained voice. "My father didn't break into people's homes and steal their belongings, he stole information and profited by it. But the end result was the same. I thought I could balance the scales. Alliance de Securité Internationale was my effort to protect people from unscrupulous people like my father."

"And like me?" he asked softly, staring at her.

Turning her head, she met his eyes. "Yes. I'm not a thief, Paul. Until you and I stole the Empress Catherine tiara, I'd never stolen anything except in the line of work."

His mind raced. "Were you hired by DeWilde's to steal the tiara?"

"No." She seemed to shrink in on herself as if the balmy, warm day had suddenly turned icy. "That was an actual theft." Focusing on a point in space, she shook her head, as if she were watching a replay of the theft, unable to quite believe it.

He made himself open his clenched fists. "Do you have an office?"

"Yes." Her gaze swung toward the park's harbor exit. "Not far from here." She drew a long, unsteady breath and looked at him. "Since meeting you, I've taken a leave of absence. I wanted to be with you and I doubted that would be possible if you knew what I really did for a living."

Paul stared toward the buildings at the end of the park, trying to guess which might house her company. She owned and operated a security testing business. She was not a thief. She was not like him. In fact, she tried to protect her clients from people like him. He was the enemy. "Do you work with the Monaco police department?"

"Sometimes," she said after a minute, dropping her head.

Anger iced his tone. "Weren't you tempted to give them The Ghost?"

"I won't lie to you," she answered finally, studying her hands. "I considered turning you in."

"You won't lie to me?" His voice rose. "You've done nothing *but* lie to me! You let me believe . . ." He stopped, biting his tongue. Shouting served no purpose. He would only draw attention. A flood of acid poured a bitter taste into his mouth. "Is your name even Allison Ames?"

"Oh, Paul." Despair darkened her eyes to a stormy navy color, and she placed a hand on his sleeve, but he drew back from her. "I'm sorry. I didn't mean to deceive you. I just . . . I fell in love with you. One thing led to another and . . ."

His stare deepened into a scowl. Anger pulsed at the base of his throat. "You claimed you were always honest. You said you never lied. Like an idiot, I believed you."

She cringed as if he had struck her, and her face went white. "I didn't lie to you. Not really."

Amazement vied with fury in his expression. "Letting someone believe an untruth is the same as a lie! God, everything I thought I knew about you . . . it was all a lie!"

"No," she protested, staring up at him with a plea in her eyes. "I love you. That isn't a lie."

"You have a damned strange way of showing it. Or should I be grateful that you didn't turn me in? Should I thank you that I'm not behind bars right now? Is that an example of your love?" Disgust twisted his lips. "How did you think this would end, Allison? Would you have told me about your firm if we hadn't run into that woman at DeWilde's?"

"I . . . of course."

"Of course?" His tone was bitter. "When?"

"Very soon. I was trying to find an opening, a good time to tell you. . . ." She covered her face with a shaking hand. "Oh, Paul. I didn't want you to find out like this."

Because he wanted to shake her until her teeth rattled, because he wanted to punish her for lying to him and destroying his image of her, he stood and paced before the bench, walking through bright sunlight and shadow.

Then he remembered and spun toward her. "Stealing the tiara was your idea." Accusation shook his voice. "Allison, you claim you're not a thief, but *you're* the one who wanted to steal the DeWilde tiara. You thought of it—you suggested it."

"Paul, please." She cast a pointed glance toward a couple inspecting a flower bed not far from them. "Can we go somewhere else?"

"No," he said roughly. "We finish it here. Now." He stared at her, hardening his heart to the moisture shining behind her eyes. "Why the tiara, Allison? Why did you say stealing it was all for nothing? And no more lying, by implication or otherwise. I want the truth."

She winced again as if he had struck her. Despite everything, the accusations of dishonesty hurt her more than anything else he said. What she didn't grasp was the irony of it. He had believed everything she said without question because he thought she was a thief like him. He had believed that she *could* be totally honest because they were alike. He had questioned nothing.

She pressed her fingertips to her eyelids. "The tiara..." she repeated, then drew a deep breath. "There was a man...I told you about him."

"He hurt you."

Dropping her hands, she met his gaze. "His name is Jeffrey DeWilde."

Paul felt as if he'd received a blow to the back of his knees. Almost staggering, he moved to the bench and sat down. "Jeffrey DeWilde."

Like pieces of a puzzle fitting together, bits of information melded in his mind. And a picture began to emerge. All their careful planning to steal the Empress Catherine tiara had never had anything to do with the tiara itself, not really. The theft had not been a career caper or one last job before retirement.

Stealing the tiara had been about revenge. With bitter clarity, Paul recognized the truth. Stealing the tiara was intended to rock the DeWilde empire. The theft was meant to unnerve the shareholders and give Jeffrey DeWilde a nasty shock. That explained why Allison had been so upset when no mention of the theft appeared in the news. Without headlines to alert the DeWilde shareholders, her revenge had fallen flat.

He saw something else with equal bitterness.

"You used me."

"Paul, no!" Her eyes looked enormous in her white face. She stretched a hand toward him, then thought better of it and returned her hand to her lap. "It was never like that."

"It was always like that," he corrected her sharply, staring at her. "If you believe otherwise, then you're lying to yourself. Did you laugh when I moved the earth to find you?" In retrospect, he had played right into her hands. "When did you start planning to use me? When we were under the desk? Or did you decide later, when, like a naive fool, I suggested a partnership?" A memory surfaced in his mind. Allison watching two women, one swinging a box with the distinctive DeWilde script flowing across its side. "You played me like a fish on a line," he said softly.

When she slid across the bench and gripped his arm, he looked down at her hand, then moved away from her.

"I wanted Jeffrey to feel hurt and embarrassed as I had felt. I thought stealing the tiara would result in worldwide publicity. I thought it would startle investors in DeWilde's, maybe affect the price of the stock." She spread her hands. "I don't know what I was thinking. Then I fell in love with you and it all seemed crazy, but I couldn't stop it once we got started. Maybe I didn't want to stop it, not really. Then, when you put the tiara on my head and I realized what I'd done...I just...I felt horrified. I couldn't believe that I'd..." She dropped her head in her hands.

He stared at a curious passerby until the woman blushed, then continued on past them. Images and insights pummeled his mind like blows, one after another, until he ached as if he'd been on the wrong end of a bloody fight.

And he felt like a prize fool.

She'd been conducting a business right under his nose and he hadn't suspected a thing. He had believed her when she said she needed an afternoon to have her hair done, or shop, or run various errands. Instead, she'd been going to her office. Making sure her employees were still catching bad guys. He didn't doubt that he would be behind bars right now if she hadn't seen a way to use him.

That hurt the most. She had moved him along step by step, playing with his mind and his emotions, encouraging him to fall in love with her. And for what purpose? To strike back at Jeffrey DeWilde.

Jeffrey, whom Paul knew slightly, loomed in his memory, handsome, urbane, a powerful and quiet man who ceded the social stage to his wife. He stared at Allison and tried to imagine her in Jeffrey's arms. Fortunately, he couldn't. Jeffrey was too old for her, too distant, too married.

"Good God," he said suddenly, turning his head to watch Allison blot her eyes and blow her nose. "Jeffrey was still married to Grace. What the hell were you thinking of?" Anger and disbelief shook his voice. "You had to know an affair with a married man wasn't going to end well! Of course you got hurt. Any fool could have predicted it." Each word hurt him as much as it seemed to hurt her. Right now he wanted to hurt her.

She started to tell him about Jeffrey, but he cut her off. "How do you dare claim that honesty is an essential part of your character? Is an affair with a married man honest? Is using a man who loves you honest?" He shook his head in disgust. "I'm a thief, but you're the most dishonest person I know. The items I take can be replaced. But you take trust and love and honesty, and when those things are stolen, they're gone forever."

"Please, Paul—" her eyes begged him to believe her "—I never told you an outright lie."

"And nothing you implied was the truth!"

"I love you, that's true. It's true that I'm sorry about the mess I've made of things." She straightened her shoulders with an effort. "And it's true that I deeply regret stealing the tiara. I wish to God that we hadn't taken it."

"I wouldn't believe you if you said the sun rose in the east!" There was more he wanted to say. Accusations scalded the back of his tongue, demanding expression. But what was the point?

It was over. A relationship he had believed would endure forever had ended.

They were not alike. What they shared was merely superficial. She had deceived him about everything important. She had used him. She had used his expertise to plan the burglary of the tiara and would have let him be the person who actually stole it. He had no idea if she'd told the truth about her background or if she had borrowed someone else's history. Everything he had believed they meant to each other was merely a charade.

He had fallen in love with a chimera, a woman who didn't exist except in his own romantic imagination. Everything about her was a lie.

In that uncanny way they had of seeming to read each other's minds, she looked up at him with reddened eyes and whispered, "Loving you isn't a lie, Paul. You must know that. You have to know it. Please. Isn't there some way for us to start over?"

Right now, all he knew was that he wanted the betrayal to end. He wanted to get as far away from her as he could.

"Keep the tiara. You've earned it and I don't want it," he snapped.

Then he turned away from her, hurting so badly that even the air seemed to choke him. Without a backward glance, he walked out of her life.

CHAPTER TWELVE

ALLISON PLACED her elbow on the kitchen table and dropped her head into her hand. With her other hand, she held the telephone pressed close to her ear.

"I'm sorry," she said for the fourth time, staring at the calendar mounted beside her refrigerator. Three weeks had passed since that terrible moment in the park when Paul had walked away from her. Three intensively introspective weeks. "Monique, I wish I could explain, but...I can't." Monique protested for five minutes, but Allison eventually heard the beginnings of acceptance. "I know it's asking a lot, but can you continue to hold the fort for a while longer?"

There was a pause opened on the line, then Monique sighed. "How much longer?"

"I don't know," Allison admitted reluctantly. Opening her eyes, she stared at the tiara sitting on the table in front of her. Bright overhead light caused the rubies and diamonds to wink as if they shared a secret with her. Allison supposed they did. "I'm leaving Monaco tomorrow. I'll be gone at least a week." She drew an unsteady breath. "It's possible that I might not return." In fact, it was probable. What she intended to do would almost certainly lead to a prison term.

She smiled sadly. People could not escape their destiny. Despite every good intention, she had followed in the family tradition by committing a criminal act, and would undoubtedly spend the next few years in prison paying for it. The shock of it numbed her.

During the last three weeks she had thought hard about this eventuality and had finally come to terms with it. If a prison term was required to help her regain her self-respect and the integrity she'd lost along the way, then she was prepared to pay that price.

Monique gasped. Then she and Allison repeated the conversation in which a frustrated Monique demanded explanations that a thoroughly miserable Allison could not supply.

"Things have begun to deteriorate here," Monique said at length. "If you stay away much longer, you might not have a business to return to. And I refuse to accept that you won't return! I'll do what I can to hold things together, but..."

"I appreciate everything you've done. You're a good friend, Monique."

"You sound so depressed. I'm worried sick about you. I've never heard you talk like this. Can't you tell me what's happening to you?"

Allison looked away from the winking tiara. Each accusing flash shot a dagger into her heart. "Someday I'll tell you everything," she promised, but she knew she wouldn't.

A cramp tightened her stomach. Here was another lie in what she had begun to recognize as a long chain of deceptions. The insight made her feel ill, and she finished the conversation with Monique as quickly as she decently could.

After hanging up the telephone, she poured a glass of Montrachet and listlessly returned to the table, pulling her terry robe around her body.

Since that awful moment when Paul had walked away from her, she had spent hours staring at the damned tiara, having retrieved it from the top of her closet. It represented everything wrong in her life. And oddly enough, the jewels seemed as lifeless as Allison felt. When the light wasn't hitting them directly, the gems lost their luster and sparkle. The jewels faded the same way that her own honesty and integrity had faded.

"It started with Jeffrey," she murmured aloud.

She had known he was married, but she had pursued him anyway, placing her own needs above any thoughts of right or wrong. She had wanted a man as powerful and strong as her father had been, but unlike her father in every other way. She had wanted a wonderful man in her life badly enough that she willfully ignored the fact that he belonged to another woman. She had chased a decent, honorable man, chipping at his resistance until he surrendered his honor.

In the process, she had compromised everything she would have sworn she believed in. Worse, she hadn't even recognized what she was doing to herself. Excuses? She had a million of them to justify an affair with a married man, to prop up her sense of integrity, to explain how wrong was right in her case. If she had let herself think about the hurt that she and Jeffrey might cause Grace DeWilde, something she hadn't let herself do, she would have explained that away, too.

But she hadn't spared Grace DeWilde a single thought. She hadn't wondered how an affair might impact Jeffrey's children or even Jeffrey's image of the man he thought himself to be. She hadn't permitted any analysis that might damage her opinion of herself as honest and straightforward, as different from her father and grandfather as marble from mud.

She had raced into the affair, searching for an indefinable something and with no thought for consequences. And she had ended by hurting a lot of people, herself most of all.

Sitting alone in her kitchen, with the tiara winking merrily at her misery, she made herself remember every detail of her affair with Jeffrey.

The hardest admission was recognizing that she had blamed him instead of placing the fault where it belonged. Squarely on herself. *She* had instigated the affair. *She* had placed expectations on the relationship. Jeffrey had never lied to her, had never made any promises. He had been a reluctant participant from the beginning.

If Allison had truly been as honest as she had insisted to Paul that she was, she would have admitted that she knew from the beginning that Jeffrey loved his wife and would never voluntarily leave Grace. Allison had been an anomaly in his life, an event that occurred at a time when something had made him uncharacteristically vulnerable. It saddened her to realize that she knew him so little that she couldn't even guess what might have left him susceptible to a younger woman's admiration and desire for love.

Paul was right, as he had been right about so many things. The affair couldn't have ended happily, and deep inside she had known that. All the while she had been trying to draw Jeffrey closer, he had been gently pushing her away.

The trouble with wielding honesty like a blade was that the blade didn't stop at one layer but cut ever deeper. If she conceded that she had known the affair with Jeffrey wouldn't last, then the ending couldn't have been a surprise. Or an offense. Jeffrey had bungled their goodbye scene, but Jeffrey had been happily married for thirty years. He wasn't experienced at ending affairs.

The bottom line? Jeffrey DeWilde didn't deserve Allison's anger or her quest for revenge. He hadn't wanted an affair in the first place, and in his own way, he undoubtedly believed he had tried to end it kindly.

Jeffrey's parting gift had not been a thoughtlessly cruel act on his part. Now Allison could admit that his gift was a touchingly naive gesture from a man who was sophisticated but not worldly. A man who understood one woman—Grace DeWilde—but not women in general. Now that her thoughts were clear, she realized it probably had never entered Jeffrey's mind that such a gesture would be deeply offensive. He hadn't thought about tarnishing a beautiful relationship because their relationship had not been beautiful to him. She guessed that for Jeffrey, their affair had been a shameful episode in an otherwise happy and successful marriage.

At some point during these introspective days, it had occurred to Allison to worry and ponder what should have been obvious. Had her affair with Jeffrey been the cause of his breakup with Grace DeWilde?

The possibility haunted her.

She cringed at the thought of being responsible for another woman's pain. And if her liaison with Jeffrey had ended in the dissolution of his marriage, then he had suffered greatly for his dalliance with Allison.

And all this made stealing the tiara as unnecessary and unjustified as her thirst for revenge. She had committed a crime that was not only stupid but senseless.

A moan issued from her throat and she raked her fingers through her hair. Paul was so right. She had lost her integrity, her personal philosophy, her sense of honesty. And the person she had deceived most had been herself.

Paul. God, she missed him every minute of every day.

Laying her head on the kitchen table, she surrendered to a storm of helpless weeping. She who had always been so controlled, so cool and self-contained, wept as she hadn't wept since the police had arrived and shattered her world by snapping handcuffs on her father's wrists.

She no longer knew who she was.

She only knew that she hurt inside. And everything she believed in was gone. Including Paul. She longed for him with an ache that was physical; she wanted him every night and missed him every day. But she knew they could never have had a truly successful relationship. How could they? How could she have an honest relationship with any man until she started being honest with herself?

His rented villa was empty. A To Let sign had been posted outside the gates.

When the storm of sobbing passed, she gripped the tiara in her hands, turning it between shaking fingers. The gems sparkled up at her reddened eyes, winking recrimination.

After a time, she carried the tiara to the suitcases spread across her bedroom and carefully packed it in a carry-on case.

She couldn't change the past. But she could atone for it. And when she had paid for her mistakes, she would begin again.

After she got out of prison.

ALLISON HAD BEEN IN TIGHT spots before, but none had wreaked such havoc on her nerves as walking into Jeffrey DeWilde's London office. The handle of the case she carried felt slippery against her damp palm. Flames roared in her stomach, and one eyelid twitched.

Firmly reminding herself that she was a professional, she walked directly to the desk of Jeffrey's secretary, a woman whose name flew out of her memory. Summoning an award-winning performance, she gave the woman a coolly expectant look and announced crisply, "Nick Santos has an appointment with Mr. DeWilde—" she consulted a slim gold wristwatch "—in exactly three minutes. Mr. Santos could not attend the meeting and sent me in his stead."

Deception was an integral part of Allison's professional life. She could see how the habit could spill into her personal life, as well. Occasionally, like now, the lines blurred between personal and professional. But she knew Jeffrey would never have agreed to see her if she had made the appointment in her own name.

Jeffrey's secretary smiled uncertainly. "Mr. Santos didn't inform us that he intended to send an associate."

"A last-minute conflict arose," Allison explained smoothly. "Now, if you'll show me to Mr. DeWilde's office..." She knew exactly the imperious tone to employ, the confident expression to convey. Maneuvering secretaries was a snap compared to circumventing sophisticated electronic devices.

At the heavy doors to Jeffrey's office, his secretary paused. "I don't believe you mentioned your name...."

"It isn't necessary to announce me. Mr. DeWilde and I are acquainted." Placing a hand on the latch, she smiled a cool dismissal, waiting until the secretary turned away with a doubtful expression.

Then she drew a deep breath. This was it. The flames leapt higher, into her throat. Her lips trembled. She wished she wasn't wearing a linen suit and could stretch into her warm-up routine and ease the tension drawing her muscles. Suddenly she wished she had worn the green silk that Jeffrey had once complimented, wished she had not dressed her hair into a severe French twist.

She shuddered lightly, then straightened her shoulders and her spine and opened the door.

For an instant the light falling through the window overlooking Bond Street cast a glare across her eyes, then she saw Jeffrey look up from his desk, a half smile on his lips.

Not a flicker of recognition lit his eyes. Realizing that he believed he was greeting a stranger confirmed everything Allison had so recently accepted about their affair. That he didn't recognize her saddened her so that she felt tears sting her eyes.

Abruptly he stiffened and frowned, rising behind his desk. "Good Lord. Allison!"

"Nick Santos is a friend of mine. I made the appointment in Nick's name without his knowledge or permission because I know he's doing some work for you, and I knew you wouldn't see me if I gave my own name."

Taut with the awkwardness of former lovers, they regarded each other across the length of Jeffrey's office. Had they met at a cocktail party or during intermission at a theater, they would have had nothing whatever to say to each other. There was something terribly painful in this realization.

Jeffrey touched his tie and buttoned his coat. He cleared his throat, then fell back on good manners to guide them through these first tense moments. "Will you have a seat? Would you care for coffee or tea?"

"Nothing, thank you." Grateful to ease her shaking legs, Allison took the chair in front of his desk and placed her case on the floor beside her. Silence rang loud in her ears. Her mouth was too dry to speak.

Jeffrey was as handsome as she remembered, and as cautious and controlled. Curiosity and alarm flared in the depths of his eyes, but his expression revealed neither. Allison gazed at his trim body and confident stance and understood why she had been attracted to him. But she no longer understood why she had fallen in love with him.

He was not a spontaneous man as Paul was. She could no more imagine Jeffrey DeWilde hiding under a desk and whimsically making love to a stranger than she could imagine him climbing the wall of a building. Jeffrey had been a wonderful and considerate lover, but he wouldn't have dreamed of taking her hand or embracing her in public. He didn't care about or understand her business and she didn't understand his. In retrospect, Allison wondered what they had found to talk about. They had virtually nothing in common.

They were simply strangers who had slept together, two wounded souls who had found brief comfort in each other's arms. The relationship could not have gone deeper because Allison was not Grace, and Jeffrey was not Paul.

"I've come to apologize," Allison whispered through dry lips. If she hadn't rehearsed her opening, she would have been struck dumb. Suddenly, she found him intimidating.

Jeffrey's eyebrows rose, and his hands, folded on top of his desk, tightened. Clearly her presence distressed him. He didn't know what to say to her.

"After you broke off our relationship, I told myself that I hated you."

Knots stood out along his jawline and he pushed back from his desk. Despite the distress she read in his eyes, his voice emerged calm and controlled. "Perhaps coming here was a mistake," he suggested politely, glancing at the door.

"Jeffrey, please. Hear me out." Before he could protest, she quickly sketched her perception of their last meeting. When she had finished, he sank back into his leather chair and stared at her with a genuinely appalled expression.

"It is I who must apologize," he said stiffly. "I never intended any offense. The bracelet was meant as a token of affection and farewell. It's stupid really, but I had an impression that it was the done thing to present a gift when leaving a . . ." Points of color highlighted his cheekbones and he waved a hand in lieu of saying the word *mistress*.

"I understand that now," Allison said in a low voice. The conversation was more painful than she had anticipated. "But I didn't then. I wanted you to suffer."

For the first time since meeting him, she watched his characteristic emotional control drop like a mask to reveal unmistakable anguish. "My dear girl, you have no idea how I have suffered."

"Then it's true," Allison whispered, closing her eyes. "Grace left you because of me."

Instead of answering, he spun his chair to the window. Two excruciatingly long minutes elapsed before he faced her again, once more in control. "Allison, why did you come here?"

The answer was complicated, made more so by the fact that they had never shared intimate thoughts. But Jeffrey had suffered because of her. She owed him as much honesty as she could muster.

"I've made a mess of my life," she said slowly, watching her fingers twist around themselves. "I've hurt a lot of people through accident or design." Lifting her head, she made herself look at him directly. "I set out to hurt you."

"I'm sorry," he said quietly.

"So am I. What I did was inexcusable and criminal." Standing, she placed the case on top of his desk and opened it with shaking hands. "I stole the Empress Catherine tiara from DeWilde's Monte Carlo. I did it to punish you. I hoped the loss would cause you financial difficulties and that the headlines would unsettle DeWilde shareholders."

She unwrapped the tiara and placed it squarely before him, surprised when he gave it only a cursory glance. Whatever reaction she had expected, it had not been indifference.

"I'm shamed and appalled by what I did. Stealing the tiara goes against everything I believed I stood for. I'm returning the piece with my heartfelt apology. I deeply regret whatever difficulty I've caused you."

A wintery smile brushed his lips. "So it was you. Oddly, that possibility never occurred to me. The police suspected a jewel thief they call The Ghost. They fear this Ghost has moved his field of operation to Monaco."

Allison's heart contracted sharply. Paul had left the area none too soon. "Do the police know the identity of The Ghost?"

He gave her a curious look. "I don't believe so, no."

She released a breath she had not realized she'd been holding. Paul was safe. "But the police were notified of the theft at DeWilde's?" A flush of color stained her throat. "There was no mention on the news."

A shrug lifted the shoulders of Jeffrey's Savile Row suit. "The authorities respected our request for no publicity."

"But the theft of a piece worth at least six million dollars . . ."

He glanced at the tiara, sparkling in the light that fell over his shoulder. "The police were informed that this is a replica worth about a quarter of a million dollars at most."

Allison's mouth dropped. "A replica?" Not once had she doubted the authenticity of the piece. DeWilde's claimed the tiara had belonged to Catherine the Great, and DeWilde's reputation was such that she had never doubted the claim for an instant. "No wonder it seemed curiously lifeless. And the security was so..." Her mind raced. "But the store manager replaced it at once. Are there *two* replicas of the original?" Confusion darkened her eyes.

Jeffrey's expression was unreadable. If he had been a man given to sighs, Allison sensed that he would have sighed heavily. "It's a long story, but yes. As the original tiara is...unavailable...there seems to be a general perception that this piece is the original." He glanced uncomfortably at the profusion of fake rubies, diamonds and emeralds. "Therefore, we have treated it as an original, hence the second replica."

What he wasn't saying fascinated Allison as much as what little he did say. She sensed a family mystery here, one that intrigued her professional curiosity. At once she guessed that her friend Nick Santos had been privately employed to unravel a secret Allison had inadvertently stumbled onto, a secret tied to the astonishing fact that at least part of the fabled DeWilde jewel collection was fake.

Relief began to flow through her as she gazed down at the tiara. She had not stolen an immensely valuable historical piece, after all. Still, a quarter of a million dollars was not an insignificant amount. The police would consider the theft worth prosecuting.

Bleak determination darkened her eyes. The value of the piece didn't matter. She had stolen it. She was here to accept whatever punishment Jeffrey chose to mete out.

"I came to return the tiara and to turn myself in. What I did was wrong, and I'm prepared to stand trial for an unthinkable lapse of judgment." When she met Jeffrey's eyes, she saw fatigue and sorrow there that had not been present when she knew him in Paris. What a fool she had been to assume he had suffered no consequence as a result of their liaison. Her suffering had dissipated when she met Paul Courtwald. But Jeffrey's punishment continued.

"Oh, Jeffrey. Is there any chance that you and Grace can reconcile your differences?" The blurted question appalled her.

To her surprise, he answered. "I doubt it," he said quietly.

"I'm so sorry. That is a tragedy."

"Yes. It is." After a moment he cleared his throat and smoothed slim fingers over the knot in his tie. "Allison...what is it that you expect me to do?"

The question surprised her. "I expect you to phone the police and demand that they arrest me for stealing the tiara."

"I see." He studied his hands for a moment, then looked up to meet her eyes. "I'm not going to phone the police."

A fierce tide of relief sucked at the marrow of her bones. If she had been standing, she would have fallen to her knees. "Thank you," she whispered, swallowing a hot lump in her throat. "I felt certain you would have me arrested. May I ask why you've chosen not to?"

For several minutes he studied her face, but Allison had an impression he didn't really see her. "One of the reasons is selfish. I'd prefer not to testify in public court that DeWilde's has been exhibiting a fake tiara as genuine. The second reason is equally selfish. I'd rather that my children don't hear in court that I had an affair with a woman young enough to be my daughter." He touched his fingertips to his forehead. "Finally, enough people have already been hurt by what I did. It seems gratuitous to add another casualty to the list. I don't wish to bear that additional burden."

"You're not to blame. What happened between us was entirely my doing."

"Not entirely. I could have said no."

The awkwardness returned to embarrass them both. It occurred to Allison that there were things Jeffrey wished to say to her but couldn't. There were things she wanted to say to him, but it was too late. Her foolish act of revenge and his decision not to prosecute opened an abyss between them.

Jeffrey cleared his throat. "As a point of curiosity, how did you get the tiara through customs?"

"I packed it with an ornate costume," she said with a slight shrug. "The gown filled my carry-on bag and padded the tiara. If I'd been questioned, I would have said I was attending a masked ball. The tiara was part of the costume."

She doubted Jeffrey cared about the problems involved in transporting a stolen tiara. But his question and her answer filled a silence that had grown painful.

"You're young, bright, talented. Your life is ahead of you." Jeffrey rose behind his desk, a signal the interview had ended. Allison too came to her feet, thinking he looked older than she remembered. The ordeal of Grace's departure had left its mark. He rubbed a hand down his jaw, then spoke softly. "You've been given a second chance, Allison. Use it well."

Because she couldn't speak, she only nodded. At the door, she turned back to him. "Thank you. I hope that you and—" But he had turned to the window and she saw only the back of his head.

Quietly, she closed his office door behind her and stood in the corridor for a moment, thinking.

She knew what she had to do next. In many ways it would be harder than this interview had been.

CHAPTER THIRTEEN

A LIGHT SPRING RAIN canceled Allison's plans for spending the day sightseeing. Instead, she passed the afternoon in her hotel suite placing telephone calls. To her surprise, the transatlantic call to Monte Carlo went through without delay.

Immediately Monique demanded, "Where are you and how are you?"

Allison laughed for the first time in weeks. "I'm in San Francisco, and since you ask, I'm nervous as hell."

"San Francisco? In the United States?"

"The very same," Allison confirmed, watching raindrops slide down the balcony doors opening off her suite.

"I don't think I've ever heard you admit to being nervous before...."

"I have a—difficult—interview later this afternoon."

When Allison didn't explain further, Monique sighed. "So. When are you returning? Or is the real question, Are you coming back at all?"

"I'll definitely be returning." Allison went limp with relief every time she thought of Jeffrey's reprieve. "But it won't be immediately. While I'm in the States, I plan to spend a week with my mother."

It was a visit that was long overdue. There were things she wanted to know about her father, questions she had never asked or discussed with her mother. They had handled the embarrassing headlines and their humiliation by holding their heads high and pretending nothing was amiss. In retrospect, Allison recognized that her skill at deception had begun early. She had been deceiving herself for a very long time.

Although she felt a greater understanding of her father now than ever before, it was time to reverse the pretense, time that she and her mother let themselves discuss what had happened to them. Surprisingly, when she telephoned her mother and broached the subject, her mother had readily agreed to talk about the past. She had even sounded relieved. It was doubtful that Allison would uncover new information, but already she sensed that talking frankly about her father and what he had done would draw her and her mother closer.

She spoke to Monique about business matters, sounding more like her old self than she had in weeks, and they settled several matters that only Allison could decide. Before she hung up, she couldn't stop herself from asking, "Has Paul Courtwald phoned the office by any chance?" She could have kicked herself for inviting a painful response.

Monique hesitated. "No. Were you expecting him to call?"

"Not really." The raindrops seemed grayer than a minute before. She watched them slipping down the panes like tears.

After hanging up from Monique, Allison telephoned her mother to confirm their plans, then spent the remainder of the day phoning friends in the States whom she hadn't spoken to in much too long.

After a late room-service lunch, she thumbed through her address book and stopped at the section marked C. She could call him in London. The number for Paul's parents was right before her. If he wasn't staying with his parents, surely they would know where he was. A momentary burst of sunlight pushed through the clouds and Allison took it as a sign of approval. She had actually begun to dial the Courtwalds' London home before she questioned what she was doing and abruptly replaced the receiver.

Paul didn't want to see her. He knew her home number, knew the name of her company. He could have reached her at any time. But he had chosen not to. As far as he was concerned, what had happened between them was over.

Tears glistened in her eyes. It hurt to recall their last moments in the park. The only thing that helped was to remember what Paul had said at the beginning. He had promised that no matter what happened, he would always love her...that would not change. She clung to those words, holding them close to her heart. But hope faded with each passing day that she didn't hear from him. Sometimes love wasn't enough.

"Oh, Paul," she whispered, watching clouds blot the brief glimpse of sunlight. "If Jeffrey can give me a second chance, why can't you?"

It was beginning to appear that she and Paul were destined to end like Jeffrey and Grace DeWilde, loving each other but separated by pride and wounds that could not be healed by time and distance. Thinking about it broke her heart.

Allison wasn't sure how long she sat at the table, drinking cold coffee and watching the rain cry against the windowpanes. But when she finally roused herself to glance at the time, it was nearly four o'clock.

Startled, she blinked and hurried to the closet to stare at a row of clothing, none of which seemed suitable.

What did The Other Woman wear to meet the wife of her former lover?

It was a ridiculous dilemma, Allison thought with a sinking feeling. Regardless of how she presented herself, Grace DeWilde would see a bimbo.

ALLISON WAITED INSIDE an idling taxi, watching people walk in and out of a chic apartment building at one of San Francisco's better addresses. Most carried umbrellas that occasionally concealed their faces, and she feared she wouldn't recognize Grace DeWilde. She needn't have worried. She recognized Jeffrey's wife at once.

With a sixth sense that made her stomach tense, she fastened her gaze on a smartly dressed woman emerging from a limo. This was Grace DeWilde, looking younger and more vivacious than the posed photograph Allison had clipped from a newspaper and now held in her lap.

Before Grace dashed for the awning and then inside the building, Allison caught an impression of a trim figure beneath a stylish English raincoat, slightly tousled blond hair and tremendous energy. Clearly the limo driver, who watched with admiring eyes until Grace was safely inside, had been charmed by her. A smiling doorman rushed to open an umbrella over her head.

Closing her eyes for a moment, Allison touched a shaking hand to her forehead and reviewed all she knew about Grace DeWilde.

During her years with the DeWilde Corporation, Grace had made herself a legend among marketing and merchandising people. Whenever the success of the DeWilde stores was lauded, Grace's name followed in the same breath. Her methodology was famous enough to be studied internationally in university business courses.

Articles published about Grace DeWilde never failed to mention her generosity and skill at organizing charity functions. According to Allison's research, Grace was also famed as a hostess, one of those rare people possessing a genius for combining guests and menus in exactly the right mix. She had conquered both business and social worlds, and she had done it while raising three successful children.

Now she was creating international shock waves with her new store and undoubtedly giving DeWilde's upper management gigantic headaches. That her store would be hugely successful was a foregone conclusion.

Altogether, Grace DeWilde was an admirable and formidable woman.

Allison's heart sank. But she hadn't traveled more than five thousand miles to cut and run. Steeling her nerves, she paid the taxi driver and made herself step out of the cab and cross the street.

The doorman watched her approach before he brushed rain from the visor of his cap and offered her a polite smile. "Can I help you, miss?"

"Indeed you can." Allison shook drops of water from the sleeves of her raincoat and smoothed back her hair, which was starting to curl in the humidity. "I have an appointment with Miss Edna Pink on the fifth floor. Would you inform her that I've arrived, please?"

The doorman handed her a sign-in sheet, then headed across the marble tiles toward the house phone. "What's your name?"

"Tell Miss Pink that Leigh Burns is here." She signed the page, then returned the sheet to the top of his desk. "From the Internal Revenue Service."

The doorman grinned, rolled his eyes, then picked up the phone. A minute later, he waved Allison toward the elevators. "Be gentle. Miss Pink is a harmless old soul. Wouldn't hurt a fly, let alone cheat the IRS."

Allison stepped into the elevator and touched the button for the fifth floor. Once she had learned Grace's address, it was simplicity itself to obtain a city directory that listed others living in the same building and on the same floor.

Next, she had studied the names of the fifth-floor residents and asked herself under what circumstances would each instruct the doorman to permit a stranger upstairs. Posing as an IRS auditor offered a workable solution. Two days ago Allison had phoned Miss Pink and experienced no difficulty making an appointment.

Stepping off the elevator, she paused a moment, then entered an elegantly appointed corridor and slowly approached Grace DeWilde's door. As she was anxious to put the confrontation behind her, she might have risked facing Grace immediately despite her assumption that if she didn't arrive at Miss Pink's door, the woman would alert the doorman, who would call security. The decision was made for her when a door farther down the corridor opened and a gray head appeared.

"Miss Burns? Is that you?"

Allison continued down the hallway, limp with a combination of relief and anxiety. "You must be Miss Pink?"

The little woman's face puckered into worried pleats. "I have the records you requested. Come in, come in."

"Thank you." Edna Pink's apartment was packed wall-to-wall with large, dark Victorian furniture. Where a bit of blank space might have relieved the oppressive heaviness, Miss Pink had hung a picture or placed a weeping fern. Lace draped the windows, the arms of chairs, the tops of tables, the backs of matching sofas and much of Miss Pink.

"The records are in the dining room." Wringing her hands, Edna Pink led the way, trailing the scent of lavender and rouge. "I've spread them out on the table for you."

"Actually, I didn't intend to conduct the audit here," Allison explained, scanning a hutch filled with valuable antique silver. She frowned, thinking the best security systems in the world didn't help when people voluntarily opened their doors to strangers. With an effort, she resisted giving Miss Pink a lecture about safety measures. "In fact, this won't take a moment. I'll just collect your records, if I may. I can review them at the office and get back to you next week."

A mixture of relief and disappointment deepened the wrinkles lining the older woman's brow. "Oh." She peered through her glasses at a plate of petit fours. "I'd hoped we might visit a little," she said wistfully.

Any other time Allison would have given in to the tug at her heart elicited by the little plate of petits fours and Miss Pink's old-fashioned lace collar. But right now, she couldn't have swallowed a bite of anything. "I really can't stay," she said gently, gathering the records into a manila envelope already addressed and ready to mail back to Miss Edna Pink. "I have another appointment. In this building, in fact."

Within five minutes of edging toward the door while refusing to sample one of the tiny cakes, she had bid Miss Pink goodbye and again stood in the silent corridor before Grace DeWilde's brass doorbell. Something had happened to the air in the corridor; she felt as if she were choking.

Bending slightly, Allison inhaled deeply and fought to control her nerves. She was in the right building on the right floor. No one was alarmed, no one had phoned security, no one was looking for her. She had crossed an ocean and a continent to reach this place and this moment. Now she was here.

She owed Jeffrey an enormous debt for so generously giving her a second chance. If she could—if it were at all possible—she hoped to repay him by giving him a second chance, too.

But, dear God. This was the hardest thing she had ever made herself do. Her finger shook so badly that she barely mustered the strength to press the bell. When she heard a distant chime inside the apartment, her instinct was to bolt and run.

Before she could surrender to the urge to flee, the door opened and she stood face-to-face with Grace DeWilde. It surprised her to discover that she was the taller of the two. Somehow, she had assumed Grace would be taller.

A second shock came when Allison suddenly realized that she might have been looking at an older version of herself. Grace's clear blue eyes mirrored her own, as did the honey blond hair. They both had stubborn chins, a proud posture and trim bodies that radiated the vibrancy of good health and energy. Finally Allison grasped why Jeffrey had felt drawn to her. She would have reminded him of Grace as a younger woman.

Grace's smile vanished abruptly, and her eyes flashed glacial fire. "How did you get into the building?"

Allison sensed she had only seconds before Grace closed the door in her face, so she didn't pause to question how Grace had recognized her. Grace DeWilde was a competent, resourceful woman. Of course she would have learned all she could about the woman who had destroyed her marriage.

Allison spoke quickly, her words tumbling over one another. "I've traveled a very long distance to speak to you,

Mrs. DeWilde. I beg you to hear what I have to say. It's important."

Like Allison, Grace was not a woman who easily hid her emotions. She trembled with the urge to slam the door and shut Allison out of her life. But, Allison realized, Grace was also fascinated by the woman who had seduced Jeffrey, and deeply curious. Allison counted heavily on that curiosity to buy her enough time to say what she had traveled thousands of miles to say.

Grace reluctantly moved backward a step, opening the door wider. Icy contempt blazed in her eyes. "You have five minutes, Miss Ames. No longer." Spinning on the heels of sleek Italian pumps, she led the way to her living room, stopping beside a small fire that crackled cheerily in the grate.

Between the cool rain and Grace's demeanor, Allison felt chilled to the bone. She would have liked to warm her shaking hands at the fire, but she stopped near the sofa. Grace did not invite her to sit down.

She had a moment to appreciate the airy spaciousness of the apartment, the clean, strong lines of the furnishings. Then it was time to begin.

"The clock is ticking, Miss Ames," Grace said coldly. Dots of high color burned on her cheekbones and she clasped her hands tightly together. Otherwise, she presented a picture of controlled and icy composure.

"This isn't easy for either of us," Allison began, speaking in a low voice.

"I don't care in the least about making anything easy for you, Miss Ames. Please say what you came to say."

It was a poor beginning. Allison lifted her head and pulled back her shoulders. She would not let this woman intimidate her. In her own way, she too could be formidable.

"I came to tell you that I am solely to blame for what happened between Jeffrey and me." Grace's eyelid flickered, otherwise she didn't react to the bald statement. "I knew Jeffrey was married, but I pursued him, anyway. What happened was not his idea and he resisted involvement."

"Do you expect me to condemn your lack of morality or to applaud your taste in men?"

Allison bit down on her back teeth and pressed her shaking fingertips together. "I deserve your condemnation and your sarcasm, Mrs. DeWilde." She lifted her head. "But Jeffrey does not. I don't know what occurred between the two of you that resulted in Jeffrey feeling vulnerable when I met him—he never talked about you— but I'd be willing to stake everything I own that he was never unfaithful before and won't be again."

The color deepened in Grace's cheeks. "I have no intention of discussing my marriage with you," she snapped. "Did Jeffrey send you here?"

"He doesn't know that I've come to see you. I . . . I saw him in London last week. On a professional matter," she hastened to add when Grace flinched and drew back. "He's suffering terribly. He loves you, Mrs. DeWilde. He's always loved you and no other woman. I meant nothing to him. He didn't even recognize me when I entered his office."

Grace stared at her. "Why should I believe anything you say?"

Allison returned her gaze. "I didn't travel this distance to lie to you. I made a mistake, Mrs. DeWilde, a bad mistake that resulted in hurting many people who didn't deserve to be hurt. I acted selfishly and, yes, immorally. I didn't think of it that way at the time, but you're correct. I can't change what happened, and I can't make amends.

But I can tell you the truth. I am entirely to blame for the very brief, insignificant affair I had with Jeffrey."

It was the most humiliating, hardest speech Allison had ever delivered. But each word was true, even if Grace DeWilde doubted it.

"My husband could have said no, Miss Ames," Grace replied sharply, echoing Jeffrey's comment. "He could have refused you. He could have remembered that he had a wife and children. He could have turned his back on you and walked away."

"He tried, but I can be very persistent," Allison answered levelly. Her face felt as if it were on fire. "I met Jeffrey at a moment when he seemed lonely and vulnerable." She drew a shallow breath. "Why he felt that way is perhaps a question you could answer better than I."

Her last statement appeared to penetrate Grace's defenses in a way that Allison's previous words had not. Closing her eyes, Grace swayed on her feet as if she had swallowed something painful.

When she lifted her head, she had regained control. Only the flush on her throat and cheeks betrayed the strong emotions burning behind her patrician features. "This interview has ended, Miss Ames."

"I'm sorry, Mrs. DeWilde. I am so sorry that my thoughtlessness and selfishness hurt you. If I could alter the past, I would do so in an instant." The words poured out in a heartfelt rush. "If you can find it in your heart to forgive Jeffrey, I beg you to do so. He loves you. He's suffering without you. Surely you still feel something for him. If only—"

"Goodbye, Miss Ames," Grace said in a husky voice wrapped in steel.

Allison bit off the flow of imploring words. Helplessly, she stared at the woman who resembled her so greatly, the

woman she had betrayed. She sensed that she and Grace
DeWilde might have become good friends in different circumstances. They were both ambitious and capable,
lauded as experts in their fields of endeavor. They were
energetic, intelligent, sympathetic and caring women who
might have found much to admire in each other. Suddenly Allison regretted Grace's contempt more than she
had ever regretted losing Jeffrey.

"If I'm forced to telephone security, it will embarrass
both of us," Grace stated quietly.

"That won't be necessary. I'm leaving." But she didn't
move. Allison thrust her shaking hands deep into the
pockets of her raincoat and looked at Grace. She owed
Jeffrey one more try.

"He loves you, Mrs. DeWilde. He always has and I believe he always will. You and Jeffrey have invested over
thirty years in each other...don't throw that away, I beg
you. Jeffrey deserves a second chance. You both do."

There was nothing more to say.

She left Grace standing before the fireplace, staring after her.

Once in the corridor, Allison sagged against the wall and
pressed trembling fingertips to her eyelids. If she lived to
be one hundred, she would never again undergo anything
as humiliating or as upsetting as facing Grace DeWilde.

Later, she couldn't recall taking the elevator to the lobby
or hailing a cab. Couldn't remember posting Miss Pink's
tax records or returning to her hotel room.

Allison stood in the center of her suite, watching darkness gather beyond the draperies. She had done what she
could. She had cast pride to the winds and told Grace
DeWilde the truth. There was nothing more she could do
to repair the damage she had caused to Grace and Jeffrey

except remove herself from their lives and get on with her own.

Somehow, some way, she would have to rebuild a life without Paul. That would be the most difficult part of her future. Maybe if she immersed herself in work she would forget how lonely the nights were without him, how pallid and listless her days had become without his smile and spontaneously passionate kisses.

Standing at the window, she watched the persistent rain, tears flowing down her cheeks.

In an apartment not far from Allison's hotel, another woman leaned against a window and wept.

CHAPTER FOURTEEN

SPRING BLOSSOMED into summer, and the evenings became sultry and warm enough that many of Monte Carlo's international residents foolishly left their windows open all night.

Allison sighed as she pulled herself over the window ledge and dropped lightly onto the terrazzo floor of the DeJardines' bedroom suite. She hoped Monsieur and Madame DeJardine were enjoying their evening at the palace, because they were going to be very upset tomorrow when they learned how easily she had entered the grounds and subsequently their home. She had not encountered a security system this inadequate in years.

After giving herself a moment to adjust to the darkness within the bedroom suite, she decided to begin by checking the paintings. Unless she'd lost her instincts, the DeJardines' were overconfident enough to place the safe in the most obvious location. She figured the combination would be 6-14-19-4-5, which translated to Madame DeJardine's birth date, another common mistake. The only surprise would be if the combination were keyed to Monsieur DeJardine's birth date instead.

Making a sound of disgust low in her throat, she crossed the room, deciding to begin at the far door and work her way around the suite until she located the painting that would click open.

She found the correct one almost immediately and swung it away from the wall safe it was intended to conceal. Exactly as predicted, Madame DeJardine's birth date opened the combination lock.

Allison released a breath of exasperation. These people were innocents. Babes in the wood. With security this dismal, they might as well have painted a target on their house with a neon sign flashing: Thieves, Help Yourselves. Already she was writing her report in her mind. It would be lengthy. Her recommendations would be costly.

Rising on tiptoe, she scanned the contents of the wall safe. Ignoring the files and stacks of securities, she removed a broad, flat jewelry case, which would contain the Stamford pendant, a perfectly cut, twenty-carat blue diamond suspended on a pearl chain. This was her target item. It was like stealing candy from a baby.

Except, when Allison opened it and looked inside, the case was empty. For an instant, she stared at the velvet cushion in disbelief, then with growing anger.

The DeJardines were playing games with her. They must have removed the pendant and hidden it a second time. Hands on hips, she frowned, scanning the room, thinking about the size of the house and where she might hide something if she were less sophisticated and more confident that she could outsmart a determined thief.

"Looking for this?"

Her heart lurched. Then she whirled toward the sound of a familiar amused voice. "Paul!"

He stepped out of the deep shadows draping a sitting area, the Stamford pendant swinging negligently from one extended finger. "These people are pathetic. My ten-year-old nephew could steal this pendant. The DeJardines keep the combination written on a slip of paper in the bedside table. I hope you blister them in your report." He stepped forward and a bar of moonlight revealed the frown on his handsome face. "What the hell kept you, Just Allison?

I've been here three nights, waiting for you to put in an appearance.''

"Paul." She stared at him, her heart in her eyes. "Oh, Paul. I thought I'd never see you again."

"I thought so, too. But it seems I can't get a certain black lace negligee out of my mind. And the woman who wore it."

She wanted to run into his arms, wanted to press her thudding heart against his and cover his mouth with pent-up kisses. But there were things to say, a past that had to be dealt with before tomorrow was possible.

Allison wet her lips. "How did you know where to find me?"

He rolled his eyes and flipped the pendant around his finger, watching the diamond catch the moonlight. "How quickly they forget." He released an exaggerated sigh. "I'm the best second-story man in Europe, *chérie*. I broke into your office, of course, and studied your schedule. You're late."

Her chin rose along with her competitive nature. "I was delayed on the Rome assignment."

"Because," he said lazily, looping the pendant around his finger again, "you need a partner. Someone to take up the slack."

Her heart stopped, then rushed into overdrive. There was a lot to settle between them, and some of the issues would be thorny. But suddenly, dizzyingly, she knew it was going to work out for them. This fabulous, wonderful man was going to be hers forever.

"Is that right?" she challenged, grinning at him. She felt as if she were fizzing and blazing, lighting the room with the brilliant radiance of her happiness.

"I have in mind, say, a retired person. Someone who knows the business. Maybe someone who used to be the best damned jewel thief on either side of the pond. Someone who has a lot to atone for, and wants to do it by providing the best possible security against thieves such as he used to be. This someone might miss the thrills and excitement of his former life unless he had something similar, but law-abiding, to do with his life. That creative someone could be a big help to you, Just Allison.''

"Someone like you, cowboy? Is that the partner you have in mind for me?''

"Possibly. If I remember correctly, you and I make a hell of a team." He advanced another step, then stood with his weight on one leg, his hip jutting forward, twirling the pendant and looking at her. "There would have to be some changes, some new rules...."

"Such as?''

"You don't ever lie to me again, Allison. Not by word or implication. We start over from ground zero, and this time we do it honestly."

A flush heated her face, but she swallowed the shame she felt because she deserved what he said. "I did deceive you, and I did use you, Paul. I regret that with all my heart."

"Part of it I understand. There would never have been a you and me if I'd known from the start that we were on opposite sides of the law. Part of it I don't understand. But I've decided it doesn't matter. People do use each other. Maybe that isn't as important as I first thought it was. Maybe it's something that's going to take a while to work out."

"It won't happen again," she promised softly. "Not without you knowing up front what's going on."

She couldn't believe he was here and they were together again. Her hands opened and closed at her sides with the need to grab him and hold him.

"Here's the hard rule." He moved a step closer. "I want your promise that you'll try to be honest with yourself. No more telling yourself that you're doing something for one reason when it's really another. No more claiming you don't love me when you do."

She itched to cling to him and never let him go. Later she would tell him all that she had discovered about herself and that she had found the Allison she had lost along the way. She would tell him about taking the fake tiara to Jeffrey and the confrontation with Grace. Never again would there be any secrets between them. "Agreed," she whispered impatiently. "What else?"

He moved another step closer, and she saw that he was dressed much as he had been the night she first met him. Black jeans, a black shirt open at the throat. His hair was longer than she remembered, and she yearned to plunge her fingers in it and pull his mouth down to hers.

"You have to promise to wear that perfume I like, and wear the black nightgown once a week and nothing the rest of the week."

She laughed softly, watching him advance another step. The scent of his skin reached her now, a scent that made her knees go weak. Her hands began to shake and her breathing grew shallow.

"I promise. What else?"

He took another step and caught the pendant in mid-swing, closing his fist around it then dropping it into his pocket. "I want your promise to stop all second-story work and become a desk jockey the instant we learn that you're pregnant."

Allison sucked in a soft breath and tears sprang into her eyes. "I promise," she whispered in a choked voice. "Oh, Paul. I love you. I've missed you so much!"

She couldn't bear not touching him for another moment. Running forward, she threw herself on him. He caught her, crushing her fiercely against his chest, and his lips covered hers in a kiss so passionate it was almost punishing.

When his mouth finally released hers, they were both gasping. He held her so tightly that Allison imagined she heard her bones crack, and she didn't care. She pressed closer, afraid if she let go, he would vanish like a dream.

"I have so much to tell you," she whispered against his shoulder.

"I want to hear everything. What happened to the tiara? What have you been doing? Did you go crazy missing me like I went crazy missing you? And I have things to tell you, too. But there's something I have in mind first," he murmured in a husky voice. Cupping her hips, he molded her against the power of his arousal.

"Here?" Astonishment arched her eyebrows.

"No, *chérie.*" He nuzzled her throat and ran his hands from her waist to her breast, laughing softly when she moaned and arched against his palms. "Stupidity may be catching. We don't want to sleep in the DeJardines' bed. Besides, they'll return long before I'm through with you."

She kissed his chin, his jaw, his nose, his eyelids. The taste and electric touch of him thrilled through her body like champagne bubbles. "I know the perfect place," she said thickly, suspecting it was where he had intended to take her all along. "Are your clothes already in my closet?"

"Still in the suitcases," he said, laughing softly against her hair. "Except for my bathrobe, which is hanging beside yours behind your bathroom door."

"Pretty sure of yourself, aren't you, cowboy." She could hardly think. What his hands were doing drove every thought out of her mind.

He caught her chin in his hand and tilted her face up to his in the moonlight. "Are you sure, *chérie?* This time is forever."

Tears of happiness sparkled in her eyes. "Very, very sure."

"Then let's get the hell out of here, partner. I'll race you to your bed. The last one naked has to make breakfast." He laughed and kissed her soundly.

Then he vanished.

Dazed, Allison smiled at the draperies fluttering gently at the bedroom window. He was amazing. One of the very best jewel thieves ever to elude detection.

Together, they would be the Grace and Jeffery DeWilde of the securities business. Unbeatable. Better together than either would have been apart.

Her smile faded, and her happiness turned to tears of gratitude.

"Thank you, Jeffrey," she whispered. "I hope you and Grace find your second chance, too."

For a moment she thought about them, two lonely people on opposite sides of the globe. She had done what she could to repair the damage she had caused. Now it was up to them. She genuinely hoped they would find their way back to each other.

Then she thought about Paul, and she felt her face flush with anticipation. Ordering herself to be careful and not to rush, she lowered herself out the window and down two stories to the ground.

And then she threw caution to the wind and ran pell-mell across the grounds, racing toward Paul, toward her love and the future, and her own second chance.

Weddings by DeWilde

continues with

A STRANGER'S BABY

by Judith Arnold

Grace DeWilde's engaged niece, Mallory Powell, was pregnant by a man other than her fiancé. She could please her high-society family and provide the child with a father and a name, or she could listen to her heart, which was pushing her in another, more mysterious direction altogether.

Available in October

Here's a preview!

A STRANGER'S BABY

"AUNT GRACE." Mallory held up her hand to silence her. Her gaze rested on the bowl of blueberries and chunks of melon. She wanted to gorge on the fruit, just to fill her mouth with natural sugars so that what she said would come out sweetly.

"What is it, dear?" Grace finally set aside her own agenda and studied Mallory. Her eyes reflected her worry. "Oh, heavens. You have bad news for me, don't you?"

"I'm not sure if it's *bad*," Mallory fibbed, smiling with more optimism that the moment could sustain. "I'm pregnant."

Grace said nothing for a moment. Then she pressed her hand to her chest and inhaled deeply. "Oh, my."

"'Oh, my' is right."

"I suppose I should be relieved that it's nothing worse."

Mallory burst into laughter. "Meaning, it's pretty damned bad?"

Grace laughed, too, a weak, shocked laugh. "Well, it certainly takes me by surprise. Whatever were you thinking of? You're a modern, intelligent woman, Mal. Surely you know how to avoid such things."

Mallory shifted uncomfortably on the sofa. "Surely I do," she said, unintentionally imitating her aunt's diction. "But even modern, intelligent women make mistakes."

Grace pursed her lips and shook her head. "I suppose it's Robert's fault as much as yours. I certainly would have expected some restraint from him."

"Robert isn't—"

"But I suppose people who put off marrying until they're thirty might behave like teenagers throughout their twenties. And I'm not so old I don't understand what hormones can do to a person."

"Aunt Grace, I—"

"When are you due?"

Mallory sighed, resigned to letting her aunt control the conversation for now. "September."

"Well. This can be dealt with. You and Robert can have a quick civil ceremony now, and then proceed with your end-of-the-year gala. Most ministers will perform a religious service for a couple who have already been married at town hall. And by December, you should have your figure back, if you watch your diet during your pregnancy. We can still proceed with the gown. This is not insurmountable."

"It's not Robert's baby," Mallory announced.

Grace lapsed into another silence. "Oh, my," she whispered, glancing at Mallory's flat abdomen. Her cheeks darkening, she lifted her stunned gaze to Mallory. "Not Robert's?"

Mallory shook her head.

"Dear God."

"I think I prefer 'oh, my.'"